Silent City

Also by James Kennedy

Armed and Dangerous

JAMES KENNEDY

Silent City

HEINEMANN : LONDON

Published in the United Kingdom in 1998 by
William Heinemann

1 3 5 7 9 10 8 6 4 2

Copyright © James Kennedy 1998

The right of James Kennedy to be identified as the author of this work has been asserted by him in accordance with the Copyright, Designs and Patents Act, 1988

This book is sold subject to the condition that it shall not, by way of trade or otherwise, be lent, resold, hired out, or otherwise circulated without the publisher's prior consent in any form of binding or cover other than that in which it is published and without a similar condition including this condition being imposed on the subsequent purchaser

First published in the United Kingdom in 1998 by William Heinemann
Random House UK Ltd
20 Vauxhall Bridge Road, London, SW1V 2SA

Random House Australia (Pty) Limited
20 Alfred Street, Milsons Point, Sydney, New South Wales 2061, Australia

Random House New Zealand Limited
18 Poland Road, Glenfield
Auckland 10, New Zealand

Random House South Africa (Pty) Limited
Endulini, 5a Jubilee Road, Parktown, 2193, South Africa

Random House UK Limited Reg. No. 954009

A CIP catalogue record for this book is available from the British Library

Papers used by Random House UK Limited are natural, recyclable products made from wood grown in sustainable forests. The manufacturing processes conform to the environmental regulations of the country of origin

Typeset in Monotype Bembo by Deltatype Limited, Birkenhead, Merseyside
Printed and bound in the United Kingdom by
Mackays of Chatham, Kent

ISBN 0 434 00383 2

To Ron Hawkins
who first discovered me under the Bells of Shandon

PART ONE

Thursday, 12 November

ONE

1

Eddie Halpin glanced at his watch and looked again through his rear-view mirror at the red Hiace van that was still climbing behind him.

There were no other cars now on the isolated mountain pass. The bleak weather that had been threatening the peninsula all afternoon had finally closed in and others, with less urgent journeys, had obviously run for cover.

The road here was dangerously narrow. Blasted and hacked out of the side of the mountain, its edge was protected only by a frail wire railing. Beyond that there was a steep descent of sheer rock and sparse heather, where even the local sheep seemed reluctant to graze. At the bottom, a thousand yards below, a deep lake was waiting to take in anything that reached it.

He glanced again at his watch. It was a little after five. The light, never the brightest in mid-November anyway, was already failing. And he needed to get beyond the town of Dingle and down to Slea Head before six o'clock. He pushed on.

He was almost at the mountain's summit, about to start the easier descent, when the rain began and the dense winter mist that was characteristic of the area settled in around him. Within seconds, it was impossible to see for more than a few yards in any direction.

He switched on his fog lights and the windscreen wipers. He dropped down to second gear and slowed his BMW 316i to a crawl.

But as he thought about pulling in and stopping, if only he could find a space that was wide enough to park in safely, the red van, like a huge and bloodied animal, suddenly loomed out of the swirling mist behind him and jolted into his rear bumper.

He knocked the gear stick into first and wondered if he should accept the contact as an accident. It would've been understandable enough in the foul conditions, he thought. And the impact had been slight. Little enough damage had been done.

He decided to accelerate away and find a spot where they could both pull over and assess the damage.

But as he pressed the pedal, the engine seemed to respond with more than the usual noise.

It wasn't only the BMW, of course. It was the van behind him, also revving furiously.

Again its flat, ugly face sprang out of the mist in his rear-view mirror and lunged at him once more.

It was only then that Halpin finally accepted that his life was in danger. The driver of the battered Hiace wasn't either drunk or panicked, he decided. He wasn't even careless. He was coldly trying to ram the silver BMW off the narrow road and down the side of the mountain to a certain death.

Halpin, in low enough gear now to quickly jump free of it, accelerated sharply.

As he pressed on, much faster than he would've otherwise risked, a horn blared suddenly in front of him. Headlights flashed repeatedly in his eyes. Another car, coming down the mountain in the opposite direction, swerved violently to squeeze past where he was holding the centre of the road.

Thursday, 12 November

His concentration wasn't totally on escaping, however.

And he was lucky.

Two hundred yards away, near the summit of the mountain, he came on a lay-by where the tourists parked their cars to appreciate the views. He pulled in and slipped between two stranded tour buses and out of sight. He switched off his lights, but kept his engine running. Peering back out, he caught staggered glimpses of the red van climbing past him on the road and disappearing around the first of the narrow bends as it began its descent.

To follow it, he had to risk shooting blindly back across the shrouded road.

But he was lucky again. And nothing came against him from either direction.

He let the BMW free-wheel down from the summit, passing thirty and edging towards a hair-raising forty miles an hour.

He reached a sharp bend, near where the undulating road climbed again for a while. Hearing another engine struggling towards him and seeing its headlights cutting through the white cloud between them, he had to brake again to slow himself.

But the sound, more audible now above his own much quieter engine, seemed to have a worrying familiarity.

He braked more sharply as he recognised it. So sharply that he lost too much power at once and the BMW skidded and stalled when he tried to accelerate from the valley. Its wheels locked to the left. And a second later, over to his right, the red van burst through the mist in front of him and, mere inches away, slipped quickly by.

He had a glimpse of its driver in the elevated cab.

It was a redheaded man, he saw. A man whose hair was thick and untidy, whose complexion was dotted with freckles.

And it was a *familiar* face. Halpin was certain of it. He had seen it before. And in a situation that had marked it out as an enemy. But he had no name for it. He hadn't even a distinct memory of the occasion or the location.

He was still scrambling for the connection in his mind, and still trying to clear the flooded carburettor and fire the BMW's engine, when he heard the van braking behind him. He heard the roaring of its engine and the crashing of gears as it crazily manoeuvred on the narrow stretch and turned to come back at him.

The BMW wouldn't take.

And he was vulnerable now. A sitting target.

He closed his eyes for a second to concentrate. He took his feet off the pedals, his hand away from the ignition key. He couldn't risk letting the car roll backwards down the slight hill in the hope of jump starting it. Chances were, he'd only meet the oncoming van without the power to escape from it.

He couldn't risk admitting his handicap at all, he decided then. So he wouldn't try to start the car again.

He thought his best option was to get out while he was still concealed by the mist and hide among the rocks along the slope to his left. The van driver would see the stalled BMW late. He might leave the cab to investigate. Might expose himself to ambush. At the worst, all he could do was push the empty BMW over the side of the cliff.

But even as he was planning it, working the angles and weighing the risks, the van loomed again in his rear-view mirror.

As he'd anticipated, its driver was moving fast and saw the stranded car late. He reacted instinctively. He swerved to avoid the obstruction.

But as he did, another car broke from the mist, coming down to the valley.

Locked on his chosen course, with the BMW inside on his left and the new arrival threatening his bonnet, the van driver kept swerving towards the only space.

Thursday, 12 November

But there was no road on his right any more.

Halpin heard the squeal of tyres. Short and sharp from the car ascending slowly towards them. A desperate, prolonged screech from the van that was now out of control.

The van's effort was useless.

There was a loud scraping as a post was wrenched from the ground. A whining scrape as the van went through the flattened wire fence. And then absolute silence as it shot over the edge of the mountain and sailed through the air. Until it crashed into a rock below and loudly bounced from obstacle to obstacle on its way down.

And then there was silence again.

Halpin stared through the spatters of rain and the still-flapping wipers on his windscreen. It was a gold Mercedes that was sitting in front of him. It had German registration plates. And it had stopped with less than the width of a wheel between itself and the BMW.

Its owner was a young man with heavy, trembling jowls and wide glasses. He was still sitting in the driver's seat. He had a stunned expression on his pale face.

When he finally followed Halpin's lead and got out to cross the road and peer into the shrouded valley below, he kept muttering, 'My God! My God! Did you see? Did you see?'

The cloud cover was still thick on the mountain. They could hardly see the broken fence at their feet and had no sight at all of the doomed van.

'Did you see?' the German cried. 'Did you see?'

He gestured wildly. A small, fat man, dressed in a charcoal-grey business suit. Standing on a mountain beside a taller Irishman who wore blue jeans and a white cotton jacket and who had closely cropped black hair and a three-day growth of beard.

Although both men were in their early thirties, the German

looked a decade older and clearly felt much less experienced. He searched for reassurance. For explanations.

'He was trying to overtake you!' he cried. '*Here!* Trying to *overtake* you!'

Halpin ignored him. He loosened a stone with his right foot and kicked it disgustedly over the edge.

He had wanted the driver alive.

Someone had set him up, he realised now. Someone who knew his schedule. Someone who knew his route. Someone who knew where his fall would look most like an accident.

Halpin was a civil-liberties activist. He'd experienced pickets outside his home before. He'd dealt with abuse and with verbal intimidation and with smears.

But attempted murder, of course, was in a higher league. And it didn't seem appropriate to his modest activities . . .

The German tourist was tugging urgently at his sleeve. 'I have a mobile phone,' he was saying. 'We must call the police. We must be told what to do.'

He was right. It was far too dangerous to stay standing there, on the edge of the cliff. Too dangerous to leave the cars as they were, abandoned in the road. It was already dark. And the ground beneath their feet was now soft and slippery from the heavy rain.

2

Roger Walcott was drinking alone in a public house on Kinvara pier when the *Grey Witch* limped back into the sheltered harbour.

The trawler's two-man crew, Bill Canavan and his teenage son, stormed angrily away from it after docking. You could

Thursday, 12 November

already hear their loud complaints before they crossed the road and entered the pub.

When Canavan aggressively pushed open the door, he brought with him a blast of cold air from the winter evening outside. And then, over a pint of Guinness, he worked on warming the place up again with his rage.

Engine trouble, he grumbled. While the rest of the fleet were still out there, happily chasing a crowded shoal of herring. Why did the poor luck always have to fall on him? And where was he going to get an engineer at this time of night? He'd have to wait and bring someone along in the morning.

None of this was addressed to Walcott, who sat by himself in a far corner of the pub.

In fact, apart from greetings and remarks on the weather, very few of the locals spoke to Walcott at all.

Three months on as curator of the nearby museum at St Kieron's House and he was still a stranger in the area.

He was an Englishman, of course. And although a devout Roman Catholic and a welcome regular at mass and devotions, he had a ripe upper-class accent that sounded gratingly superior to the fishermen and the village traders. His manner was cold and painfully reserved.

And besides, his predecessor as curator, a local historian named Tommy Folan, had died in a gruesome car accident six weeks after being presented with a company car by his bosses. There was a touch of resentment that the job had drifted away to an outsider. And a hint of the macabre about the speed of Walcott's appointment, less than a week after the funeral.

Walcott might've surmounted all these obstacles with a better personality. But he wasn't either pleasant company or pleasant to look at.

He had a pale complexion. His hair was thin and straw-coloured. He always seemed to have a slight smile playing on his narrow lips. It made him look disdainful. And it annoyed almost everyone who talked to him.

There were a few exceptions. Dominick Rushe and his wife, who worked at St Kieron's as groundsman and cook, found him formal but decent. For an Englishman, as Rushe always hurried to add.

Otherwise, people tolerated Walcott. They were courteous to his face. Behind his back, they pitied his dullness and his loneliness.

An hour or so after Canavan's arrival at the pub that night, when Walcott checked the time and finished his drink and left, no one paid any more attention to his departure than they had to his presence.

It was almost eight by then. Beyond the lights of the village, the night was dark and heavy with the mist that had come in off the Atlantic over Galway Bay.

At the end of the pier, Walcott turned left and walked stiffly along the narrow footpath that led for three hundred yards with the main road from the village down to the entrance gates of St Kieron's House.

When he was out of sight, he allowed himself one small expression of his frustration. He kicked a stone as it rolled in front of him off the low wall that divided the footpath from the seashore.

Stopping at the gates of St Kieron's, he drew a few sharp breaths to regain his self-control and then turned inwards to crunch across the gravel driveway.

Ahead of him, its dark silhouette barely visible against the night sky, there was a castellated tower house and a modern, two-storey extension to the tower's west wall. It was the tower that housed the museum devoted to the life of Joseph Manning and to the history of Crastina, the charity Manning had founded while working as a civil servant in Dublin in 1941 and still led today, more than fifty years later.

Thursday, 12 November

Moved by the suffering caused in the Luftwaffe's bombing of neutral Dublin that year [as the official brochure explained] *and also by the recent deaths of both his parents and his only sister, Joseph Manning responded to the poverty on the streets of his native city by opening to the poor the doors of his own private house in the prosperous Dublin suburb of Ranelagh. His extraordinary act and extraordinary message inspired an organisation that is now a major international charity and aid agency.*

With its warm approval by the new American administration in early 1997, Crastina is currently the largest provider . . .

Walcott unlocked the main door of the west wing, which was used as a retreat house by Crastina. Inside, he opened the connecting door to the tower on the right and stepped onto the cold flagstones. Switching on a light, he picked up the sign he'd already prepared, announcing that St Kieron's was closed for the next three days and would reopen after the weekend.

He looked around anxiously for a while, checking that everything was in its place. Then he turned and left the buildings and walked down the driveway again to hang the sign on the entrance gates with thin wire.

When he came back he turned right after closing the door behind him, into the tower house once more.

Again he examined the furniture inside. The oak table with its display cabinet of sacred medals and relics and the wooden cross that Joseph Manning had taken from his original home in Dublin. The high-backed dining-room chair. The hand-woven rugs.

He was concerned about their static relationships. Their order. Their neatness.

Again he calculated the straightness of the lines created by the photographs hanging on the walls.

His adjustments were minor. Almost neurotic.

But they calmed him.

When he could do no more, he climbed the narrow spiral stairway and checked on each of the four upper chambers.

Not wanting to be noticed, he didn't clamber onto the exposed battlements on top.

Instead, he descended the spiral stairs, left the tower house after locking the connecting door behind him, and walked along the corridor between the reception and the kitchen in the west wing. He passed the communal dining-hall and the narrow cells that had been built for contemplation.

Inside the small church at the end of the corridor he knelt and prayed for a while.

And that, too, had the effect of soothing him.

When he was finished he sat in darkness in the pew and glanced again at his luminous watch.

It was almost nine o'clock. And he could do nothing now except wait for Bill Canavan to make contact with him.

3

Eddie Halpin was delayed for more than two hours at the scene of the accident before being questioned by a nervous young policeman.

Halpin gave his name. He spelled out his address as the Island, Snipe Avenue, Galway city, and described his occupation as a lecturer in history at University College, Galway.

But that was as far as his honesty and co-operation stretched.

He lied casually about his presence in the area, inventing a short touring holiday for himself. He pretended that the van driver was a total stranger. And he said nothing about the Hiace's manoeuvres immediately before the crash.

At eight fifteen, already a couple of hours late for his

appointment, he was finally released by a local sergeant who had taken control.

By then, the mist had lifted and the mountain-rescue team, working with the searchlights they'd mounted, seemed almost ready to winch the body of the van driver from the shore of the lake below. Anxious as he was to identify his attacker, Halpin didn't wait. His curiosity would've seemed either morbid or suspicious.

He drove on, through Dingle and down towards Slea Head.

Three miles beyond the town of Dingle, he took a minor road on his left and immediately saw the hand-painted sign for the Gables. An unsurfaced lane of dried earth and a little grass, pitted with the tyre marks of tractor wheels, led up to the farm.

An antique Morris Minor was parked outside the porch of the whitewashed cottage.

Halpin pulled in behind the car and knocked at the cottage door after stepping from the BMW.

A middle-aged, black-haired woman answered and invited him in. Beside the coal fire in the main room, a grey-haired old woman sat in an armchair, reading a book.

This was Anna Rosen, now seventy-one years old, unhappily living with her widowed niece on this isolated farm and eternally scheming how to get back to her own Jewish community in Dublin.

Researching a short history of Crastina the previous year had first given Halpin an interest in Anna's brother Alan, who had died when the German air force, intentionally or otherwise, had bombed the capital of neutral Ireland during the Second World War – the tragedy that had first inspired Joseph Manning to establish his charity and to devote his life to the innocent victims of the world's conflicts. Other work had intervened and kept Halpin from developing the topic. But for the past six weeks, in a series of informal interviews with Anna, he'd been preparing a detailed account of the extraordinary life and early death of her brother.

The young man's uniqueness attracted him.

Alan Rosen's background was unremarkable. He was the only son of a prosperous solicitor and was diligently studying for the Bar himself.

But in early 1941, he'd somehow grown impatient with the boundaries of the small Jewish community in Dublin. One of the very few who actually believed the stories of mass executions filtering through from Europe, his intense anger had made him militant. But since he had nowhere to express his rage on an insular, neutral island, he had become aggressive about advertising his religion. Someone, in other words, who might well have made himself an easy target for abuse and physical attacks in the puritan Ireland of the 1940s.

The old woman greeted Halpin testily now, grumbling about his lateness, her own tiredness and her reluctance to start an interview.

Halpin apologised. He explained in detail about the accident on the road, assured her that he didn't want to do a formal session and stressed that he had only completed the journey as a courtesy.

But of course his motive was deeper than mere politeness.

'Has anyone else come to talk to you about the past lately, Anna?' he asked casually.

'About what?'

'About Alan.'

'No.'

'There's a lot of interest in the period at the moment.'

She angrily shook her head. 'There might be in the college you teach in. I don't hear any of it. People don't like to remember any more. Then they have to suffer, too.'

'You haven't discussed it with anyone else since I was last down with you, two weeks ago?'

Thursday, 12 November

'No.'

'Do you remember telling me then that in the months before Alan's death a stranger came several times to the synagogue, and afterwards to Alan's workplace, and finally to your home, enquiring about him?'

'That's right, yes.'

'You haven't found out who the stranger was or anything like that, have you?'

She stared at him irritably. 'How would I find out who he was? It was more than fifty years ago!'

'I know, yes.'

'I was a child. I was twelve years old. He frightened me. I closed the door in his face. I saw him only for a few seconds.'

But the face had lodged in her mind, Halpin knew.

Except that it was a face from almost six decades ago. A face that couldn't now survive in the same form, even if its owner was still alive. And her descriptions of it were useless.

Halpin stayed on for a while afterwards with the two women, sharing a pot of tea and chatting idly. But he was restless. And instead of relaxing him, the tea only increased his agitation.

When he left, it was with a sense of deflation and disappointment.

He'd hoped for more. He'd almost anticipated a direct connection between the attempt on his life and his contact with Anna Rosen.

He still believed that the two were related. It was too fine a coincidence otherwise. Too rich a chance to comfortably accept.

He made a short detour in Dingle to pay a social call on Caroline French, a solicitor who was also a civil-rights activist, a friend from older days and older struggles.

But again he was unsettled. And he left abruptly after a brief conversation. Saying nothing about the incident on the mountain.

He thought about the past once more as he drove.

There had been a small Nazi group in Dublin in 1941, when, for a short time, Alan Rosen had been politically active. They met in locked rooms at the backs of seedy restaurants. Proposed solutions to the city's grim poverty by promising to make life hard for its Jewish money-grabbers. And they waited patiently for the German army to 'liberate' the country.

And odd things had been happening to the Rosens before Alan left home in early April 1941 to rent the house on the North Strand where the bombs had killed him the following month. Nothing much. Nothing significant. Friends would stop visiting the family or neglect to return their invitations. Conversations with neighbours would sometimes get a little strained. The father's legal business occasionally became a little slacker than was reasonable.

That subtle redefining of normality, in other words, that on the Continent had steadily crept towards violence.

But this was 1941, Halpin reminded himself. This was all of fifty-seven years ago . . .

Back on the mountain, the scene of the accident was still being patrolled and cordoned by the local police. But the young guard who had questioned Halpin earlier allowed him to park again behind the line of squad cars and then step out to look.

'Not find anywhere to stay in Dingle, sir?' the guard wondered.

'What? No, I thought I'd go back to Tralee for the night . . .'

The dead van driver, Halpin saw, was taking a lot more time to come back up the face of the cliff than he had to go down. In the darkness, the rescue team was still struggling with his stretcher.

'Was he a local?' Halpin asked innocently.

Thursday, 12 November

The guard stared at him. 'Sorry, sir?'

'Probably not,' Halpin went easily on. 'Probably a visitor of some sort. Do they know who he is yet?'

The young policeman, a poor liar, looked embarrassed by his obvious concealment.

'Ah, well,' he stammered. 'No, sir. They don't, no.'

His discomfort must have communicated itself. A few seconds later, his sergeant was on his back, hounding him away to other duties, and then bustling Halpin into his BMW and onto the road again.

Which was curious, Halpin decided. A few hours ago, the same sergeant, with the same dead man on his hands, had been relaxed and sympathetic.

TWO

1

She passed the silver BMW outside the village of Kilcummin, at the entrance to the mountain pass.

Eddie Halpin had been delayed by roadworks and was now stopped under the street lighting at the edge of the village. Drifting through with the slow-moving traffic in the open lane, she saw him clearly, less than an arm's reach away.

He didn't notice her. He was leaning over the steering wheel, staring vacantly through the windscreen. And obviously thinking about something else.

Her instinct was to brake and turn.

But she resisted it.

She wondered if his presence on the peninsula was just coincidence. Or had he come for a macabre gloat, she thought. Like a ghoul chuckling to itself in the background of a funeral.

Still the same strange man, she decided.

Still . . .

There was a long tailback near the scene of the accident beyond the mountain's summit. More ghouls, she thought. Sightseers. Crowds attracted by the forming crowds.

When she finally got through and pulled over, a harassed young guard immediately rushed up to her window and waved her off again.

Thursday, 12 November

She parked and showed her ID as she stepped out. 'Detective Inspector Charlotte Rainey. Special Branch.'

He stared at her dumbly.

She seemed too sophisticated to be a guard. So far, his experience of detectives was limited to burly men in crumpled clothes from a dated style. This one was dressed in a light-grey trouser suit, fawn woollen overcoat and black woollen scarf.

She seemed too young to be an inspector, also. Her face, almost babyish in its smoothness and softness, looked ten years short of the thirty-five she actually was. She wore no make-up, he noticed. Her brown eyes and her light auburn hair . . .

'Who was the first officer on the scene?' she was asking him.

He swallowed drily and muttered, 'Ah, I was, ma'am.'

'Good,' she approved. 'Don't go away. I'll need to talk to you. Who's in charge here at the moment?'

He gestured down the line of squad cars to the grey-haired man with the stripes who was directing the final passage of the stretcher as the rescue workers lifted it clear of the broken fence and lowered it to the side of the road. 'That'll be Sergeant Divilly, ma'am.'

'I'll be back.'

The sergeant too, before Rainey introduced herself, was curt and irritated. He had the air of a man on a vital mission who just could not afford distractions. The puffed-out chest of the chosen servant, Rainey observed. And not even the grace to apologise when he was finally enlightened.

Rainey ignored his poor manners. In fact, she said nothing at all for a long time afterwards. Just deliberately left him to stew in suspension, with neither an order to gripe about nor an offered courtesy to sneer at. She knew the type. Her father had been one of them. Unimaginative little men. Left without anything to react to, they withered into a background of confusion.

She took a pair of plastic gloves from the pocket of her

overcoat. In the still, awkward silence, she loudly snapped them on. She stooped and undid the zip on the covered stretcher. As she pulled it downwards, the material folded away above her hand to slowly reveal the bruised and bloodied, but still slightly comic face that she had expected.

It was, she thought again, as if two sections of separate personalities had been unskilfully grafted together. The thick, wide lips were far too expansive for the rest of the redhead's face. They belonged to a man who was loud and outgoing. But the small features above it were those of a stunted, shifty individual.

Over the last year or so, while interrogating him occasionally, she had come to know him a little more.

Among his mates, he was known as Birdy.

For his pelican's mouth? His owl's nose? Or his wren's eyes?

It was impossible to tell. Like many nicknames, its origins were obscure.

His surname was Finnegan.

It wasn't that Rainey mourned his passing. The man had been a thug. A little robbery with menace here. A little protection masquerading as debt collection there. A lot of marching in the front line as steward at right-wing protests, beating the drum of conservatism with his baseball bat.

But she regretted the loss.

He'd meant something to her. Potentially, anyway. Lately, she'd been certain that he was on the fringe of something. She'd felt it particularly the last few weeks. Her only window into a world whose *existence* she was even uncertain of. And now it was blacked out.

The last time they'd met, for instance, at Birdy's house in Cork city, he'd been very drunk and a little careless. Wanting to impress her. Trying for the usual impossible target of the little man entangled in a bigger drama. Needing to be admired for stoic indifference and simultaneously loved for co-operation.

Thursday, 12 November

He'd dropped some obscure boast about a terrorist named Shane McKelvey before picking it up and tucking it quickly away again.

But the echoes had stayed.

McKelvey was notorious.

Or a legend. Or a myth. Or another jackal. Depending on which newspaper you were excited by.

Always wild and always extremely violent, he had drifted at sixteen from Republican terrorism in Northern Ireland into the wider arena of the extreme right on the Continent and had left a trail of death before dropping out of sight again more than a year ago. He was wanted in France for the murder of two left-wing Arab students. Wanted in Germany for torching Turkish immigrants. And still wanted in Ireland for his earliest crimes.

There were persistent rumours that McKelvey had been slaughtered in a messy sexual dispute at an isolated cabin in a Spanish forest. But also constant reports of sightings in one or other of the South American dictatorships.

Rainey wondered now if Birdy had died tonight because of his drunkenness then.

Who had been with them in the house in Cork? Only Birdy's girlfriend, she remembered. Kylie Craddock.

2

For the third time that night, Roger Walcott walked down the gravel driveway of St Kieron's House to the entrance gates. He undid the lock that he'd secured earlier. He pulled the gates open and fastened each section to the concrete posts on either side of the driveway.

When he went back he sat in the green Opel Vectra that was parked outside the west wing. He drove it quietly down and through the open gates. On the main road he turned left, away from the village of Kinvara and on towards Galway city.

He parked almost immediately again, however, and strode back along the narrow footpath to relock the entrance gates. Then he resumed his journey.

Everything he did was done with an icy self-restraint.

Walcott was exasperated.

He had no objection to the order to break into Eddie Halpin's home in Galway city that night.

Quite the contrary.

The journey was short, less than twenty miles, and would take him perhaps thirty minutes in all.

There were sensitive documents, he had been told, that had to be located and removed. There were computer files and discs that had to be destroyed. There were photographs that needed to be checked.

None of these could be safely seen or handled except by senior officials.

But Walcott had been delayed at St Kieron's. Bill Canavan had failed to contact him until late and even then hadn't been able to deliver the expected cargo from the *Grey Witch*. It was now past midnight. And what should've been done some hours ago still lay ahead of him.

His driving illustrated his problems. Awareness of the time made him accelerate anxiously. The fear of being stopped and questioned by the police immediately slowed him again. Knocked back and forth between the two, his humour was roughened a little more.

As he travelled, he wondered if Halpin's body had already been identified. He worried about the police or Halpin's relatives calling to the house before him. The prospect of being too late both chilled and irritated him.

Thursday, 12 November

He entered Galway city from the south and took the ring road to the north-west suburb where Halpin lived.

He turned in off University Road and onto Snipe Avenue.

To his left was a high wall. To his right, the line of bungalows.

Halpin's was the last in the row.

Walcott cruised past. The house was in darkness and seemed deserted.

He drove down the length of the cul-de-sac, turned at the end and came back. Before he reached the bungalow again, he swung into a clearing on his left and parked there in front of locked gates and beside a red Nissan Micra.

He turned out the Vectra's lights.

He waited until his eyes had attuned themselves to the darkness.

There was no movement along the length of the avenue. No lights inside Halpin's bungalow. No one concealed in the surrounding shadows.

He stepped out of the Vectra and gently closed and locked its door behind him before turning to walk towards the house.

A week before, while cautiously casing the area, he'd decided to break in through the rear.

It had the advantage of not being overlooked. It was separated from the neighbours' garden by a high wall. And the pathway to it, around the side of the house, was obscured by hedges.

Best of all, there was no alarm in the house and the sash window at the back was protected only by a frail security lock.

3

Eddie Halpin was almost safely home before he felt the first tremors of the aftershock.

For more than three hours, on the journey up the west coast from Kerry, his mind had been elsewhere, raking through memories for a lead to the redhead who had tried to kill him.

But now, less than ten miles from Galway city, he looked out through the windscreen and the side windows and found that he had no idea where he was. Nothing was recognisable. And he couldn't remember when or why he'd joined this stretch of road.

He was instantly threatened with panic.

For a few seconds he actually lost his self-control. He looked desperately in the rear-view mirror. But the sight of distant headlights behind him only brought back the sensation of being hunted. He accelerated to draw clear of the other cars. He slowed to let them overtake. They seemed to just sit there, taunting him.

The interior of the BMW became airless and stuffy. He turned off the heating. It made no difference. He was still drenched with sweat.

Convinced that the system wasn't working, he looked anxiously at the instrument panel and saw that he was travelling frantically, at over ninety miles an hour.

He had to stop, he decided. He had to rest a while. His mind needed time to get his nerves back under control.

He pulled over and parked on the hard shoulder.

One by one, the cars that had been behind him all passed indifferently.

He had no rest, though. Instead, he was almost overwhelmed by a new dread.

He was too vulnerable here, he feared. Too isolated. Alone and unprotected. If anyone was watching him . . .

For the first time, a grim realisation sunk fully through. His survival had left him still in danger. Those who wanted to kill him would inevitably try again.

He wondered if he would've told the truth to the police in Kerry if the risks had been obvious to him earlier. And should he tell them now?

In the darkness, he vigorously shook his head to himself.

He didn't trust the police.

It was more than mere suspicion, he reminded himself. It was past experience. And his reading of the past.

His panic subsided gradually while he was shifting his fears to the more familiar target of the police. But he was still extremely tense. For the rest of the journey, after easing back into traffic, he drove with a rigid grip on the steering-wheel. And when he finally pulled in towards home, along Snipe Avenue, his shoulder muscles ached from the effort.

It was a little after one in the morning by then.

The avenue seemed deserted. And the streets around it were quiet.

Nevertheless, he drove slowly along its length, worried that someone, somewhere, might be staking it out. He passed the row of bungalows on his right and the high wall opposite that had been decorated with a children's mural. Beyond these there was the loading bay of a disused supermarket. And at the end of the cul-de-sac, a pedestrian entrance to a modern housing estate.

Apart from a few parked and empty cars in the loading bay and outside the houses, it seemed all clear.

He turned and drove back. He parked in his own driveway and got out.

The bungalow was in darkness. The curtains in its front room were still open. The paperback novel was still sitting on the window-sill inside.

The way he'd left the place early that afternoon.

He walked across and slipped the latchkey into the lock.

But as soon as he opened the front door, he was certain that there was something wrong.

He heard a slight noise from inside. A chair or a floorboard creaking.

He stopped.

To the left of the hallway, there was his study and then the bungalow's two bedrooms, separated by the bathroom. To the right, the kitchen and the living-room.

It was from the last that the noise had come.

4

Charlotte Rainey zipped up the cover over Finnegan's face and thought ironically that the only chance Birdy now had of posthumous relevance was the discovery that his death was no accident. Accidents were dead ends. Murders left trails. Tracks as distinct as human footprints. Leading up to the corpse. And leading away from it again.

She stripped off the plastic gloves and asked the truculent sergeant to fill her in. Briefly.

He didn't mention names in his dismissive account. The German tourist, he said. The Irish driver.

It was only when she tired of him, went back to the younger guard and asked if a man named Eddie Halpin, driving a silver BMW, had stopped any time at the scene, that the look of astonishment alerted her.

Thursday, 12 November

'But he was the witness, ma'am.'
'Witness? Who?'
'Mr Halpin, ma'am. Edward R. Halpin.'
'Yeah? Who took his statement?'
'I did, ma'am.'
'Right. Let's hear it.'
She listened politely.
But she found the story incredible.
When it was finished, she took a torch for illumination and the young guard to hold the traffic and went onto the road to examine the tyre marks on its surface. Those that were there seemed to support the statements of the witnesses.

She walked slowly back up the slope, towards the summit of the pass. Looking for somewhere that the van could've hidden and emerged from.

'That'll be the car park at the top, ma'am,' she was told when she asked.

But she never reached the car park.

One hundred and fifty yards on, she stopped and looked at a post that had been bent slightly backwards at the road's edge. And then opposite that, on the other side, she examined a smear of red paint that had been left on a jutting rock.

She must've drifted into a reverie between the signs.

When she looked around her again, the young guard was apparently returning to her position, although she hadn't noticed his departure in the first place.

'The sergeant says they're ready to take the body into Tralee hospital, ma'am,' he told her. 'He wants to know if it's all right to go ahead.'

She nodded absently.

Birdy wouldn't tell her anything else now. And neither would the autopsy on his corpse, she decided.

But others might.

27

5

Eddie Halpin left the front door open behind him. He slipped past the old mahogany telephone table and dropped his hand to the brass knob of the living-room door. The thing turned in his palm before he could grasp it.

He let it go again.

He watched the door being slowly pulled away from him. He saw a shadowy figure behind it easing itself into the gap. At a certain point, the orange street lighting through the front window caught the intruder's face for an instant. The man seemed to be wearing a balaclava.

Halpin, still mostly concealed by the wall, didn't wait to let his advantage slip. He sprang out and reached for the lapels of the stranger's jacket or the loose material of his shirt or sweater.

But there were no clothes to grasp. Only bare flesh.

The man was naked.

He cried out in surprise and fear as Halpin's nails caught and cut his chest.

There seemed to be an answer to his call from somewhere deeper in the house.

And Halpin decided that he had to move quickly before he was outnumbered.

He grasped the man's hair and dragged him from the doorway across the hall. But as he swung, he lost his footing on the loose rug that was under his feet. His thigh knocked painfully against the sharp edge of the telephone table. His hold loosened while he struggled for balance.

The intruder swung at him as they crossed, catching him with a blow to his chest.

Thursday, 12 November

But Halpin was in no mood to take such petty restraints. He drove back into the other's face with his forehead. At the same time, he landed a combination of left and right punches to the unprotected stomach.

The man began to scream. But the breath was knocked too quickly from him. And only a grunt emerged before he crumpled against the wall and slid downwards to the bare floorboards.

Halpin stooped and raised his fist again to finish the business.

To his right, he heard a bedroom door being opened.

Light spilled out from the room into the darkened corridor.

And a woman's voice screamed nervously, 'Tom! Tom!'

Halpin abandoned his attack, confused by the sound. He looked anxiously down. Above him, the hall lighting was switched on. And standing there in the corridor outside the bedroom, wrapped in a green sheet, with a white desk lamp held aloft in her right hand, was his own sister, Linda.

She'd been staying with him on and off for the last year, of course. But not for the previous month, he calculated rapidly to himself. And not at all since . . .

'Jesus!' she cried now. 'Eddie!'

She stared in disbelief at the naked man who was slumped by the open front door, at the blood that was streaking through the thick growth of hair on his face.

'What the fuck are you doing, Eddie?' she demanded. 'Tom! Tom! Are you all right, Tom?'

Halpin stepped away, frowning. The balaclava was a heavy beard, he noticed now. Not a mask at all. 'Do you *know* this guy, Linda?' he asked.

'Of course I fucking know him,' she snapped.

'Who is he?'

She was at the man's side, desperately trying to revive him. 'He's my boyfriend, Eddie. Tom Tomkin.'

'Tom Tomkin?' Halpin repeated incredulously. It seemed impossible.

'You met him three weeks ago. He was here for a meal. Don't you remember?'

'He mustn't have enjoyed it, did he, Linda?'

'What?'

'Why was he trying to attack me?'

'We thought you were a burglar.'

'I came in through the front door. With my key.'

'We were in bed. And someone tried to break in earlier. We thought he'd come back.'

'Someone tried to break in?'

'Through the window at the back. He didn't get in. He ran off again when Tom turned on the light and he realised that there was someone here.'

'Did you see who it was?'

'No. He was gone before we got out.'

Tomkin was stirring under the attention and starting to regain consciousness.

'Right,' Halpin muttered. 'I didn't know you were here. I thought it was a burglar, too.'

'Eddie, you're not supposed to be back until next week yourself. Remember? You told me you were going on a holiday. In Kerry. I could use the place.'

'I had a change of plan, though. Your car's not outside, by the way.'

'It's parked around the corner, in the loading bay.'

'The red Nissan Micra? I didn't know.'

'I've had it three months now, Eddie.'

Tomkin was conscious again by then. He was still slumped. His eyes were clouded. A little comically, he was trying to decently cover his groin with one hand. The other was gingerly exploring his bruised face. When he spoke, his voice was

Thursday, 12 November

distorted. As if he'd just come from the dentist with his mouth swollen by anaesthetic.

Linda translated for him. 'He thinks you've broken his jaw, Eddie. Or his nose. Or something.'

'Right,' Halpin muttered again. 'We're going to have to get him to casualty, then, aren't we? For an X-ray. Do you want to drive? I'll help get him dressed and get him outside.'

'Fuck off, Eddie,' Linda swore. '*You* broke his nose. We'll go in the BMW. We'll get his blood all over your car.'

He thought it a bit unromantic of her.

6

Two miles short of Kinvara, while still tense and frustrated after the aborted raid on Halpin's house, Roger Walcott pulled in to redial a phone number he'd tried a number of times already. He wasn't hopeful. But instead of ringing out, as it had done before, the receiver was lifted now.

A youth, very drunk and very irritated, slurred at him heavily. 'What is it?'

'I need to speak to Cormac Lowry,' Walcott told him.

'Who?'

'Cormac Lowry.'

'Oh, right. Hang on a minute, will you?'

Walcott held his breath while he listened with distaste to the gross confusion in the background at the other end of the line. As if the stench of alcohol and sweat would travel across the distance to him if he inhaled. As if the smell of tobacco would tempt him to return to the habit he'd crushed before coming to Ireland.

Lowry, too, was drunk and sore-headed when he finally came to the phone. 'What?' he snapped. 'What? Who is this?'

'Roger Walcott.'

'Walcott? What do you want? You're not supposed to be ringing me, are you?'

'Many things that are, Lowry, weren't supposed to be.'

'Jesus! Where did you get that? In a fortune—'

'Our friend's house, for instance, was not unoccupied tonight. As you promised it would be.'

'What?'

'I think perhaps you heard.'

'Well, I don't know anything about that, do I?'

'Quite clearly not.'

'Did you see who was there?'

'No. I left.'

'Well, it's not our friend himself, anyway. That's for certain. He's happily departed, isn't he?'

'Has that been confirmed?'

'Of course it has, yeah.'

'To you personally?'

'Who the fuck else do you think?'

'What source?'

'A little fucking bird told me. Know what I mean? Jesus!'

'Don't make the mistake, Lowry, of becoming impertinent with me.'

'I'll get anything I like with you, Walcott. I don't have to report to you. I don't even have to talk to you. I shouldn't be, anyway. You're not in charge of this, are you? You're not—'

Walcott sharply disconnected.

Already unsettled by failure, he didn't need to be reminded that he could now do nothing to rectify it.

For three whole months, since coming to St Kieron's, he'd been dwelling bitterly on how the crude and unpredictable

Thursday, 12 November

McKelvey had been given the major role in the present operation and how he himself had been trusted with less.

McKelvey was considered a hero, of course, he scoffed. McKelvey had a colourful reputation. McKelvey was well-known to the police and the media.

But wasn't it at all appreciated, Walcott complained, that the *silent* killer was more effective? Wasn't it understood that the *faceless* assassin was more efficient?

What was wrong with the present operation, Walcott knew, was that he himself hadn't planned it and didn't now control it. He was relying on the intelligence and competence of others. How little these could be trusted had already been exposed by the disruption with Bill Canavan's trawler, the *Grey Witch*, and by the fiasco at Halpin's house tonight.

Walcott sat back in the Opel Vectra. He didn't start its engine. He opened the glove compartment. And for a long time, until he took more pleasure from the strength of his own will-power than from the contemplation of relief, he stared at the packets of cigarettes and the lighter inside.

THREE

1

Five past two in the morning, Charlotte Rainey drove up to Birdy Finnegan's house in Mayfield, in Cork, armed with a warrant and a small search party.

She wasn't expecting trouble. At least, not from Finnegan's connections.

Otherwise, you never knew.

Mayfield was a local-authority housing estate, built and neglected in the same decade. Now more than thirty years old, it was still bleak and unserviced. What little colour, and what little hope it had seemed to come from the pin-ups in the windows of the Manchester United soccer player Roy Keane, who had been born and reared there.

Finnegan's house was tucked away at the back of the estate. Without a local cop, it would've been difficult to find. All the roads looked like sections of the same depressing maze and the numbering system was erratic.

Like most of the others, the house was now in darkness.

Rainey left the two local uniforms guarding the cars and went with the rest to the battered door. Its green paint had flaked and fallen away a long time before. The exposed wood was damp and rotting in places. The knocker was broken, and useless. And the electric bell didn't work.

Thursday, 12 November

Rainey pounded with the heel of her fist on the wood.

Along the night air, the sound seemed to carry more outwards than in. And as usual, it woke everyone except the one it was intended for.

Other windows were opened along the row. A few isolated curses and calls of abuse were heard.

Around her, her team was getting restless and nervous. They were also Special Branch officers, but stationed locally. They'd advised against a raid in the area so late at night. But Rainey was anxious to pick up trails before news of Birdy's death alerted his masters.

And he had masters, of course. Birdy wasn't one to act alone. He needed the approval that a group gave him.

Someone was tugging at her sleeve and directing her attention upwards.

At the bedroom window above the door, the curtain had been lifted back and a face was pressed against the glass.

Rainey knocked again.

The window above was opened slightly and a voice called down, 'What do you want?'

'Gardai, Kylie!' Rainey shouted. 'We have a search warrant. Open up.'

Kylie, she thought. You imagined slim young girls. But names were given to infants, without foreknowledge of the adults who'd bear them.

Kylie Craddock, who opened the door a minute later, was not only a big, strong woman, but overweight as well. She had unevenly cut short black hair that some amateur had hacked away at, no doubt in return for a pint as payment. Her face was very pale, very large and very squat. But like her boyfriend, her features seemed to have been borrowed from someone else. They were all rather petite. Particularly her tiny, rounded eyes, which stared unblinkingly outwards, understanding nothing. Her breathing was asthmatic. Not helped by the four mangy cats in the living-room, whose loose hairs were everywhere, and whose stench pervaded the house.

Once she'd let them inside, Kylie followed the police around at their tasks. She didn't seem either surprised or excited. And her questions were almost dull. So perhaps she was used to it all.

'What's he after doing now? It's Birdy, isn't it? Do you hear me? He's always into something.'

She had a strong Cork accent. Her syllables rolled rapidly up and down and then rose to a screech at the end of each sentence.

Rainey took her aside. Out from under her colleagues' feet.

She knew that she should tell the woman about her lover's death. Decency demanded it. But Kylie was prone to hysterics. So she also knew that she'd get nothing but screams from her once she was informed of her loss.

'Do you remember me?' Rainey asked. 'I was here a few weeks ago.'

The woman nodded vaguely, not quite sure one way or the other, but willing to swallow someone else's word on most things.

'My name is Charlotte. Charlotte Rainey.'

'That's right. I remember that. You were talking to Birdy.'

'You made me some tea.'

'Did I?'

'Any chance of another cup, Kylie?'

'What? Right now, you mean?'

They went to the small, untidy kitchen. There were grease stains on the mugs, cat hairs on the table and unwashed crockery on the draining-board.

But Kylie seemed to forget their objective once they were there. She leaned back against the sink and folded her arms. And she waited.

'What's Birdy up to lately?' Rainey asked her.

'Birdy? You're asking the wrong one there, girl. He wouldn't tell me, you know.'

'Do you know where he is tonight?'

'He's not in, anyway. That's all I know.'

'What's he driving, Kylie?'

'Driving?'

'What car does he have?'

'The one that's always outside in front there. Except when he's off in it. The old Ford Escort.'

'Does he own a Hiace van?'

'He wouldn't be in a van. Not unless he was helping Batty with the chip van.'

'When was the last time you saw him, Kylie?'

She screwed up her eyes, covering them with the fat off her cheek-bones. 'I can't remember now, to tell you the truth.'

'A few days ago? A week ago? Longer?'

'Longer than what, like?'

It was like trying to do maths with a two-year-old child, Rainey decided wearily. There was no obstruction as such. No resistance. Just that the capability wasn't there.

2

Whatever lightness Eddie Halpin might've felt after escaping a second assault was quickly chilled by the skinny, humourless nurse who was on duty at the hospital's reception and then crushed by the tedium of being stuck in the waiting-room afterwards.

Even at two on a Thursday morning, casualty was crowded with victims of the city's recklessness. Most of them were local characters, brought there by the combination of drinking and any one of a hundred other dangerous pursuits. Like most characters, they transformed themselves into bores after about five minutes.

On the television, *Sky News* had an item on the American President's forthcoming visit to Ireland, due to start in about ten hours, at noon the following morning. Since the President was the first black man elected to the White House and since this was his first visit to Ireland, the comments were all predictable.

'They say he has this Secret Service fellow by his side all the time, to take the scissors from him after he cuts the ribbons opening things. And do you know why? *In case* . . . it said this on the news . . . *in case he accidentally finds a vein with it.* Do you get it? The blacks. They have their finger on the nuclear button now, but *they can't even use a pair of scissors properly* . . .'

'John F. Kennedy was a great man for cutting ribbons. Did you ever see Kennedy cutting ribbons?'

Dulled by boredom, Halpin went to the toilets.

He found a tourist magazine that someone had abandoned in one of the cubicles. Since it seemed to be the only reading material in the entire hospital, he brought it back to the waiting area with him and skimmed through the features.

Yeats Country. The Burren. Joyce Country. The Ring of Kerry . . .

He stopped. But not for the Ring of Kerry, where he'd almost lost his life. Instead, he went back to the previous article. He read its title and its opening paragraph again. And again something niggled at his dulled mind. Some association. Some distant connection.

He reached for it. It seemed to elude him. But only barely, he felt. Only a fingertip away.

He reached again.

And then, as if in a dense nightmare, the pieces suddenly flew at him with apparent absurdity.

The man who had tried to kill him, he remembered, the man

Thursday, 12 November

who had died in his plunge off the Kerry mountains . . . his name was Finnegan.

He felt a surge of triumph. But then a colder sensation as he also recalled where he had seen the man before and realised what his discovery meant.

He stood up from the hard plastic seat in the waiting-room.

He touched Linda's arm and said, 'I've got to go back home.'

She turned and stared up at him, frowning with bewilderment. 'What?'

He was already walking away from her. 'I've got to go. I've got to check something at home.'

She had to call him back. 'The car, Eddie! We need a lift home!'

He turned. He detached his house keys from the ring and gave her the remaining car keys. 'You take the BMW,' he said. 'I can get a taxi. Or walk. It's not far.'

He'd walk, he decided as he left the casualty unit.

He needed to clear his head. He needed time and space to think. He needed to work the implications through.

3

To Charlotte Rainey's right, the sergeant appeared in the kitchen doorway to summon her. 'Inspector?'

'Coming,' she sighed. She turned to the woman still leaning against the sink. 'Excuse me, Kylie.'

The sergeant led. They went upstairs, past the bathroom, into the bedroom that Kylie and Finnegan obviously used. The room was untidy with discarded clothes, but otherwise clean. Unlike the rest of the house.

The top drawer of a bedside locker was lying open for Rainey's inspection.

She took plastic gloves again from her pocket and slipped them on.

The drawer had an assortment of papers and writing instruments. But on top of the pile was a wad of banknotes.

Rainey took them up and flicked through them. All tens. All used. About thirty of them, she estimated. Three hundred pounds.

Near the end, the sequence was broken by a single cheque.

It was dated the previous Friday. It was made out to Finnegan. It was drawn on a Crastina No. 3 Account. It was countersigned by a Harry Fame. And its amount was one hundred pounds.

Rainey held her breath for a moment. This was dangerous, she already knew. Extremely dangerous.

The sergeant was lifting a second bundle of papers from the drawer.

She took them from him.

They were weekly pay slips. Computerised. All for the same small and rounded amount of one hundred pounds. All issued by Crastina. Which wasn't a commercial company, as she was well aware. It was a registered charity. Religious. Patriarchal. And now with an international profile.

So much she knew about the organisation led by Joseph Manning. What she *suspected* was that its donations were partly siphoned off, not only to fund conservative pressure groups, but also to finance more violent extremists. Unfortunately, no one else in Special Branch shared her view. And her isolation had made her suspicions look increasingly personalised, until her superiors had lost patience with the investigation and assigned her to other duties.

But now?

Thursday, 12 November

The pay slips, she noticed, went backwards from the previous Friday for a period of about six months.

They probably explained the neatness of the bedroom, she thought. If nothing else for the moment. In relation to certain things, Birdy clearly had a tidy mind.

She handed the pay slips for checking to a young detective.

She turned, intending to descend the stairs and question Kylie in the kitchen again.

But the woman had climbed behind them and was now standing in the bedroom doorway, staring curiously at the activity inside.

'Do you know where Birdy was working the last few months, Kylie?' Rainey asked.

The woman shook her head and shrugged.

'*Was* he working?' Rainey persisted.

'What?'

'Did he go out every morning, come back every evening? Was it regular?'

'Are you having me on, girl? Birdy wouldn't have a job like that.'

'Right. Did he ever mention anything about Crastina?'

'Crastina?'

'That's right.'

'What's that?'

'It's a charity. Its founder is Joseph Manning. It, ah—'

'No.'

'It works as an aid agency, Kylie. You know, famine in Africa. Have you heard of it?'

'I think so.'

'It also has, ah, *foundations* here in Ireland. You know what I mean? Drug-rehabilitation centres. Shelters for the homeless. That sort of thing. Did Birdy work for any of those?'

Kylie's face was blank again.

Frustrated, Rainey turned to the sergeant. 'What does Crastina have here in Cork?'

'Birdy isn't working in Cork, if that's what you're saying,' Kylie put in suddenly. 'He'd go up to Galway sometimes. I know that.'

'Galway. Right.'

Rainey looked again at the cheque among the banknotes. The signature belonged to Harry Fame, a director of Crastina. Crastina's headquarters were in Galway.

From behind her, the detective who was still sifting through the pay slips grunted with sudden interest. 'Huh!' he cried. He extracted a small page that had been torn from a ringed shorthand notepad and read from it. 'In what year did Columbus discover America?'

'1492,' someone muttered automatically from behind him.

'No, that's not right,' Kylie told them casually from the doorway.

For a while, no one said anything to her.

For a while, no one even looked at her.

For a while, everyone in the room, except for Kylie herself, shared the same perception.

Her interjection had given some mysterious significance to an item they would otherwise have ignored.

They had no idea what that significance might be. They only sensed that Kylie could have no reliable awareness of dates, no detailed knowledge of history, no casual interest in explorers. The question and the historically inaccurate answer had stuck in her mind because she had either heard them repeatedly or caught them once in unforgettable circumstances.

It had that scent of concealment about it that cops always get hooked on.

In the tense silence, Rainey worked with her eyes to get the young detective who had responded to the question to pick up the thread again.

Thursday, 12 November

Kylie was like a child, she knew. She'd talk innocently off the top of her head all night and then clam up at the first sign of a direct question. Like all children, she felt that questions had answers which she would inevitably get wrong.

Finally, the young detective took the hint. 'I *thought* it was 1492.'

Kylie stared at him blankly from the doorway. Not holding out. Not even thinking. Just not *engaged* any more.

The silence lasted again for another minute or two afterwards. And then became too heavy. And too intimidating.

Rainey broke it.

She called the sergeant from the room and went downstairs to talk to him, asking another detective to keep Kylie from dogging her footsteps again.

'You're going to have to take her in for questioning,' she told the sergeant. 'You're going to have to work around this Columbus lark. To be brutal about it, if you break the news of Birdy's death at the right time, it might flow out of its own accord. It might all be nothing, of course. You can never tell with Kylie. I'll keep in touch. I'm going up to Galway.'

'Crastina, is it?' the sergeant guessed.

Something in his tone make Rainey stare at him.

And he seemed to have a knowing, cynical look on his face.

PART TWO

Friday, 13 November

ONE

1

Eddie Halpin watched the fax printing slowly from the machine in his study.

It was a little after noon the following morning.

About two hours earlier, he'd sent a photocopy of an old photograph to Caroline French in Dingle. The photograph had a handwritten caption, *Dublin, November 1940*, in the bottom right-hand corner and showed in close-up a group of four young men in army uniforms with their arms around each others' shoulders.

The pair on the outside had never been identified by Halpin. The two in the centre were Joseph Manning and Harry Fame, serving as reservists in the Local Defence Force at the time.

On the covering sheet, Halpin had requested Caroline French to drive the few miles out to Anna Rosen's farm and ask the old woman if any of the four was the stranger who had come looking for her brother Alan before his death.

Now the same photograph was coming back to him along the line.

And presumably with the answer.

But the machine, outdated anyway, was struggling to cope with the large amount of graphic. The photograph had been fed from the top. And apart from the hairstyles of the four young men, nothing was apparent yet.

Beside him, his sister Linda was waiting for an answer to the question she'd just asked.

She'd passed most of the previous night in accident and emergency, only to learn that her boyfriend had nothing more serious than heavy bruising.

Tomkin hadn't come back with her to Snipe Avenue. And hadn't wanted her to return, either. But she was anxious about her brother. And she was still driving his BMW.

Halpin had given her a brief account of the incident on the Kerry mountains and some idea of the original purpose of his journey.

'His name is Finnegan,' he told her now. 'The guy who tried to push me off the mountain. I saw him at St Kieron's House in Kinvara, about two weeks ago. He has something to do with Crastina.'

'What were you doing in Kinvara?'

'I had a short meeting with Joseph Manning.'

'About what?'

'I was looking for background. Ireland's attitude to its Jewish citizens during the war in Europe. The Catholic Church's attitude. Also, Manning anonymously helped Rosen's family after Alan's death.'

'You must've talked about other things.'

'We talked a little about Manning's recent travels. It was a brief meeting.'

'I mean, more sensitive things. Like the finances of Crastina, for instance.'

'I dealt with all that a year ago, Linda, when I was researching the essay on the history of Crastina. Manning's personal life. The founding and development of the organisation. Manning's family. No one objected to it then. This time,

Friday, 13 November

we talked about Rosen, about the Jewish community in Ireland.'

'So what are you saying, Eddie? That Manning didn't want you asking about Rosen and told Finnegan to blow you off the side of a mountain just to keep you quiet?'

'You can't assume it was only Manning who might have reacted. I don't believe he did, anyway. There was a group of them in Kinvara. Manning's driver and bodyguard, Jimmy Kyne. His personal secretary, Michael Carter. Harry Fame. Finnegan. The curator of St Kieron's, Roger Walcott.'

'Roger *Walcott*?'

'He's an English Catholic. And also ex-British Army, apparently.'

'Strange combination.'

'Not really. It's common enough. But he's a strange *character*.'

'So why did Finnegan come after you? And which of the others knew about it?'

Halpin didn't answer. Because he didn't know. Not yet.

Beside him, the uncovered heads of the four young men were now visible on the fax paper. Joseph Manning at twenty had been tall and dignified, with a pale complexion and features that seemed too severe ever to fully relax into laughter. The young Harry Fame had been plump and pleased with himself, his face rakish and bright-eyed.

Contrasting types, Halpin thought. According to popular perception, they were saint and rogue, mystic and joker . . .

'I've got to get a faster machine,' he muttered irritably.

Through the open doors, across the hall from the front room, they could hear the television coverage of the American President's arrival at Dublin Airport. The military bands. The noisy crowds. The excited commentator drawing attention for the hundredth time to the wonder of an American black man boasting nineteenth-century Irish ancestors. 'When General Sir John Lenfesty was appointed Governor of Jamaica in the early

1800s, his secret liaison with a black slave girl called Sarah may well have raised eyebrows back at his ancestral seat in County Clare . . .'

And ironically, the loud cheering from in there coincided with the page finally dropping out of the fax machine in the study.

Halpin picked it up, noticing immediately the thin handwriting under the images of Manning and Fame.

He looked first at the caption for Manning.

It read, *Anna Rosen says this the young man who was so generous to family when brother Alan fell ill with pneumonia and later when killed in German bombing.*

Halpin glanced sharply across, under Fame's jovial image. *Anna Rosen says this the stranger who called to their home. Doesn't know name.*

He gave the page to Linda.

Fifty-seven years ago, he thought. A long time. A *lifetime*. How much could he now rely on Anna Rosen's memory and her judgement?

But he knew, deep within himself, that she was certain, and that she was right. He'd talked before to Jewish survivors of the Holocaust, preparing an essay on their post-war settlement in Ireland. They all carried faces with them in their minds, as clear as the snapshots in other people's wallets. And though Anna Rosen hadn't suffered like them, she'd obviously shared the same watchful dread and the same immediate recognition of the enemy.

'Harry Fame rang me a few days after I met him in Kinvara,' Halpin confided now. 'On some pretext about wanting to help with my research. I had no interest in him, really. But he was very nervous. And he claimed that he'd never actually known Alan Rosen. I still had little interest in him. But I suppose I must have stumbled across something down there then.'

'Are you sure it's worth killing you for?' Linda asked him. 'It was over fifty years ago. Whatever it was.'

'It must be, Linda. Money, perhaps? Fame lives in luxury. Presumably from the public's donations to Crastina. Or reputation, maybe? He's a director of the charity, a childhood friend of Manning's. It must be worth killing for.'

'Are you going to tell the police?'

He shook his head. 'No, no. No police. When it comes to conservative politics mixed with a lot of religion, I don't really trust our guardians. Too many bad experiences in the past.'

'You mean Char—?'

'I mean the lot of them!'

'You're wrong about that, you know. I told you you were wrong at the time.'

'I don't think so, Linda.'

'So how are you going to protect yourself?'

'Not with the police. I don't have the evidence. All they'll do is alert Fame to my suspicions and put him on his guard. I need to flush him out first.'

'How are you going to manage that?'

He took the fax back from her and slowly shook his head while considering it. 'I don't know.'

'I do,' she asserted casually.

'How?'

'*I'll* do it.'

He looked up at her. Ten years before, when she was twelve, their parents' separation had badly scarred her self-confidence and she'd been full of reckless enthusiasms ever since. For causes. For self-improvement. And for boyfriends.

'Let's get some breakfast,' he suggested.

He went to the kitchen, put on toast and boiling water, and took out a couple of Rombauts coffee filters, butter and marmalade.

She followed him, irritated by his dismissiveness.

'Didn't you hear me?' she insisted. 'I said I'll do it.'

'How?' he demanded.

'I'll ring Fame up. Put the wind up him. I don't need to say anything definite, just hint. Then I'll arrange to meet him.'

He took the toasted bread, put it on a plate and brought it to the table. He dropped two fresh slices into the toaster. He poured boiled water into the coffee filters and put a lid on each.

'He tried to have me killed, love,' he said gently. 'I don't think he's going to crumble before either your charm or your muscle.'

'I've done this before, you know, Eddie. I did a big drug dealer in Dublin. If you do it properly, it's perfectly safe.'

He raised his eyebrows in disbelief. 'Come on, Linda. You're a trainee journalist. They're not going to let you loose on unprotected drug dealers.'

'It's true! So what do you say?'

'What do I say? Let me have some breakfast. And let me think about it.'

2

In front of the dressing-room mirror, Jimmy Kyne brushed his hair and the trouser legs of his grey suit and polished his brown shoes.

He thought about wearing the shoulder holster and its Walther semi-automatic pistol, but threw them instead into the open suitcase on the bed.

He slipped on his jacket, made a last adjustment to his pale blue tie and left the bedroom to climb down the oak stairway of the medieval town house in the centre of Galway city that was Crastina's temporary Irish headquarters.

At the bottom, he looked through the stained-glass door of

the small chapel and saw the distorted image of Joseph Manning, kneeling at the altar with his arms spread wide and his head lowered in prayer.

As always, Manning was dressed in a plain white robe and brown sandals.

Kyne gently pushed the door and stepped quietly in. But he didn't stay. He just satisfied himself that the old man was safe and undisturbed and that the place was otherwise empty. Then he left again.

Kyne was forty-eight years old this year. And he was a model testament to the charity's claim that those who sought its help invariably learned to help themselves and became members of Crastina's wider community while doing so.

In the early seventies, the young Kyne, born into inner-city poverty, had been a tearaway driver for a gang of Dublin bank robbers. But the same comfort with excitement that had made him sharp behind the wheel had also hurtled him into an addiction to heroin in his late teens.

Somewhere along the road he'd lost a younger sister. She was eighteen years old when he smashed into a wall while racing a stolen BMW.

But somewhere along the way, and maybe only a few days short of suicide, he'd also crawled into a drug clinic Crastina had just established in Dublin's inner city. And he'd had the luck to meet a strange, middle-aged character who dressed in white robes and brown sandals. A man who took no pity on him, but who actually demanded something from him.

In the world of Crastina, as he'd quickly learned, everything could be put to good use. Even a life of crime.

Joseph Manning hadn't tried to change the young Jimmy Kyne. He'd just redirected his muscle and his sharpness behind the wheel into the roles of bodyguard and driver.

Like most reformed criminals, though, Kyne was now a little over the top.

He was fiercely protective. And he was fiercely watchful. Even in Crastina's own headquarters.

Not that Kyne had much to do with Crastina's general security these days. Over twenty-five years, the organisation had slowly outgrown both him and his personal touch. His mind had stubbornly refused to expand along with it. He knew nothing about the dangers of supplying aid to a turbulent African nation. And nothing about the hazards of drug rehabilitation on the streets of New York.

Security now was the responsibility of a commercial firm that called itself Javert International.

Opportunists, Kyne dismissed them sourly. Unreliable mercenaries. And totally impersonal.

Because, like most reformed criminals, Kyne was also scornful of anything less than true devotion and total dedication. It was the *intensity* that measured the worth.

All in all, he didn't much like the new breed of Crastina employees. Particularly those who had scrambled on the gravy train during the hectic last decade. All the accountants and public-relations people. The analysts and the spin doctors. All the ones, as he described them contemptuously, who thought that there was nothing wrong with them before they joined . . .

3

Eddie Halpin drank his coffee, but forgot about the toast. He stared vacantly through the open door at the television in the front room, but without registering any of the images.

'You can ring him,' he said finally to Linda. 'Harry Fame. See what his reaction is. But that's all. We'll figure how to take it from there.'

Friday, 13 November

'Is his home number in your book?'

She was already gone, making for the telephone table by the front door, before he'd finished nodding.

He took his coffee with him as he followed her. He stood in the doorway of the study and watched her.

She dialled. But as her expression went from expectant to dull, it was obvious that there was no answer from the other side.

'Try Crastina's temporary headquarters here in the city,' he suggested. 'They've built a new one in Kinvara, but it's not open yet.'

She checked the number in the book and dialled again.

'Oh, hi!' she said suddenly. 'Could I speak to Mr Harry Fame, please?' She listened, then winked across at Halpin. Her face tightened with concentration once more, though, as she said, 'Hi! Look, you don't know me yet, but I think I've got a little problem you could help me with . . . what? . . . well, you see, I know what your little secret is . . . what? . . . well, the name Alan Rosen must mean something dangerous to you, does it . . . ?'

She listened, smiled and gave a thumbs-up sign to Halpin with her free hand.

She said, 'Well, we won't talk about that now. Maybe later. But it must be worrying you, mustn't it? Otherwise you wouldn't go to the extremes you have, would you?'

As she laughed and drew a breath, the front doorbell rang.

She was so absorbed in her pursuit that she reacted naturally. Without thinking.

With the receiver crooked between her shoulder and her face, she reached out to open the door.

Still too trusting. And still not in the groove of being careful and suspicious.

Halpin was too slow to stop her. Retarded by his wariness about revealing his presence to Fame at the other end of the line, he watched her helplessly as she got to the latch before he could even push himself away from the study doorway. So that he was straining uselessly forward, with his right arm outstretched, while the front door was already swinging inwards towards him.

Linda was still talking animatedly. 'Well, I don't know if that's the best idea, you see, because I don't . . .'

She tailed off. Her face betrayed astonishment. Her shoulders slumped, allowing the phone to slip from under her chin and drift away from her.

Halpin caught the door. He pulled it wider. And looked around it.

Standing outside in the weak morning sunshine, dressed in a blue denim jacket and jeans, was Charlotte Rainey.

She stared inwards at the pair in the hallway.

'Hi, Eddie,' she said finally. 'Hi, Linda.'

Linda dragged the telephone back and muttered faintly into it. 'What? No, no. What? Hold on a minute, will you? I, ah . . .'

She clamped her palm over the receiver and looked appealingly at Halpin for directions.

4

Jimmy Kyne's unhappy reflections in the corridor outside the chapel were broken by the voice of the receptionist over the PA system, summoning him to the main desk.

He weaved slowly through the packing crates that were cluttering the passageways, thinking again to himself that this move, from the medieval style here in Galway to the sterile new headquarters just completed in Kinvara, pretty much

Friday, 13 November

summed up the wrong paths that had been taken over the last few years.

Harry Fame was already at the desk before him, talking on the telephone, and Kyne thought at first that it was the old man who wanted to see him.

He liked Fame. It was true that the old rogue was a little flashy in his clothes for a man in his mid-seventies and a little showy in his lifestyle for a director of a charity. But he had one virtue that outweighed the faults. He came from the old days. He was a childhood friend of Joseph Manning's and had been with him for the length of the long journey.

The old man looked uncomfortable now, though. He had his back to the receptionist. His head was tucked into his hunched shoulders, so that only his thin white hair was really visible, and he was mumbling self-consciously into the mouthpiece.

When he saw Kyne approaching, he twisted again. Like a dog protecting a bone from circling thieves.

Kyne still overheard a little of the conversation.

'No, no,' Fame was muttering. 'Not at all, no . . . Why don't I ring you back? . . . Well, no, you'd have to go through the switchboard again, you see . . . It would be better if I could ring you directly from my office . . .'

Kyne took a note from the receptionist and left. He walked back again through the central hall, but turned right and under the stairs at the doors of the chapel. He opened the back door and stepped outside into the small secluded garden at the rear of the house.

Manning's personal secretary, Michael Carter, was sitting on a white bench under an elm tree, waiting for him.

Another of the dry professionals, Kyne thought disdainfully. And another that he didn't much take to.

'Ah, Kyne!' Carter said. 'You got my note. Sit down. Sit down.'

He indicated a single garden chair that he'd placed opposite the bench. But Kyne ignored the offer and sat down next to him.

Carter was one of those who found the physical closeness of others distressing.

He was a small man, who didn't seem to enjoy very much in life. His pallid face, its roundness exaggerated by circular spectacles and a smooth bald head, seemed set in a permanent look of distaste.

Kyne, with his squat and powerful build and his lined face that had the colour and the texture of a hazelnut kernel, looked like a different species beside him.

And it always pleased Kyne to make the shrivelled little secretary squirm.

Carter tried to manoeuvre a space for himself, but found the armrest of the wrought-iron bench too painful against his ribs when he moved. He smiled weakly, and decided to get the business quickly over with.

'Now, Kyne, the schedule,' he said sharply. He detached a typewritten sheet from the sheaf he held in his hands and passed it to Kyne. 'You already know about today, I take it?'

Kyne nodded. 'Yes.'

'This afternoon we're going to inspect the progress of the new headquarters in Kinvara. We'll stay the night at St Kieron's House.'

'I already know about today, Carter.'

'Quite. Yes. In any case, we travel to Dublin for the ceremony at North Strand tomorrow afternoon. The reception at the American Embassy is tomorrow night. The times are listed there. Sunday morning must be kept free.'

'What for?'

Carter sighed. 'What for?' he repeated haughtily. 'For the official opening of our new headquarters, Kyne. That's what for. Now, if you would kindly—'

Friday, 13 November

They both looked up as the back door of the house was noisily opened.

Neglecting to close it again behind him, Harry Fame strode into the garden, carrying an old-fashioned walking stick that had a crooked brass handle. He didn't immediately notice the others. He looked distracted and seemed to be heading for the end of the garden, where a locked gate led to a lane way outside.

Carter coughed. Very loudly. His breath quite visible in the crisp November sunshine.

It wasn't intended as a polite warning. It was an expression of annoyance at being interrupted.

Fame started and pulled up when he heard the sound. He stared for a while, totally bewildered, at the pair sitting on the bench. Then he raised his stick in greeting, turned sharply and walked back to the house.

5

Charlotte Rainey assumed that the stiff behaviour of Eddie and Linda Halpin at the doorway on Snipe Avenue was just natural embarrassment and she squeezed between them when neither returned her greeting.

The strong smell of fresh coffee and toast in the hallway immediately triggered memories for her. Nothing specific. Not a particular day or a particular incident. More a way of life. The feel of mornings as they used to be. And weren't any more.

She turned right, into the front room, without waiting for the invitation.

She glanced quickly around. Bare pine floor. Light oak

bureau-bookcase. Glass coffee-table. Black leather couch. And that gross, commanding television.

Nothing much had changed, she saw.

Not even the photograph of herself and Halpin in hiking gear on the summit of Mount Brandon in Kerry. It was still hanging in the alcove to the right of the chimney-breast.

A thought struck her. Was it just coincidence? Or had their humour really improved with elevation? Mount Brandon. The Comeraghs. The Pennines in England. Had it been so *rare*, whatever they'd once shared between them?

Because the toast and coffee, pleasant in themselves, hadn't brought back purely happy memories. Breakfasts had never been *easy* in this house. Unlike . . .

They'd camped, she remembered now, that weekend they'd climbed Mount Brandon. They'd been woken at six on Sunday morning, by a dumb sheep chewing on the guy-ropes. They'd laughed about it. And accepted the chance to make love before the dawn. And before the coffee . . .

When Halpin followed her in and closed the door behind him before switching off the television, she was still standing in front of the photograph.

'Doing any climbing lately, Eddie?' she wondered.

'Physical or social?' he asked.

The question was phrased as a joke. In his usual style. But the tone was sharp.

Light banter, she understood, was going to be discouraged. Along with gentle laments for the past.

'What brings you to Galway, Charlotte?' he asked directly.

She sat on the couch by the coffee-table, slipped off her jacket and folded it over the armrest. 'Oh, you know . . . concern, Eddie.'

He smiled dubiously. But he said nothing. He finished the coffee he'd brought in with him and placed the mug on the wooden mantelpiece.

Friday, 13 November

'Anything on your mind, Eddie?' she wondered.

'On yours, surely,' he said. 'If concern brought you here.'

She leaned forward in the couch, ready to question him more closely. But Linda, who'd been talking quietly on the phone in the hall, opened the door at that point, stepped in, and swept a totally different atmosphere along with her.

'God, sorry, Charlotte!' she apologised loudly. 'I couldn't get away. I like the jacket. Is it new?'

Rainey stared at her.

She and Linda had been friends. She knew that Halpin's sister was an educated, intelligent woman, with no more than a casual interest in fashion, and that she very rarely made remarks on people's appearance.

It must be embarrassment again, she decided.

And she wondered if she could play on it.

'I was just talking to Eddie about Crastina, Linda,' she said.

'Oh, yeah?' Linda confirmed.

Before Halpin's warning gesture could reach her.

Rainey watched the two of them exchange rapid glances. His was loaded with caution and disappointment. Hers was apologetic and regretful.

Good, she thought.

She said, 'What did you find out about them, Eddie, that's got them so annoyed?'

He wearily shook his head. 'What are you talking about, Charlotte?'

'You're the historian, aren't you?'

'Uh-huh.'

'You research the development of organisations like Crastina.'

'That was last year's work.'

'You dig up things that people would sometimes prefer to leave buried.'

'No, you were right the first time. I'm a historian.'

'But at least you get your dates right.'

'I try.'

'Do you know when Columbus discovered America?' she threw in.

'1492.'

'I don't think that's the right answer, Eddie.'

She watched them both again.

There was silence. But only a puzzled one.

There was no recognition. No fear. No anxiety.

All she saw in their eyes was the new realisation that the question had significance.

'Hey!' Linda said breezily then. She laughed, looked at her watch and shrugged her shoulders. 'I've got to go out, Charlotte. And I'm late already. I have to change.'

As soon as she'd left the room, Halpin offered coffee.

He went immediately to the kitchen, taking the response to the question for granted. And hoping, Rainey thought, for a private conversation with Linda.

He didn't manage it.

Linda stayed in the bedroom, and then, as if being deliberately perverse, reappeared only when Halpin was juggling mugs and jugs and sugar bowls and was back in the front room. She'd dressed in blue jeans, a red and yellow rugby shirt and a black leather jacket and was holding a small brown rucksack in her right hand.

'I was going to have coffee as well,' she announced. 'But you've only got one filter left, Eddie. I put it back in the fridge for you. See you, Charlotte!'

'Bye, Linda.'

The crockery in his hands delayed Halpin.

'Linda!' he called.

But she was already gone, opening the street door and skipping through and closing it behind her again.

'Excuse me a minute,' Halpin said to Rainey.

Friday, 13 November

He hurried after his sister, leaving the doors swinging open.

When he came back, it wasn't necessary to ask whether he'd caught her or not. He obviously hadn't. His face was creased with irritation.

He sat in the armchair opposite Rainey, forgetting to return to his coffee.

And apparently forgetting about Rainey, too.

'Eddie?' she summoned him.

'Uh-huh?'

'Are you with me?'

'I'm here.'

'I heard you were involved in an accident, Eddie,' she told him. 'A man died, going over the side of a mountain in Kerry.'

'I was on a little touring holiday.'

'And now you're back.'

'I didn't feel like continuing afterwards.'

'I was down there last night as well, you know. I checked the scene. I know that there was more to the incident than what you told the local guards. You want to share it with me?'

'Share it with you?' he repeated incredulously.

'Uh-huh.'

'Have you been in America, Charlotte?'

'The van driver. He passed you coming in the other direction, didn't he? Then he turned and came back at you. Why did he do that?'

'You've been on some police course in America, haven't you?' he persisted. 'With the FBI or something.'

She sighed, sat back in the couch and asked irritably, 'What about it?'

'That's where they *share* things, don't they? In America.'

'It's a phrase, yeah.'

'Except they don't, of course. Share anything. It's a culture dedicated to acquiring. The cute *phrase* conceals the reality.'

'Forget I used it, Eddie.'

'Have you ever noticed, Charlotte, that the less there is of something in the modern world, the more it's talked up. Like employment. The less jobs there are, the more career guidance there is. There's an inverse relationship. And on that point. As I remember it, Charlotte, the last time we shared something—'

'It was a bed,' she interrupted. 'In the bedroom across the hall here.'

'There was also the small matter of a confidence.'

She shook her head, preparing to object. But his momentum was already irresistible. He was too quick for her.

He went on, 'I told you I had information about an illegal demonstration by right-wing students. The next morning, myself and half a dozen other activists were arrested for questioning. The demonstration went ahead. We spent the night in jail.'

'That wasn't my fault, Eddie,' she claimed.

'Come again?' he invited.

'It wasn't my fault.'

'*Nothing's* ever your fault, Charlotte. This is your burden in life. You're an angel born into a secular world.'

'I make mistakes. Like everyone else.'

'It's not about making mistakes. It's that *your* mistakes are genuine human errors; *mine* are expressions of a darker character. *Your* intentions are always pure; *mine* are sometimes sullied. Like I said, you're an angel condemned to a secular world.'

For the first time, she felt emotionally upset.

He was misusing privilege, she thought.

In their year-long relationship, one of the things she'd confided to him was that her hopeless father's term of affection for her had been *angel*. It was an expression that she'd grown to hate. Like the word *share* that Halpin himself had objected to earlier, it had become a useless substitute for attention and responsibility.

Friday, 13 November

Which was part of his point, she supposed. As also was the demonstration of how hurtful a misuse of confidence could be.

The two of them, they hadn't actually seen each other since that awful muddle of a separation six months before. There was unfinished business. There was accumulated bitterness. There were speeches and jibes that had been sharpened over months of lonely resentment.

It was, she realised, their shared passion for civil rights that had first brought them into contact with each other. And it was the same intensity that had driven them apart again. His suspicions about her colleagues. Her knowledge of extremists among his associates.

And what else could they do now but return to the same unanswered accusations?

'Have you ever written down, Charlotte,' Halpin asked, 'the names of the people you discuss things with? Your colleagues. Your superiors.'

'Hasn't it ever occurred to you that the Judas might be in your *own* group, Eddie?'

It registered with him, she saw. His face, tense with rage, suddenly loosened into concern, into puzzlement. As if a vague worry had just clarified.

They stared at each other for a while. Tense. And heated with anger.

'Crastina, Eddie,' she said then. 'You haven't told me what you found out about them.'

'Nothing to find *out*, Charlotte. You're even flogging the wrong dead horse.'

But she always knew when he was concealing something from her. The effort to hold a neutral expression always pressed his lips together into what looked like a small, but slightly pained smile.

She put her empty coffee mug on the glass table between them, stood up and skirted the table to cross to him. Standing in front of him, she stooped and placed the forefinger of her right hand across the tense lips that had betrayed his secrecy.

'You'd better be careful, Eddie,' she cautioned. 'If what I think happened in the Kerry mountains last night actually did, then you'd better watch your back very closely. Or learn to trust me again.'

TWO

1

In the small church at St Kieron's in Kinvara, a little after two o'clock that afternoon, Roger Walcott knelt by himself in a side pew, praying intently for guidance.

The morning newspaper lay on the seat beside him, over to his right. It wasn't open at the article that interested him, though. Even here, his caution was habitual. But he'd already read and studied the item. A short paragraph on page five, simply reporting that a man had died in the Kerry mountains near Dingle the night before when his car had plunged off the side of the cliff in heavy fog. The dead man's name hadn't yet been released, but it was believed that he was holidaying in the area and originally from Galway.

And yet, Walcott was still on edge. Still unsettled and depressed. Still brooding on the incident at Halpin's house.

He was deeply uncomfortable with failure. It hung around him like a hair shirt. A constant taunt. A constant irritation. It revived old resentments. And it sharpened the permanent ones.

He might've contacted McKelvey to report the problem. But his instructions were rigid. McKelvey was not to be approached.

He might've gone again that morning to Halpin's house. But again, his orders were simplistic. And dangerously inflexible. He was to hold St Kieron's all that Friday.

So he held. And waited. And prayed.

But it seemed as if McKelvey's crude arrangements had a genius for unravelling.

A little after two fifteen, as he lifted his bowed head to the crucifix in front of him, Walcott caught a blurred glimpse through the window at his side of someone slipping past along the gravel driveway outside.

The window he was kneeling beside had stained glass. He rose and walked immediately to the next window. But that too was opaque. And again he saw only a shadow moving quickly out of sight.

Unable to put a face to it, he imagined the worst of intruders.

He genuflected, hurried down the aisle and tugged at the church's heavy doors. He ran through the corridor in the west wing, past the dining area and small reception, and turned right towards the main entrance.

He stepped out, on to the gravel driveway, and searched immediately to his left.

A figure was disappearing around the tower house, about thirty yards away from him.

But it wasn't anyone he'd feared or expected.

It was a thin, short-haired girl, dressed in black jeans and a faded yellow T-shirt.

Walcott stopped and cursed softly to himself. Partly with relief. But mostly with astonishment.

The girl's name was Josie Thomas. And he had inherited her from his predecessor. Damaged or abused in some way that he still wasn't familiar with, and adopted by Crastina when her parents had failed her, she now used St Kieron's as more or less a permanent refuge.

But she shouldn't be there this weekend. He'd already arranged for her to stay in Kinvara village with the Rushes. He'd seen her off the afternoon before, watched her clinging

Friday, 13 November

tightly to Margaret Rushe's hand as they walked down the driveway . . .

Exasperated by this new complication, he called out to her sharply and set off in pursuit.

An unsurfaced footpath, beaten into the grass by visitors, looped around the tower itself. And the thing changed its character as it went. At the back of the tower, above a sheer descent of a hundred yards to the rocks and the sand and the breaking waves, it suddenly turned into a narrow ledge overlooking Kinvara Bay. Only a frail wooden fence offered any protection from the drop.

The girl wasn't there.

Remembering stories of her threats and her previous suicide attempts, Walcott leaned cautiously on the fence and looked over and down.

Below him, the *Grey Witch* was heading back out to sea.

And from its deck, Bill Canavan was waving at someone on the beach below the tower.

It had to be the girl, of course. She hadn't walked around there, after all. Instead, she'd taken the steep path down the side of the headland to the beach.

Walcott cursed again.

But before he could get off the ledge and follow her, a voice startled him.

'Hi, there!'

He swivelled, grasping the wooden rail to steady himself.

At the edge of the tower, leaning against the corner, was a long-haired young woman. She was wearing a black leather jacket and blue jeans and she was carrying a small brown rucksack on her back.

2

This nonsense with the last coffee filter in the fridge. It irritated Eddie Halpin.

He stacked up on coffee filters. He *hoarded* the damn things. There was an entire press in the kitchen slavishly devoted to an impressive range of brands.

So of course, there had to be a note awaiting him.

And that was what annoyed him. The *style* of communication. The taste for artificial excitement, for juvenile adventure and subterfuge. It was typical of Linda's palate. Typical of her appetite for the new and the sensational.

But Halpin was in the mood for being easily irritated that afternoon.

Charlotte Rainey's reappearance had unsettled him. Deeply. As only someone he still had intense, irrational feelings for could manage to.

It was just a revival of the old complication, he knew.

How could he relax with her? He was a civil-rights campaigner. She was a policewoman. How could he trust her? What dubious tricks was she getting up to when he closed his eyes while kissing her?

She was devious.

And paradoxically, he thought, she was too honest as well. Having given her oath to uphold the law, what weight would the testament of love carry afterwards? Could he rely on her vow at the altar to relinquish all masters except the new one?

Like hell he could.

And yet . . .

Friday, 13 November

Always that *yet*. That ugliest of the language's short qualifiers.

He yanked open the door of the fridge, disturbed an egg, but caught it in mid-air before it shattered.

The single coffee filter was inside its foil wrapping on the upper tray, concealed by a wall of yoghurts. The note inside, written in faint pencil in Linda's small hand on a blue index card, said, *I've arranged to meet Harry Fame. I'm going to drop down to Kinvara as well. I have to call in on Tom, so I'll probably ring you from there. See you later.*

For a moment, Halpin was distracted from anxiety by further annoyance.

What did it mean, he wondered. Did it mean that she was going first to meet Fame? And *where* was she meeting him? At Crastina's headquarters in Galway? Or at his home in Clarinbridge? Or had Kinvara, on the other hand, just belatedly occurred to her as a handy filler before a later meeting with Fame?

She had to be stopped, in any case, he decided.

It was the point to her childish elusion earlier. She knew that he'd restrain her.

But she had to be saved. If not from embarrassment at St Kieron's House, then at least from the obvious danger of blundering into Fame.

He looked at his watch. It was well past two o'clock.

Rainey had stayed more than thirty minutes after Linda, he calculated. Enough for Linda to comfortably reach any of her intended destinations. The city centre. Clarinbridge. Kinvara.

He went to the telephone in the front hall and rang the number of Crastina's Galway headquarters, reading it from the book Linda had left carelessly open on the table. Had Rainey also taken note on her way out?

Of course she had, because . . .

A woman with a high-pitched voice eventually answered his query. 'Mr Fame's line is busy at the moment, sir. Will you hold?'

'I just want to find out if he's still there.'

'Just a moment, sir.'

The switch played *Adeste Fidelis* for him while he was on hold.

He cursed its monotony. Once. Very vehemently. And the line instantly went dead.

Grumbling with frustration, he disconnected and redialled.

Another, younger operator took him this time. He went through the same routine. And waited again. And again listened to *Adeste Fidelis*. Although silently now.

'Mr Fame has just left, sir,' he was told then. 'If you had rung five minutes earlier—'

'Did he say where he was going?'

'Is this Mr Walcott?'

'Yes.'

'He's been trying to get through to you, Mr Walcott, since—

'Where is he going?'

'He said you could contact him at his home all afternoon. Do you have the number of—'

Halpin hung up and paced, constantly checking his watch, impatiently allowing time for Fame's Mercedes to make the short hop between Galway and Clarinbridge. If that was where the old man was going and where Linda had arranged to meet him.

Because Fame, too, he accepted, also had a history of elusiveness.

He'd disappeared from Dublin, for instance, after the end of the Second World War. No one knew to where. Or to what.

The last time he'd been seen in the city was September 1941, at the funeral of Joseph Manning's older sister, Bridget. The young woman, only twenty-three at the time, had killed herself and was therefore denied a Roman Catholic burial in consecrated ground. Another of the great personal tragedies that had impelled Manning towards a life of reclusive self-sacrifice.

Very few had attended Bridget Manning's removal. But among them was Harry Fame, incongruously dressed in a flashy woollen overcoat and a fine silk scarf, and with a strange, fur-coated woman on his arm.

Halpin had photographs of the burial. All monochrome, of course. But Fame still seemed too colourful for the occasion in all of them. He seemed out of place. Not belonging any more to the world that had reared him. As if he was *celebrating* rather than mourning.

Shortly afterwards, he'd emigrated. And he hadn't returned for almost twenty-five years, apparently. Until 1969. Lured then, no doubt, by Crastina's new-found wealth and prestige . . .

At two thirty, abandoning his reflections, Halpin finally tried Fame's home number. The phone was engaged. When he tried again, it rung for only half a tone before being snatched up.

The old man's voice said urgently, nervously, 'Fame. Yes?'

'Sorry,' Halpin mumbled. 'Wrong number.'

He hung up immediately, collected his jacket and his car keys from the front room, and left.

3

'You must be Roger Walcott, are you?' the young woman asked. 'The caretaker here.'

'Curator,' Walcott said stiffly.

'Right. Curator.'

Walcott immediately sensed danger. The woman's manner, her tone of *superior* knowledge, made him instantly wary.

And besides, he wasn't comfortable with belligerent women. No more than he could've been comfortable with a rebellious, disruptive child. Both were unsettling to him. And distracting.

'How did you manage to get in here?' he demanded.

She smiled at him breezily. 'Oh, I did all the conventional things. I rang the doorbells and I used the knockers. There was no answer. I thought I'd look around.'

'I mean, into the grounds.'

'From the road. There's no other way, is there?'

'You must have missed the sign on the main gate, then. I'm afraid St Kieron's is closed to visitors this weekend.'

'Is it? Why's that?'

He gestured and strode briskly towards her. Once beside her, his hand swooped down to guide her elbow. 'Please. Allow me.'

She walked with him silently until they reached the grass in front of the tower, at the edge of the gravel driveway. But she asked casually then, 'How do you find it here?'

'I beg your pardon?'

'You're English, aren't you? Ex-British Army. Come across any prejudice at all?'

'I'm afraid you may be confusing me with someone else,' Walcott told her with icy courtesy.

He had no need to lie. Some of the locals already knew and accepted his background. And yet he was cautious. The woman was an enemy, he felt. She did not accept his guidance, as she should have done. His courteous hand on her arm was an irritation to her. He could feel her strong resistance to it.

'I am English, of course,' he conceded. 'But I never served in my country's army. My career since leaving university has been in charity.'

'What did you study?'

'History.'

'Is that right?' she exclaimed. She crooked her long black

hair behind her ear with the fingers of her right hand and said, 'You must know when Columbus discovered America then, do you?'

Walcott frowned, baffled by the question. If the woman was an enemy, he thought, how could she know the password of friendship?

'November,' he said quietly. And waited for her to supply the next response in the sequence.

She only laughed and asked, 'Yeah, but what year?'

And Walcott realised immediately that his reaction to her failure betrayed him.

He didn't lose control for very long. Maybe only a second or two. But in those few moments he felt he compromised everything.

Her partial knowledge was so unexpected. So devastating.

His resistance was so weakened by recent disruption.

He was so off guard.

Inside, he felt confusion. He felt fear and a defensive anger.

But looking at the sudden surprise on the young woman's face, he knew that the emotions must also have shown, however briefly, on his outer expression.

He tried to reel in the damage. 'Columbus?' he repeated.

'Uh-huh.'

'The Spanish explorer—'

'Yeah, right,' she interrupted quickly. She laughed again, with knowing and nervous humour. She shrugged her shoulders to settle the rucksack, glanced at her watch and suddenly moved to slip away from him. 'Got to go,' she said.

But now he wanted to detain her.

Now he desperately needed to sound her out. The depth of her knowledge. Her sources. Her intentions. Her contacts.

Her *name*. Who was this outsider who seemed to know of Columbus?

He'd intended reaching out to take her arm again.

But as he smiled, coldly and briefly, the telephone rang in the reception room behind, distracting him.

And then there was a group of late American tourists on the footpath below, pointing up and taking photographs of the tower.

And she was safe.

Without looking back, she raised a hand as she hurried away from him down the gravel.

He turned from her, still wondering what her gesture meant, and strode inside.

Through the window in reception, while he picked up the receiver, he watched her climb the locked gates at the end of the driveway and chat for a while with the Americans.

'Hello?' he said into the phone.

'Walcott?' the voice on the other side enquired.

'This is Walcott.'

'Harry Fame here,' the voice explained. 'I've been trying to ring you. I've only just got home—'

'What is it?'

'Listen. Was there a woman there in St Kieron's earlier, looking for—?'

'Yes,' Walcott interrupted impatiently.

He looked out the window again and saw her glance nervously back as she left the Americans and took the footpath that arced from St Kieron's down to the village.

'What about her?' he demanded.

'She knows, Walcott,' Fame warned quietly. 'Do you hear me? I'm almost certain that she knows.'

THREE

1

Charlotte Rainey was already on the road, driving towards Harry Fame's home in Clarinbridge after establishing that Fame had left Crastina's headquarters, when the summons came from the local station over her car radio.

Her boss, Chief Superintendent John McQuaid, head of Special Branch, was also in Galway and wanted to talk to her.

She'd expected a tug of the leash. But not so early. And not straight from the top.

Her first testing of the murky waters had already caused some ripples.

All that morning, she'd been trying without success to contact the sergeant in Cork, looking for an update on Kylie Craddock's interrogation. The responses had been suspiciously evasive. The sergeant was out, supervising security for the American President's visit to the city, she'd been told. The guard on the switch had only just come on duty himself. Offhand, no one knew anything about a Ms Craddock . . .

Rainey turned now on the outskirts of Galway, drove back through the city, and left her black Alfa Romeo in the car park at Mill Street garda station.

Needing an inside track on why McQuaid had obviously

flown from Dublin by helicopter that afternoon, she called first on Jarlath Burke in his office.

Burke was a family friend of her mother's. Fifteen years earlier, when she herself had joined the force, he'd already been a detective inspector. Now he was close to retirement age. And still at the same rank.

She remembered him as fatherly from her childhood. And he had probably influenced her choice of career.

He was also a gruff, bad-tempered man, though, who seemed to suffer permanently from an unsettled stomach.

Instead of welcoming her on her rare visits, instead of enquiring about her mother's health and her own progress, he usually had a criticism already prepared.

'What are you after getting yourself into now?' he'd snap at her irritably.

Rainey found him more direct than unsympathetic, however. Once he'd greeted you sourly, he actually listened to you. She liked his toughness, and his expectation of strength in others. The shoulder he offered was less for crying on than for using to regain your balance against.

But today, Burke already had two other detectives sitting in his office when she went to see him.

'Pat Lawlor and Gerry Donahue,' he introduced them. 'Have you met?'

She didn't know either of them.

Lawlor was an old-fashioned man, dressed in brown cords and a check jacket with leather patches on the elbows. Donahue was a young blond in blue jeans and an open-neck shirt. And both had obviously settled in for a long stay.

Rainey stood. Listening impatiently to their banter. Looking uneasily at her watch as the minutes passed. And having to avoid the one topic she'd come to ask advice on.

'I've got to move, Jarlath,' she said finally.

'Well, don't pass the door again on your way back,' Burke

grumbled at her. 'Like you usually do.'
'I'll drop in.'

2

His head was completely shaved and a large swastika had been tattooed on his right forearm. He was wearing a green sleeveless singlet, green camouflage trousers and black Doc Marten boots. The image he'd worked on was one of uncompromising aggression. But when he opened the front door of Harry Fame's house to answer the bell and saw Eddie Halpin standing on the steps outside, he shuddered violently with fright.

His name was Cormac Lowry.

He had one criminal conviction for assaulting a doctor with a baseball bat and another for breaking and entering the home of a left-wing politician. The doctor was supposed to have referred pregnant young Irish women to English abortion clinics. The politician was divorced himself and favoured extending the facility to others.

Most days, Lowry put in his time trying to peddle racist propaganda to an indifferent Galway public. Most nights, he slouched across the city's streets, hoping for trouble.

Halpin described him as one of the more basic building blocks of the conservative right in Ireland. But he was also one of the easiest of the blocks to knock over. Already hooked on booze and drugs, his need now to conceal his addictions from his political friends was just as desperate as the cravings themselves. And Halpin, who had known him since Lowry first dropped out of college a couple of years back, had used him often for information in the past.

'Cormac,' Halpin said casually now. Not betraying his own

astonishment. As if he'd *expected* Lowry to open the door of Harry Fame's house.

Lowry shifted his weight from one foot to the other and stared nervously out of his watery blue eyes. He looked ill. And he had reason to.

A couple of months back, a respected Catholic businessman had died unexpectedly of a heart attack. Less than an hour after handing over a substantial cash donation to Lowry for transfer to Lowry's mysterious political masters.

Lowry's masters had never seen the loot, though. Whoever they were, they could hardly be cynics. They seemed to have swallowed Lowry's tale that the businessman had died before Lowry himself had reached him.

But *Halpin* had seen the money. Accidentally. Coming on Lowry in the street and escorting him back to his local-authority flat to pump him about something else.

The only thing Halpin still didn't know was the intended destination of the lucre. The identity of Lowry's shadowy superiors. The cause the money was meant to serve. Everything else he'd either traced by himself or squeezed out of Lowry.

So Lowry's mouth was fairly dry now when he finally spoke. 'Mr Halpin?' he croaked.

'I'm looking for Harry Fame, Cormac.'

'Mr Fame isn't here.'

'I talked to him on the phone fifteen minutes ago,' Halpin pointed out.

'Right now, anyway,' Lowry qualified. 'He's not here right now.'

Halpin gestured towards the car that was parked on his left, beyond the hedge separating the driveway from the steep garden he'd climbed through. 'His car's still there. That's his, isn't it? The gold Mercedes?'

'He's not here, though,' Lowry repeated. 'Right now.'

'Could I come in, Cormac?'

Friday, 13 November

'What?'

'Do you mind if I step in?'

'Ah, well, you see, it's just—'

'Is there anyone else in the house?'

'No, no, not at the moment. But I can't—'

'Thanks,' Halpin muttered.

He pushed the heavy door and stepped past Lowry.

Fame's place was one of those grey, featureless buildings constructed by landlords on the outskirts of Irish towns in the nineteenth century. All its character was on the inside.

The central hallway Halpin now found himself in, all marble below and delicate plasterwork above and leading towards an oak stairway, had been decorated and furnished with a lot of taste and a lot of expense.

The crude Lowry, his heavy boots sounding noisily as he scurried after Halpin, and his green camouflage clashing with every subtle tint around him, seemed totally absurd in the surroundings. And only capable of wrecking them.

In fact, he'd already started in his own small way.

In the front room to Halpin's right, an open and now half-empty bottle of rare Middleton Irish whiskey and a Waterford glass tumbler were on the mahogany coffee-table.

'What are you *doing* here, Cormac?' Halpin asked.

He kept walking as he spoke, into the front room. And immediately he saw the photograph and the frayed old sheet of personal notepaper lying on the bureau-bookcase in the alcove to the left of the open fireplace.

Lowry followed. And then, seeing the point of Halpin's movement, he tried to squeeze past and get in front. 'Just helping Mr Fame, that's all.'

'Helping him do what, Cormac?'

'Odd jobs, you know. I do that. I work for him.'

A second before Lowry also reached for them, Halpin picked up the photograph and notepaper from the bureau.

The photograph had been taken on a windy day in mid-April 1941, on the broad sands of Sandymount Strand in Dublin. The date and location were written in the bottom right-hand corner. The weather conditions were obvious.

In it, the plump young Harry Fame, overdressed as usual, had his arm around the shoulders of an attractive black-haired woman that Halpin recognised from other photographs as Joseph Manning's older sister, Bridget.

The couple seemed carefree.

But the note revealed otherwise.

It, too, was dated April 1941. It read, *You can't torture me like this, Harry Fame. You simply can't. You can have what you want. Don't make me despair.* It was signed, *Bridget*.

Halpin turned. He poured whiskey into the tumbler on the coffee-table and brought the glass across to where Lowry had slumped in an armchair. But he didn't offer it yet.

'How did Fame travel if he didn't take his car, Cormac?' he asked.

Lowry shook his head. Only his eyeballs didn't move. Because they were locked on the booze. 'I don't know.'

'What do you mean, you don't know?'

'I mean, he must've taken a taxi or got a lift or something. I didn't see him leave, that's all.'

'Did he have a woman with him?'

'Woman? I don't think so, no.'

'When did he leave?'

'Only about ten minutes ago.'

Halpin passed over the drink then. 'Don't move from there, Cormac,' he warned.

Lowry's blue eyes stared at him with sullen fear over the rim of the tumbler as he gulped the alcohol.

Still carrying the photograph and faded notepaper, Halpin left the front room and checked the others on the ground floor,

Friday, 13 November

searching only for people and not noticing any more of the fine detail or impressive furniture. All the rooms were empty. As were the bedrooms on the upper levels.

In one of them, Halpin checked Tom Tomkin's number in the local directory and used the bedside telephone to dial.

When he answered, Tomkin still sounded as if he'd just had dental treatment. 'Hello?' he slurred. 'Yes?'

'This is Eddie Halpin, Tom.'

He could almost *feel* the receiver getting chillier.

'What is it?'

'Has Linda been in touch with you?'

'She rang me earlier.'

'What time?'

'She rang me from the pier in Kinvara. That's where she said she was. Can you believe that?'

'What *time*, Tom?'

'She rang me to tell me she wouldn't be able to get back to me, she wouldn't see me until the party tonight. What's she doing on the fucking pier in Kinvara?'

'Tom—'

'This is another one of your schemes, is it?'

'What *time* did she ring you, Tom? It's important.'

'I told you. Just now. About twenty minutes ago. Why?'

'No, that's OK. I was supposed to meet her. Where's the party tonight, by the way?'

'Why? Are you going?'

'No.'

'A house called Inish. It's in Grattan Court. Here in the city. Do you know it?'

'Vaguely. Thanks, Tom. And I don't know if I properly apologised. For the misunderstanding last night.'

'Huh!'

Halpin replaced the receiver.

Still sitting on the bed, and still thinking intently, he didn't hear the creaking as someone put their weight on a loose board while climbing the stairs on their way up to him.

He heard nothing.

His first warning of danger, in fact, was a cold breeze on the nape of his neck as the bedroom door was pushed fully open behind him.

3

East from Kinvara, through the village of Ardrahan and into the Aughty Mountains, Roger Walcott followed the red Nissan Micra without being noticed.

When the woman pulled into a clearing in a wood, he stopped below her, out of sight, and watched her movements through binoculars.

She stepped out of the car. She looked around. Then glanced at her watch. It was a little after three. Ten minutes before appointment time. Looking quickly around again, she walked away from the car after locking its doors, into the darkness of the pine trees.

Walcott knew that she'd arranged to meet Fame a little further up the road. He guessed that she now intended checking that the old man was alone as he passed. But he knew also that Fame wouldn't make the rendezvous and that she'd have to return disappointed to her car.

He eased the Vectra back onto the narrow road and drove quietly up the hill and into the forest clearing. He parked the bonnet tight against the rear bumper of the Micra. And then he waited.

Five minutes into the vigil, he finally gave in to temptation.

Friday, 13 November

He broke the plastic wrapping on a fresh packet of cigarettes and lit up for the first time since he'd tried to kick the habit three months before. The smoke felt harsh inside his mouth and caught so drily at his throat that it made him cough.

He wasn't comfortable with what he had to do.

He remembered the only other time he'd killed a woman, three years before. A small, fat creature, with lank black hair and heavy spectacles. But a real enemy. An anti-fascist agitator. Not a soft, irrelevant target, like the Turkish immigrants Shane McKelvey had burned in Berlin.

Walcott had called at night to the woman's apartment in Berne when she was alone . . .

But of course, on that occasion his planning had been meticulous. He was already known to her as a fugitive, posing as a member of the British National Front who had become disgusted with the right wing and who had a great deal of valuable information to pass on. Their meeting was a dark secret between the two of them.

He remembered the look in her pale brown eyes when her glasses had been knocked off and she finally knew that he was going to strangle her. It was one mostly of regret, he thought. She'd realised at last that her entire life had been devoted to mistakes. Too late.

But he hadn't enjoyed killing her.

When he was a child, on his parents' farm in Sussex, a deformed calf had been born to the herd one February. Its destruction was inevitable. But not a cause for celebration . . .

Stifled by memories, he opened the Vectra's door and stepped out, onto the grass and into the fresh air. He crushed the rest of the cigarette under the sole of his shoe. Irritated by his own weakness with the smoking, he walked to the front of the Micra and sat on its bonnet to wait there.

Two minutes later, he felt the craving for tobacco again.

It distracted him.

He'd expected the woman to come back along the same route, on the same narrow footpath beaten into the wood, but instead, when it was too late to conceal himself, he heard the rustling of branches and fallen leaves to his right. He swivelled sharply. And as she stepped into the open, holding her ignition key in her right hand and slightly in front of her, like a useless, miniature sword, they saw each other simultaneously.

She stopped immediately. He had no time to take advantage of her surprise, or her fear, or her struggle to understand. He was too far away. By the time he'd slipped from the bonnet of her car to rush at her, she'd already turned and darted back to the cover of the trees.

She was fast. But also an easy quarry. She'd taken off her black leather jacket. Her red and yellow rugby shirt was clearly visible against the darker colours of the trees. And he gained on her with every pace.

A yard behind her, as he reached to bring her down, she made a last desperate effort and swung suddenly left. He thought it was only to evade him. And so he didn't see the slope she'd swerved to avoid. His right foot pounded only on air. He went over, tumbling down a sharp descent. Fir tips and fallen cones and broken branches tore at him as he fell. Unable to change his course, he crashed against a broad trunk and was spun painfully sideways.

As he came to rest again, he heard the roaring of a car engine from the nearby clearing. He pushed himself to his feet and scrambled back up the slope. But there was pain in his left knee. The joint was too weak to take his weight at speed. And he hobbled more than ran now.

The Nissan was still manoeuvring frantically in the tight space between the trees and the Vectra and was almost clear.

But not quite.

Taking the last of its turns, its front wheels caught the

exposed roots of a felled tree and the whole car was jerked violently backwards on its springs.

Walcott went immediately to the driver's door. It was locked from inside. He raised his elbow to smash the glass in on the woman's face. But she quickly knocked the gear stick into reverse and accelerated with the force that was already rocking the Micra backwards.

The door handle was ripped from Walcott's hands. He spun along the front wing and around the radiator grille and was left with little choice when she braked and started driving forward again. He dived to his right, springing off the strength of his uninjured leg.

He'd intended rolling and coming back up. But his head knocked sharply against a stone or a tree-trunk. The blow stunned him. For a few moments, he drifted out of consciousness.

4

Chief Superintendent John McQuaid was sitting behind the desk in the office he'd borrowed from the local superintendent.

He was a tall man, with straw-coloured hair and a smooth, youthful face that more than three decades of fighting crime seemed to have left unetched.

He actually stood up as Charlotte Rainey entered. A gallant courtesy. Maybe he even bowed a little as well.

It encapsulated what she most disliked about the man. He was over-sweet. Over-attentive. The surface was so perfectly glazed that it was impossible not to suspect the barbs it was sugaring.

'Ah, Charlotte,' he greeted her now. Always the first name.

Always the personal touch. 'Sit down. I wouldn't have called you in at all, you know, except for your usual record of prompt and comprehensive reports. I was getting a little worried about the lack of one.'

Here we go, Rainey thought as she sat. The way her own experience went, a compliment from a man was only safe if he was a genuinely casual friend. Within a sexual or professional relationship, it always preceded a demand.

She took the only line that subverted it. She accepted blame for inefficiency.

'I'm sorry, sir. I travelled up from Cork late last night. I should've contacted you this morning.'

'Yes, I heard about Cork.' He leaned forward and put his elbows on the desk. He interlocked his fingers as if in prayer and stared over his hands at Rainey. 'Not very good PR, Charlotte, is it? You call at a woman's home in the middle of the night to inform her of the accidental death of her common-law husband, but instead arrest her for questioning. *Insensitive* will be the mildest of the headlines, I think.'

'I believe she has information that may explain the death of Finnegan, sir.'

'According to the newspapers, there is no death of Finnegan.'

'It's only customary, sir, not to release the name of the deceased until the next of kin have been notified.'

'I'm not referring to that. I'm referring to disinformation. The dead man appears to have been driving a car instead of a van. He seems to have changed his home in mid-fall, from Cork to Galway. Did you authorise that press release?'

'Yes, sir. But I believe—'

'No doubt you do. But don't you think you might be letting your personal prejudices run away with you a little on this one, Charlotte?'

She stiffened. 'How do you mean, sir?'

He unlocked his hands to gesture. Throwing both apart.

Friday, 13 November

Inviting her to take advantage of the gap he offered. Then he sat back and pulled thoughtfully at his lower lip with the thumb and forefinger of his right hand.

She understood, of course.

Because Rainey knew all about Irish charities. And from the inside, so to speak.

In the 1950s, her own mother, the illegitimate child of an unmarried domestic servant, had been born in a laundry workhouse run by one order of nuns, separated from her parent within hours, and then reared in an orphanage by a second order of nuns. Conceived in sin, stained at birth, and burdened by the black soul of the bastard, she had wilfully resisted every method of cleansing then known to the more scientifically advanced charitable religious orders. Ice-cold water to wake her on winter mornings. Canes and rulers to beat it out of her. Soap to wash her mouth. And words to wash her brain.

And, of course, feeling useless herself, she had also married uselessly once she was free of the place. Rainey's worthless father.

'Finnegan worked for Crastina,' Rainey said now. 'Finnegan was a thug.'

McQuaid sighed wearily. 'I thought we had closed the file on Crastina some time ago.'

'Could I suggest that this opens it again, sir?'

'Have you asked in what capacity Finnegan was employed?'

'I was on my way to interview Harry Fame, the Crastina director with responsibility for that area.'

'But there's nothing necessarily sinister about it as far as I can see. It may have been ignorance of the man's character. It may have been rehabilitation. To jump immediately to suspicion might, as I say, be allowing the personal to intrude.'

Rainey knew, of course, that McQuaid himself was a patron of many Irish religious charities. Including Crastina. Just as she knew that he was a member of the Legion of Mary, the Catholic lay organisation founded by and for men in 1932, with the spiritual salvation of women as its main objective. The same organisation that Joseph Manning had joined as a devout fourteen-year-old in 1934 and was still a member of today.

Even the name of the thing provoked her. Half of it the maternal figure, symbol of protection and nourishment, image of purity and modesty. A particularly male view and a particularly male expectation of women. The other half a military unit of the ancient Roman army, symbol of strength and virility, of victory and conquests. A particularly male view of men.

Looking across the desk at the almost priestly concern of McQuaid, she suddenly remembered Eddie Halpin's caution about talking idly to friends and colleagues. And so, despite the danger it placed her in, she stopped herself short of mentioning either Halpin or her suspicion that Finnegan had been tailing him in the Kerry mountains.

It was extremely risky, she knew. But as long as she was withholding opinions and not actual evidence...

'Harry Fame,' McQuaid was asking her. 'Where does he live?'

'Clarinbridge, sir.'

'Famous for its cut glass, eh?'

'It's less than ten miles away. I can easily make it this afternoon.'

'Yes, well...' He reached out and played absently with the leather gloves and soft hat he'd left on the surface of the desk. 'No matter how I put this you'll take it wrongly, Charlotte; so I may as well put it bluntly. You'll not be able to interview Harry Fame, or anyone else associated with Crastina. At least for the weekend.'

'May I ask why, sir?'

Friday, 13 November

'This is a question of timing, Charlotte.'

'In what sense?'

'The American President, to tell you the truth.'

'American President? I'm sorry, I don't see the connection.'

'Special Branch is already overstretched. The American Secret Service is difficult. Things will settle down again when he's gone. But not this weekend.'

She didn't believe him. It seemed to her a puny excuse. Ill thought-out. And badly formulated.

To make it worse, she could also see that he noticed her scepticism. And for a while, he didn't seem to care.

'Crastina, as you know, has been recently endorsed by the current American administration,' he said finally. 'A hasty investigation into the charity during the President's visit would hardly be diplomatic. I'm sure I don't have to labour the delicacy of the situation any further.'

'No, sir. You don't.'

She rose to go, impatient to breathe more freely again.

'One more thing, Charlotte,' he detained her.

'Yes, sir?'

'I'll put this pleasantly, but naturally it's an order. I don't want you talking to anyone outside about either your current assignment or this conversation. I know you have something of a reputation as an individualist. For once I'd like you to live up to it.'

'May I ask why, sir? Again.'

'Because I want my officers reporting directly to me, Charlotte, not to anyone else. Incidentally, I'll be here for another couple of hours before flying back to Dublin. See if you can catch me with a written report of last night's events in Kerry and Cork.'

Her parting salute, she saw, disappointed him. It was too correct. Too cold and formal.

Burning with anger, she passed Jarlath Burke's office on her way out, without being able to look in at the inevitable surprise and disappointment and misunderstanding he must have experienced. It made her feel furtive, and slightly cheap. And she resented it. While she drove from the car park, through the city without a destination in mind, she thought of it as warping her natural instincts.

5

The flooring in the bedroom was pitch pine, lightly polished and uncovered except for a couple of loose rugs.

Again, Cormac Lowry's heavy boots betrayed him on the hard surface.

Eddie Halpin turned, alerted by the rushing footsteps.

Lowry was almost on top of him already. Sweat was dripping from the youth's bald head, across his pallid face and falling away behind him to the floor. His bulging, drunken eyes had trouble focusing. His right arm was raised above him as he charged and was grasping the now empty whiskey bottle as a weapon.

Halpin swerved. And then rolled desperately across the mattress.

The bottle sliced through the air beside him. He felt its movement where his body was uncovered, on his cheek and along the back of his hand. He heard the savage *swish* as it cut its way down. And then a crash as it met the bed frame and shattered noisily.

Lowry would still be holding its neck, he thought. And its end was now jagged. An even more lethal weapon.

Friday, 13 November

As he rolled off the bed on the opposite side, he grasped the arm of a metal reading lamp on the bedside locker.

Lowry had unbalanced himself. He was sprawled face down across the bed, his knees on the wooden floorboards, his right arm twisted a little awkwardly where the broken bottle had snagged on the covers.

Halpin brought the lamp down hard on Lowry's wrist. In the one movement he drew it back and got ready to strike with it again, but into the other's face this time.

Lowry yelped with pain. His fingers loosened their hold on the bottle's neck and drew away from it. As he raised his head, he saw the shade and bulb of the lamp, like a monstrous eye socket, hurtling towards him.

He hadn't either the speed or the guile to avoid it.

But the lamp never made contact with his face.

Its flex was fully extended before it got to him, and although Halpin's movement jerked the plug from the socket, the tug was enough to retard the momentum and shorten its arc. It passed in front of his face.

Halpin grasped the bedclothes in his left hand and yanked them towards him, pulling the broken bottle and the fragments of glass over to his side. He dropped the lamp to the floor and went round the base of the bed to finish with Lowry.

But he could see that the fight was gone from the other by then. Lowry was sobbing drunkenly, with his head buried in the bare mattress and covered by his arms.

Halpin prodded him with his right foot. 'Get up!' he told him. 'And shut up, too! Don't try my patience. Sit in that chair over there.'

Lowry struggled to his feet and slumped in a frail bedroom chair that almost buckled under his weight. He tried not to look at Halpin.

Halpin gave him a few minutes to rest. And then he asked quietly, 'What's worth having a go at me for, Cormac?'

Lowry didn't answer.

'Look, Cormac,' Halpin said coldly. 'I don't want to bear any grudges. Now that you've failed to get rid of me, I want our relationship to be the same as it always was. You tell me everything. I don't tell anyone anything. Do you understand?'

Lowry nodded jerkily.

'You'd better,' Halpin advised. 'Now. Do you know where Harry Fame has gone?'

'No, I don't.'

'Is he coming back?'

'I don't know.'

'The photograph and letter from downstairs. Did he tell you to pick them up?'

'He told me they were in the bureau.'

'And he wanted you to bring them to him?'

'No, no. To get rid of them.'

'Why?'

'That's Joseph Manning's sister—'

'I know who it is.'

'She killed herself.'

'In September 1941. I know. What about it?'

'It was Mr Fame who discovered her body.'

Halpin started. 'Why do you say that?'

'He told me.'

Bridget Manning had died on a Thursday morning, dangling from a curtain cord that she'd tied to the brass centrepiece in the high ceiling of her bedroom at the family home in the prosperous Dublin suburb of Ranelagh. Her younger brother Joseph was at work at the time, a civil servant at the Department of Education. Her invalid mother was asleep in another bedroom. Her father was long since dead, a casualty of the Spanish Civil War in 1937, where he'd gone with General O'Duffy's Irish Brigade to fight for Franco's Nationalist army.

According to the inquest, Joseph Manning had found his

sister's body during lunch-time. Why would Harry Fame have been calling on her any earlier? Why would he *conceal* his visit and his discovery? Why would he admit the truth to Lowry?

'What else did he tell you?' Halpin demanded.

Lowry frowned. He wiped the sweat from his eyes with the fingers of his left hand. 'How do you mean?'

'Did he tell you why she killed herself?'

'No, nothing like that.'

'Did he talk about their relationship? Were they lovers? What?'

'He didn't, no.'

'Did he tell you *anything* else? Why he wanted these things destroyed?'

'Not really, no.'

Exasperated, Halpin looked again at the photograph he still held. Bridget Manning was twenty-three years old in it. She was a tall young woman. Her complexion was a little pale, but her soft features and smooth skin and long black hair made her very attractive.

Not that anything much had ever been done, as far as he knew, to add to or highlight her beauty. The shortages of the war period didn't exactly allow for fine clothes and jewellery, of course. And also with an invalid mother and a dead father . . .

Easy sexual prey for a feckless charmer like Harry Fame?

Halpin wondered.

'Is there other material he told you to get rid of?' he asked Lowry. 'Apart from these.'

Lowry warily shook his head. 'No, that's it. That's the lot.'

He was probably lying, Halpin decided. But without his co-operation, the house would take too long to search. There were too many rooms. And too many possible hiding places.

And besides, Halpin needed to travel quickly to Kinvara to intercept Linda. Which had been the whole point of the current exercise, really.

Silent City

'Let's go,' he ordered Lowry.

He pushed the youth in front of him, down the stairs and back into the front room.

'Sit down,' he told him.

He crossed to the bureau and quickly searched its drawers and compartments. But he found nothing. And Lowry remained calm while he was rummaging. So he obviously wasn't missing anything, either.

He checked the time and went to stand in front of Lowry, glowering down at him.

'If you do happen to think of anything, Cormac,' he warned coldly, 'or if you happen to see Fame again, you'll remember to give me a ring, won't you?'

Lowry's eyes were drifting away, towards a far corner of the room, where the drinks cabinet was obviously situated. But he nodded. Even if his enthusiasm was mostly for seeing the back of Halpin.

6

When Roger Walcott came to, it was quiet again around him in the forest clearing. Except for a bird singing indifferently in a nearby bush.

He limped across to the Vectra and drove at speed down the mountain, back the route they'd travelled, until he reached the junction with the main road.

She wouldn't keep straight on, he reckoned. She wouldn't return to Kinvara. And just to confuse him, she wouldn't take a right, the shortest and most obvious route back to Galway city.

Walcott swung left. Gambling on reading her mind.

Friday, 13 November

For a while he travelled with dying hope. Seeing nothing. Frustrated by ponderous trucks.

But he'd actually called it correctly.

Five minutes later, on the outskirts of the town of Gort, he finally saw the red Nissan Micra in the light traffic ahead of him, wedged between a bus and a black Land Rover.

And he almost lost it immediately again in the town. Flashing past the opening to a shopping centre and barely catching the blur of red from inside its car park.

Four o'clock on Friday afternoon. The place was busy. And almost full.

Walcott raced up and down the lanes. Checking on everything likely. Cursing the popularity of the colour red and the commonness of make and model. But spaces were rare. The Micra had slowed while searching for one. And he finally saw it as it was turning in, a couple of rows across from him.

The woman was stopping to contact somebody. Not to hide. Because she hadn't noticed him yet.

He drove to the top of his own lane. He turned left against the one-way flow, came quickly in behind the Nissan's boot, and blocked its exit for the second time that day.

Even before the Vectra had settled, he was fumbling with his seat-belt. He swung out, hampered by the need to keep the weight off his bruised knee, and then tried to hurry across the tarmac. He went immediately to the Micra's unlocked driver's door and yanked it open.

The car was empty. The keys were still dangling from its ignition. The door on the opposite side was slightly ajar and still swinging gently back and forth.

She could only have seen him and escaped just seconds before he'd reached her. Too close to being captured to worry about her keys.

He stood up and looked over the roof of the Micra, scanning the car park.

He saw her immediately. She was hurrying through the parked cars a couple of rows ahead of him, carrying her brown rucksack by her side.

As he took the keys from the Micra and closed its doors and set off after her, she suddenly glanced behind her.

When she saw him, she pushed herself forward again, desperately trying to reach the safety of the automatic doors at the entrance to the shopping centre. She ran recklessly into the traffic lane. She didn't check to right or left. A white Ford Escort, speeding to snatch a nearby parking space before it was snapped up by someone else, sprang from another lane and caught her in the middle of its bonnet.

Walcott lost sight of her as she went down.

He still kept running. Towards the rising screams of the onlookers. Into the crowds being sucked by the accident.

By the time he reached her, she was encircled by people. She was unconscious. Her long black hair was thrown across her face, covering her like a blanket. Blood was seeping from somewhere and staining the bright yellow of her rugby shirt. The brown rucksack lay abandoned by her side.

But why take the rucksack and not the keys, he wondered immediately. What was in it? What was more important than her car?

He lingered. Unsettled by the outcome of the chase. Disturbed by its inconclusiveness.

But he kept hearing faint comments and questions that finally worried him. The girl had been running somewhere, the witnesses said. Someone had been after the young woman.

He became conscious of his own appearance. His limp. The leaves and the twigs still clinging to his clothes from the forest.

So he turned and slipped away, moving against the flow of the curious now being drawn to the drama. But no one challenged him.

Friday, 13 November

In the toilets inside the shopping centre, he washed his face and hands and cleaned the debris from his clothes.

When he went back outside, a team of paramedics had strapped the unconscious young woman onto a stretcher and were lifting her into the waiting ambulance.

The brown rucksack had disappeared.

And a motorcycle policeman was questioning the driver of the white Escort.

Walcott turned away. He would've preferred to have known which hospital they were taking her to. He would've preferred some confirmation of her death. Some proof of her identity. Some idea of her profession. But he didn't want to ask. Just as he didn't want to answer the questions from the newcomers who were pressing in around him.

At times, his English accent was a burden in Ireland. All too distinctive. And all too memorable.

He walked briskly back to where he'd parked the Opel Vectra.

But that, too, was now surrounded by a separate knot of people.

FOUR

1

It was already dark when Jimmy Kyne turned the black Mercedes limousine through the open gates of St Kieron's House in Kinvara.

In the rear seat, Joseph Manning and his secretary, Michael Carter, were still working carefully through the schedule for the following day.

The three of them had just come from inspecting the development across the inlet, where Crastina's new headquarters had been built.

Kyne stopped at the entrance, half in and half out of the grounds. Frowning slightly, he lowered his window to read the sign that told him St Kieron's was closed to visitors for the weekend.

He stayed too long, troubling himself with the apparent contradiction. From behind, Carter reached forward and dropped a thin, irritating hand on his shoulder.

'What's the matter, Kyne?' he asked sharply.

Kyne shook his head. 'Nothing.'

'Then get on with it, please. Mr Manning is tired and needs to rest.'

Kyne arched his eyebrows as he turned from the sign to stare through his rear-view mirror.

Friday, 13 November

For a second, Carter's sour little face and bitter eyes still filled the glass. But then he shrank away from the challenge.

Kyne sighed. His patience was wearing thin, he knew. The unwanted visit to the new headquarters had stretched it a little more. All those arrogant young suits with their mobile phones and calculators and personal organisers. Kids who wouldn't talk unless the exchanges were scripted. Executives more interested in the angle the television camera was going to settle on them than in the world's hunger and poverty.

And of course, Kyne was getting particularly tired of the self-important little secretary at his back.

He released the handbrake and drove the limousine cautiously up the gravel driveway.

Sensing unease in the air, he watched the buildings ahead of him, waiting for Roger Walcott to come out and welcome them.

Someone showed. Eventually. But it wasn't the curator. As Kyne parked and looked suspiciously around, he caught a glimpse in his right wing mirror of a slight figure in black jeans and a faded yellow T-shirt peering anxiously at them from behind the tower house and immediately disappearing again.

He turned to talk to Carter. 'Wait here,' he ordered.

'I beg your pardon?'

'Wait here. Don't leave the car until I come back for you.'

Kyne stood out. He closed and locked the driver's door, checked that all the others were secure and then walked across the gravel to the front doors.

Inside, to the right of the hallway, the overweight cook, Margaret Rushe, and her thin husband were already working in the kitchen.

Kyne stood in the doorway and stared in at them.

They didn't respond to his arrival. Neither offered him a greeting. They didn't even look up from their work.

'Did the girl come here with you?' he asked them finally.

A furtive glance between the pair, full of surprise and suppressed guilt, warned him that his own uneasiness had been justified. Something was wrong, he thought. Something was being hidden.

'Girl?' Dominick Rushe repeated nervously.

'Josie Thomas.'

'Where is she?' the cook blurted out.

'Don't you know?' Kyne asked her.

'Well, you see—' Rushe started to explain.

'As far as I'm aware,' Kyne interrupted him, 'she's not supposed to be here. Nobody's supposed to be here, apart from you two and Walcott. Where *is* Walcott?'

Again that glance was quickly shared, indicating either an ignorance they couldn't admit or a knowledge they couldn't share. They said nothing. Rushe went back to chopping vegetables on the wooden board below him. His wife kneaded dough at the table. Apart from the noises their work made, there was silence in the room.

Irritated, Kyne stepped in and loudly slapped his palm on the table. 'I asked you a question,' he said. 'Do you know where Walcott is, or don't you?'

Margaret Rushe jumped at the noise of the slap and quickly shook her head. 'No. We don't. We didn't see him today.'

'What time did you get here?'

'Three o'clock. Like we were supposed to.'

'Was the girl with you?'

'She wasn't, no. She stayed with us last night, but she slipped out of the house some time this morning. We didn't know where she'd got to. We were that worried we—'

'Was the front gate open when you arrived?'

'It was, yes.'

'And there was no one here?'

'No one, no.'

Friday, 13 November

'Right,' Kyne accepted. 'That's all I wanted to know. Is Mr Manning's room ready?'

'It is, yes.'

'Mr Carter and myself are staying the night as well.'

'Everything's ready for you.'

'Come and help Mr Manning to his room,' he said more gently then. 'He'll want to rest for an hour or so before dinner.'

He made an effort to smile and lighten the atmosphere, not wanting to make enemies with the couple.

But he still saw fear and anxiety in their eyes.

Except that the eyes weren't looking at him any more. And he was no longer the source of their considerable apprehension. They were staring beyond him, into the open doorway behind.

2

One of the group at Roger Walcott's Vectra in the shopping centre car park, a small, fair-haired man, had placed himself behind the steering-wheel and was trying to start the car with the keys Walcott had left in the ignition.

But the engine wasn't firing.

The radiator must have taken damage in the mountains, Walcott realised, and then leaked itself dry on the journey back down.

'I say,' he announced himself crisply. His sharp English accent now more of a weapon than a liability. 'Is this your car? You see, that's my Micra you've got hemmed in there and I'm afraid I'm rather in something of a hurry.'

The blond man hopped quickly out of the Vectra, disassociating himself from the piece of junk. 'No,' he said, shaking his head. 'It's not mine, no. Someone just left it there, blocking the lane.'

'Damned nuisance. I wonder if you . . .'

'Why don't you just drive out? OK? We'll push it out of your way and then push it back into the space when you've left.'

'Would you?'

'No problem.'

'That's very kind of you.'

Sitting in the Micra, Walcott took its keys from his jacket pocket, started the engine and waved cheerfully at the waiting crowd as he reversed.

He circled the shopping centre for a few minutes before parking in another space.

He checked the Nissan's glove compartment and the woman's black leather jacket. But there was nothing of interest in either. No purse. No identification. No correspondence.

When the crowd had cleared, or been drawn to greater excitement, he walked back to the Vectra to take its keys and his own papers and cigarettes from inside.

He drove from the shopping centre in the Micra. And lit up his third cigarette of the afternoon as he went.

Things were drifting out of shape, he thought despairingly. Slowly. Inexorably. And he could even pinpoint the moment when the crack had opened and chaos had started to seep through.

He turned right and travelled north through Gort, back on the main road to Galway city.

Once he was comfortable with the Micra's controls, he tried to work his way through to a resolution of the problems. Step by step. Examining the consequences of each decision and every action.

But his bitterness kept intruding and distracting him.

There was a natural order to all things, he thought. A natural form. To disturb it was to weaken its native strength. Its immunity. To expose it to disease and decay and death.

But even those who preached this truth sometimes forgot that it also applied to themselves and to their own organisations.

'Shane McKelvey is in charge,' Walcott had been told. 'You will place yourself at his disposal and function as cover for him.'

But McKelvey was a street fighter. Walcott was a strategist. McKelvey was addicted to the thrill of fighting. Walcott knew that violence was only a necessary cleansing.

To place McKelvey in control, planning an operation of such importance . . .

It was to *invite* failure.

Its consequences were already evident. The bungling with Halpin's papers. This girl with mysterious knowledge.

And yet, who in the organisation was even *aware* of such dangers, apart from Walcott himself . . . ?

On the outskirts of town, the flashing blue lights of a police car appeared in his rear-view mirror and then its wailing siren cut through his self-absorption.

He slowed and steered to the left, allowing it space to pass. But it pulled sharply across in front of him and indicated that it wanted him to stop.

His first thought was that the Micra had been reported stolen.

Tensing himself for conflict, he lowered his window to take the questions from the young officer who approached.

'Could you tell me the registration number of your car, sir?'

'Ah!' he exclaimed. He had no idea, of course. He said, 'I'm afraid I don't really know. This is my sister-in-law's car, you see. I merely borrowed it.'

'Are you a visitor, sir?'

'Yes. Short winter break.'

'From England, are you?'

'Yes, quite. Sussex, actually.'

'Could I have your sister-in-law's name?'
'Grant. Vera Grant.'
'And her address?'
'Tavistock, Clarinbridge, County Galway. I'm returning there now.'
'And your own name and address? Your home address in England.'

The policeman wrote everything down. Slowly. Diligently.

If he also returned to the squad car to check the details over the radio . . .

But he didn't.

'You haven't been drinking, sir, have you?' he asked.

Walcott smiled. 'Not at all, no.'

'Do you know why I pulled you over?'

'I'm dreadfully sorry. I'm afraid I have no idea. Was I travelling too fast?'

'You've been driving without any lights on, sir. Could you test them for me now, please?'

Startled, Walcott looked down at the darkened instrument panel and cursed his own stupidity.

Why search for an outside source of disorder, he wondered furiously. It was his *own* failings that were helping to unravel the pattern. His easy betrayal of his fears when the young woman had first mentioned Columbus at Kinvara. His carelessness now.

The self-disgust must have shown on his face. When he glanced back after struggling desperately to locate the lighting controls, the policeman had put his notebook and pen in his pockets and was chuckling quietly to himself as he turned away.

Walcott watched him spin the squad car in a U-turn and drive past on his way back to Gort before he himself pulled out and continued on to Clarinbridge.

However much he was grateful for his own release, he felt nothing but contempt for the policeman's indifference to his country's laws. It was characteristic of a slovenliness he found distasteful.

Friday, 13 November

And so his mood worsened as he drove. His dissatisfaction. His self-loathing. His anger at the accumulation of small obstacles. His rage at the untidiness of the world.

But Harry Fame's house, the Tavistock Walcott had offered the policeman, was in darkness and already seemed deserted when he reached it. Fame's gold Mercedes was no longer in the driveway.

And the sight eased his worries.

He parked and walked around to the rear of the house, still needing to confirm that both Fame and Lowry were gone and lying low.

Fame's fawn Labrador bitch, recognising his scent before she even saw him, waddled around the corner of the house with her tail wagging at him in greeting.

'Hello, Jess,' he called softly.

Crouching to fondle her, he saw that she was already lonely and hungry. It worried him. She might draw attention to the empty house, he thought, if she was left there unattended.

So when he took the key from the flowerpot on the back window and opened the rear door with it, he brought the dog inside with him.

3

Jimmy Kyne was edgy. In the kitchen, when he swivelled to check behind him, it was half with the expectation of defending himself. But only the slight, apologetic figure of Michael Carter was standing in the open doorway, fingering his rounded spectacles and peering distrustfully inwards.

Kyne's aggression slipped quickly into irritation. 'I told you to stay in the car,' he snapped.

Carter's weak blue eyes, enlarged by the glasses, blinked rapidly a number of times. 'Quite,' he said coldly. 'But Mr Manning has already come in and is praying in the chapel.'

Kyne wearily shook his head as he stepped past the secretary.

He no longer felt really at home in Crastina, he thought sadly. No one thought him important any more. Perhaps not even Mr Manning himself.

Outside, he turned left along the gravel driveway and took the beaten path around the tower house.

The girl was in darkness on the narrow ledge at the back, leaning against the frail wooden railing and staring into the water below, where the lights of a local trawler could be seen manoeuvring for the pier.

Kyne stopped at the corner of the tower, not wanting to startle her.

He knew that she felt drawn by the sea. He knew that the sound of a trawler coming into the bay sometimes brought her out to stand and dream on the driveway with her brown teddy bear, even in the middle of the night.

Maybe it suggested some sort of escape to her, he thought. Some sort of illusory freedom. Like his own addiction to high speeds and heroin when he was young.

But he also knew that half the attraction was the temptation of self-destruction.

Because he'd been there himself.

Josie's mother had been a drug addict and a prostitute. Further back, Josie's grandmother had been an alcoholic and also on the game. When she was eight, Josie herself had been raped by one of her mother's clients. At sixteen, three years ago, she'd had a daughter of her own. The state had taken the child, and Crastina cared for Josie.

She was never going to make it in the outside world, Kyne accepted. Not now. But at least she had comfort and protection at St Kieron's. At least it broke the awful cycle that had trapped her mother and her grandmother.

'Josie,' he called her gently.

She turned sharply, anxiety on her face, but then smiled shyly when she saw who it was.

She didn't greet him. She seldom spoke to anyone. Instead, she hugged the soft toy in her left hand and pointed with her right to the trawler below. 'The *Grey Witch*,' she muttered.

Kyne looked over the railing. He couldn't read the name on the side of the boat, but its captain and crew were visible enough on deck. 'No,' he said. 'That's the *Prince Killeen*, Josie.'

She shook her head, deeply disturbed by the contradiction. 'The *Grey Witch*,' she muttered again. 'The *Grey Witch*.'

Kyne shrugged, not wanting to upset her. 'Where's Mr Walcott, Josie?' he asked.

She glowered and again shook her head. Not knowing where Walcott was. And not caring, either.

Her agitation was intense and obvious, but its cause remained uncertain.

And as he watched her exaggerated reactions to his questions, Kyne started to worry again.

She seemed too close to that wooden railing, he thought. She seemed to be pressing much too strongly against it.

He stepped slowly forward, trying to think of something to take her mind away from whatever was troubling her, but then, above the breaking of the waves and the trawler's engine, he heard the sound of a car turning in to St Kieron's from the main road and rolling up the gravel driveway.

He thought it was Walcott returning.

And so did the girl, obviously. She suddenly frowned, clutched her soft toy with both arms, and looked over nervously at Kyne.

When he smiled and beckoned to her, she scurried across to him anxiously. He offered her his hand, but she didn't take it.

She didn't really trust anyone enough to leave herself open to their touch. But on the way back around the tower to the front of the buildings, she stayed as close to him as possible without actual contact.

It wasn't Walcott's Opel Vectra that had pulled in behind the limousine in the driveway, however.

It was a silver BMW. And stepping out from its driver's seat was a tall, black-haired man dressed in jeans and an oatmeal waistcoat. Even in darkness, his face seemed vaguely familiar to Kyne.

The man came across, his hand outstretched in greeting. 'You're Jimmy Kyne, aren't you?' he said. 'My name is Eddie Halpin. You might remember. About two weeks ago, I was down here for a meeting with Mr Manning.'

Kyne nodded and took the offered hand. 'That's right. What can I do for you, Mr Halpin?'

'I noticed the limousine,' Halpin said. 'Is Mr Manning here at the moment?'

'He's in church.'

'Right. Have you been here long?'

'In what way?'

'What time did you arrive today?'

Kyne frowned. Was it just his own uneasiness again, he wondered, or was the enquiry actually peculiar? 'Is something bothering you, Mr Halpin?' he asked.

Halpin smiled and gave a slight shrug. 'Actually,' he admitted, 'there is. I don't want to disturb Mr Manning, obviously—'

'No, no,' Kyne interrupted. 'I'm sure he'll be glad to see you. Let me check first.'

The girl had stayed by his side all the time, although more relaxed since discovering that it wasn't Walcott returning.

Kyne turned to her now and indicated that she should lead them through the main doors to the west wing.

Friday, 13 November

'We finished our new headquarters, Mr Halpin,' he chatted, 'since you were down here last. Have you seen it? We've just come from there ourselves...'

4

Eddie Halpin waited in the tower house, among the items on permanent display in the museum, while Kyne went off to talk to Joseph Manning.

The connecting door to the west wing had been locked when Halpin had broken into Kyne's pleasantries to ask if he could visit the museum, and the key hadn't been hanging from its usual hook. But Kyne had finally located a spare in the small reception area.

Looking around it now, Halpin couldn't immediately understand his own persistence.

He'd been here before, of course. At least on three occasions. And all the objects were already familiar to him.

The scythe that Manning's father had used in the fields of County Dublin in the 1930s, for instance, was still propped in the same gloomy corner. The carved oak table with its glass case containing relics and medals and the simple wooden cross from the previous century that had once belonged to Manning's mother still dominated the centre. Underneath it lay the hand-woven rug that his sister Bridget had completed shortly before her death in 1941. Even the signs warning visitors not to touch the exhibits or disturb the table were undisturbed.

It was the photographs on the walls, however, that eventually attracted him.

And one in particular that held him.

It was another copy of the print he'd faxed to Kerry that

morning, showing the four young men in their army uniforms late in 1940.

And what had drawn him back to it, he realised now, was a problem with it that he'd suppressed or ignored. *Anna Rosen says this the young man who was so generous to family when brother Alan fell ill with pneumonia and later when killed in German bombing*, Caroline French had written on the fax. But Rosen, he remembered, had suffered from pneumonia in February 1941.

He thought . . .

'Mr Halpin!' he was summoned.

He turned.

Joseph Manning was coming through the open doorway, onto the cold flagstones of the tower's floor, his stick tapping a slow rhythm as he walked. An old man, bald and stooped, and wearing only a plain white robe and brown sandals.

Halpin felt guilty. 'I'm sorry for disturbing you so soon after your arrival.'

Manning waved away the apologies. 'Not at all, Mr Halpin, not at all. I've just completed a dull journey, and had nothing to look forward to but further dullness.'

They shook hands and exchanged greetings. They warmly remembered the last time they'd met. They gossiped for a while about the weather and about the American President.

And then Halpin, still standing by the wall, tapped the glass on the photograph above him and said, without apparent relevance, 'Whenever we talked in the past, Mr Manning, you never mentioned that you actually knew Alan Rosen before his death.'

The old man tensed a little. 'I don't think the occasion ever really arose, did it?'

'Not when I was researching the history of Crastina last year. Rosen was one of many victims of the German bombing. He wasn't individualised. Our focus was on the tragedy itself as the inspiration for Crastina. But you may remember that I

Friday, 13 November

mentioned to you at our brief meeting a couple of weeks ago that I was now preparing a biographical essay on Rosen himself.'

Manning frowned. Without answering, he turned and walked away to sit on the high-backed chair beside the display table.

Kyne, who had followed him into the tower, helped to settle him comfortably.

Manning's secretary, Michael Carter, had stayed in the doorway. Pale and limp, and apparently without the energy to advance any further, the man looked seriously ill. He stared across at Halpin with what seemed like horror and indignation.

'What makes you think that I knew Rosen before his death, Mr Halpin?' Manning asked finally.

Halpin indicated the framed image hanging on the wall. 'Anna Rosen identified you from a copy of this photograph.'

'Anna? I tried to contact her in Dublin many times over the last few years. No one knew of her any more. I thought she must have died.'

'She's not living in Dublin.'

'Where did you find her?'

'She was interested to hear that I was in contact with you. She's writing to you. But what she told me was that you cared for Alan when he was suffering from pneumonia, early in 1941.'

Manning was gently shaking his head. 'I helped the family financially. I doubt if this is truly the same as care. Don't you? His father was a solicitor, as you know, and Rosen himself was studying for the Bar, but their practice was damaged at the time because they were Jewish.'

'The point is, you knew Rosen in February 1941.'

'This is true, yes.' Manning's dark brown eyes, famous for their gentleness and compassion, stared now with sharp concern. 'Do you know *why* I didn't tell you, Mr Halpin?'

Halpin shrugged. 'I've never known you to volunteer details of your personal work, Mr Manning,' he said respectfully, 'but there is a point, I think, where modesty obscures the truth.'

Manning smiled, having heard the compliment, and the complaint, before. He glanced to his side as his personal secretary suddenly summoned the energy to come from the doorway and stand closer to him. But when he reached behind, it was to search for Kyne's comforting hand, and not for Carter's.

'Perhaps,' he conceded.

'I understand your motives, in other words,' Halpin explained. 'I can sympathise with your reluctance. I have no absolute right to know. But I'm also curious, of course, to discover where you met.'

'It was in the army, Mr Halpin.'

'In the army?'

'Didn't you know that Rosen served in the Local Defence Force?'

'Of course, yes, but—'

'It was in late 1940, while I also was serving as a reservist.'

Halpin half-turned to the photograph again.

He didn't need to. Didn't have to look at it. The image of the four young men in uniform with their arms around each others' shoulders was already clear in his mind.

'But then,' he said slowly, 'surely Harry Fame must also have met Rosen at the same time.'

He left a silence after mentioning the name. And in the silence, he glanced at each of the three faces confronting him.

Kyne's was blank, except for a slight residue of concern for the health of the old man.

Manning's was relaxed and approving.

Only Carter seemed agitated. And outraged. And nervous.

'Is this what you came all the way from Galway to speak to me about, Mr Halpin?' Manning wondered finally. 'Or am I right in imagining that something else is troubling you?'

Friday, 13 November

5

Tense with tiredness and frustration and a craving for more tobacco, Roger Walcott turned the red Nissan Micra through the gates of St Kieron's and revved it irritably when the tyres met the gravel inside and spun a little.

He pulled in beside the silver BMW in the driveway and parked behind the black Mercedes limousine. He turned off the headlights.

Not wanting to go in immediately to confront Kyne and Manning and explain his absence, he lit another cigarette.

He glanced at the BMW beside him while he smoked. Casually. Without particular interest or worry. Assuming it belonged to someone in Joseph Manning's ever-expanding entourage.

When he'd finished the cigarette, he flicked the filter stub out onto the gravel, closed the window and stepped from the car.

Walking across to the west wing, he slotted his key into the lock and turned it, gently pushing the front door away from him.

Immediately, because it fell across the floor at his feet, he saw the strip of light that was coming from the tower house on his right.

He stopped abruptly, grabbing the door that was swinging away from him before its inside handle knocked against the wall and advertised his arrival.

Over his own muted breathing, he heard voices from inside the tower. Manning's was first. It was followed by Jimmy

Silent City

Kyne's. And then by a stranger's.

'I doubt it very much,' Manning was saying.

'He was in our headquarters in Galway earlier,' Kyne added. 'I saw him there. About one o'clock.'

'Yes,' the stranger said. 'Would it be possible that he might be here later?'

'He very seldom visits here.'

Straining to catch the details, Walcott let the door slip from his left hand and had to swivel sharply to clutch it again. He eased it back towards him, pressed it shut after stepping in, and silently turned the lock to secure it.

With the noise of his own heartbeat pounding in his ears, he heard nothing else distinctly for a few moments. He moved a little to his right, against the wall dividing the tower from the west wing, and edged up to the open doorway to peer cautiously around the frame.

Inside the tower, beside the carved oak table, Manning was sitting in the high-backed chair.

Behind him stood Jimmy Kyne.

And beside Kyne, staring fearfully across at Walcott and silently warning him not to advance and show himself, was Manning's personal secretary, Michael Carter.

Walcott instantly drew back.

6

Distracted for a moment by the secretary's fidgeting behind the seated Manning, Halpin fell suddenly silent.

Manning stared at him, absorbed by the worried expression on the other's face. 'Why would your sister want to meet Harry Fame, Mr Halpin?' he asked then.

Friday, 13 November

'Why?' Halpin repeated. 'To ask him the same question I've just asked you. When and where did he meet Alan Rosen before Rosen was killed?'

'And you think there may be some cause for concern in this? Some reason for Harry to object?'

'It's possible, yes.'

'Because you're clearly worried for your sister's safety, aren't you?'

Behind Manning, Carter suddenly detached himself from the group and drifted towards the doorway. When the others stopped talking to look at him, he muttered weakly, 'I'm sorry. Would you excuse me for a moment, please? I, ah . . . I don't feel quite well, and, ah . . .'

He left without rounding off his explanation.

Kyne frowned a little at the secretary's movements.

'How Harry and I met Alan Rosen is quite simple, Mr Halpin,' Manning said gently then. 'And really no great secret. You mustn't create an aura of hazardous mystery about it because I thought it too . . . too *private* to communicate before.'

'I don't want to intrude on your—'

'No, no. If it eases your worries . . . It is only the *significance* which is private, Mr Halpin, not the scene itself. It happened in December 1940. As reservists, Harry and I were on weekend manoeuvres with the regular army. We slept in the barracks that Saturday night, expecting to return to our homes after mass the following morning. But something extraordinary happened. Although I'm sure you're already too familiar with the incident. The entire army was put on general alert that night. Ever since the fall of France six months earlier, as you know, the country was alive with rumours of invasion.'

'I didn't realise that units of the Local Defence Force were involved.'

'That was a mistake, I'm afraid. And peculiar to our own barracks. We were woken at four in the morning, in any case, and ordered into the barrack square. The night was wet and very cold. I remember it perfectly. We stood for thirty minutes, waiting for the full battalion to form.'

'And Harry Fame was also there?' Halpin asked.

'Harry? Harry was at my side. We were next-door neighbours, Mr Halpin. And even closer friends. We did everything together. And both of us thought it was another pointless alert, to be honest. More manoeuvres. Another inspection. But then we noticed that a crude wooden platform had been put in place at the top of the square. Three narrow steps leading to an elevated floor.

'At four thirty or so, our chaplain, Father Hegarty, finally appeared. He was dressed for a service, in black cassock and white linen surplice. He climbed the narrow steps and stood alone in the rain on the small platform.

'He raised his hands and lowered them slowly again. Asking us to kneel. For prayer, we thought. It was for something more than that, however. As it turned out, it was actually for general absolution. To cleanse our souls before we went into battle to repel the invader.

'And it was then, Mr Halpin, that the really extraordinary thing happened . . .'

7

Carter had closed the door behind him after coming from the tower.

Trembling with fear, his round little face so drained of self-control that it had even lost its normal look of distaste, he grabbed Walcott by the sleeve and tugged him away, down the empty corridor. After a few paces, however, he changed his mind again. He seemed confused. Unable to decide. First he restrained the curator. Then he released his hold, gestured vaguely and slipped up to the open kitchen door and smiled inwards.

'Ah!' he grunted at the couple inside. 'Excuse me. Mrs Rushe, Dominick.'

Closing the kitchen door, he beckoned Walcott into the small reception opposite.

He slumped in a seat, exhausted by his own terrors. But he was immediately on his feet again, unable to rest.

Walcott stared at him, baffled by his agitation.

Carter removed his glasses and furiously rubbed at his aching eyes with the fingers of his right hand.

'You saw him!' he cried then. His voice was almost breaking with tears and hysteria. 'You saw him! You saw him yourself!'

'Saw who?' Walcott asked distastefully.

Whatever the cause, he hated this show, this *exhibition*, of disintegration. Dignity. Self-control. Strength and courage. These were his personal values.

'Saw who?' Carter repeated. 'Saw Halpin! Halpin!'

'Halpin's dead.'

Carter's already fragile voice cracked into a high-pitched laugh. 'He's in the tower, Walcott!' he cried.

'The newspaper reported this morning that he was dead.'

'He's not dead! He's in the tower! Talking to Manning! Asking about Fame in 1940! Asking about his sister!'

'Then where's Finnegan?' Walcott demanded.

'I don't know! I don't know where Finnegan is!'

'Why hasn't Lowry reported that there's a problem? I was talking to Lowry less than two hours ago. I wanted him to get Fame safely out of the way. He never mentioned anything about Finnegan.'

'I don't know. Lowry was supposed to contact me if there

was any problem. I haven't heard from him. All I know is that Halpin is here now.'

Carter strode away, but found the door and the wall blocking his path after a couple of paces. Like a caged prisoner, he turned immediately and paced furiously back again.

'What's this about Manning's sister?' Walcott asked.

'What?'

'You said Halpin was enquiring about Manning's sister.'

'No, no. *Halpin's* sister. His *own* sister. She came here earlier today, apparently. About what, I don't know.'

Walcott stared. 'Did he describe her?'

'Her name's Linda.'

'That's not what I asked you. Do you know what she looks like? Did he describe her?'

'Yes. He said a tall, black-haired girl. She was wearing jeans and a black leather jacket. Why? Have you seen her? Where were you, by the way? You weren't here when we arrived. Your orders were to remain at your post . . .'

Walcott was no longer listening.

He was glancing through the window, into the darkness of the driveway outside.

The red Nissan Micra, he thought. It was Halpin's sister's car.

It couldn't be seen from the tower. There were no windows on the ground floor. But of course, the man would recognise it as soon as he stepped outside.

'*You'll* have to do it, Walcott!' Carter was hissing at him, cutting across his reflections. 'You'll have to do it yourself!'

The little secretary was standing directly in front of him, jabbing an insistent, irritating forefinger into his chest.

'Do what?'

'Kill him, Walcott! What Finnegan couldn't manage. Kill him! Tonight! Before he destroys everything.'

Friday, 13 November

Walcott smiled, but more with a wry bitterness than any genuine humour.

He had no objection to the task. He saw how essential it was.

But the quivering Carter was one of those who had sat behind a table a year ago with smug expressions on their confident faces, telling Walcott that he must do as he was ordered. That he was not the man to take charge of this operation. That McKelvey was already in training for it . . .

And a week before, when the problem with Halpin had become apparent, it was Carter again who had reminded Walcott that he had no authority to act. McKelvey would take care of that. In his own, inimitable way. McKelvey was the man.

Well . . .

'Does Kyne know that I'm here?' Walcott asked now.

'Kyne? No. He didn't see you. Not yet.'

'Is he staying the night?'

Carter nodded. 'Yes. But you don't have to come back. Follow Halpin when he leaves. Don't, in fact. Don't come back. Stay away. Get out of the country when you're finished. Use the route we intended. I'll look after things here.'

'What if something else goes wrong?'

'Nothing else will go wrong.'

Walcott stared, unable to believe the assurance.

There was no handgun that he could now easily and quickly acquire, he reminded himself. He had only a stolen car in which to tail a man who was actually searching for the vehicle. And he wondered if he should mention the young woman who might or might not have regained consciousness in some hospital or other . . .

8

Half-distracted by Carter's awkward departure and continued absence, half-surprised by Joseph Manning's energy and liveliness after a tiring day, Jimmy Kyne listened only intermittently to the ancient story unfolding in front of him.

He had no great affection for the past himself. The past was a terror he'd escaped from. And he was still wary of reviving it.

But it also occurred to him, sadly, that he had little warmth for the future, either.

The door to his right, connecting the tower to the west wing, blew slightly open as he was thinking. And a cool draught came sharply through it. Offering him the excuse to leave.

'Sorry,' he muttered. 'I'll just . . .'

As he moved quickly across the flagstones, he doubted if the others had even heard him.

Carter was in the hallway outside, standing between the closed doors to the kitchen and reception. He seemed to be sweating heavily. And he seemed to be disorientated, also. He was alternately using the same cloth handkerchief to clean his glasses and wipe the perspiration from his face. A sloppiness that was out of character.

He tried immediately for his usual haughtiness. 'Ah! Kyne!' he cried.

But he couldn't manage that, either. He was too nervous. Too distracted.

'What are you up to, Carter?' Kyne demanded.

The little man blinked, his bald forehead creasing with anxiety. 'I beg your pardon?'

Friday, 13 November

'What the hell's wrong with you?'
'Why?'
'You look sick.'
'Oh! Yes. Something I ate, Kyne. Shellfish. I had to leave.'
'What are you doing standing out here?'
'Well, I, ah, thought the Rushes, you see . . . That chap's sister. If she called, they may well have been here.'
'Have you asked them?'
'No. No. I was forced to go to the bathroom first, I'm afraid.'

Kyne stepped past him to open the kitchen door.

Inside, Mrs Rushe was stooping to take a casserole from the oven. Her husband was sitting at the table, reading a newspaper. Josie Thomas was huddled in a corner, clutching her soft toy.

'Did anyone call to St Kieron's today?' Kyne asked. 'Since you got here.'

The cook and her husband both shook their heads. 'No, not since three o'clock or so. There hasn't been a soul.'

The girl stared at Kyne. Meaningfully.

He smiled at her. She didn't return it.

There was a message in her hard look, he knew. A negative one. But he couldn't interpret it. It might be resentment directed at himself for abandoning her to the Rushes. It might be pique that he'd spoken to them and not addressed her first.

He didn't have time to investigate.

He stepped out and closed the kitchen door again.

He crossed in front of the still-static Carter to open the door to the reception opposite.

Something had created the draught that had brought him out, he remembered. Either this door or . . .

He turned sharply to ask Carter, 'Have you been outside?'

The secretary frowned and put his glasses back on. As if they were going to allow him to hear better. 'Sorry?' he enquired.

'Did you open the front door a while ago?'

123

'Me? Oh, yes, yes. A little fresh air, you see. Because I don't feel so . . .'

A slight odour of the perfumed aftershave Walcott used came from the empty reception room, mingling in the hallway with the smells of Mrs Rushe's cooking. The sweetness was unpleasant.

Kyne closed the door on it. And on the reminder of the curator's irritating absence.

9

'There was a sudden rustle of clothes,' Manning remembered. 'For all the world, like a savage gust of wind, Mr Halpin. There was the splashing of our boots through the rainwater, the thud of our rifle butts on the concrete. It was very impressive, our co-ordination. Much more impressive, our commanding officer informed us later, than our regular drills. But in any case, that's what we did. We all knelt and bowed our heads to receive absolution.

'All except one soldier . . .

'It was an extraordinary image, Mr Halpin. Quite extraordinary.

'An army battalion assembled in combat fatigues at four o'clock in the morning. Darkness and driving sleet. The priest shouting out his prayers from the small platform. The wind fighting against his straining voice. And one man still on his feet in front of him, still standing to attention down there in the dark, while the rest of his flock were on their knees.

'An extraordinary image . . .

'It was Alan Rosen, of course. Also there by default, by the way. A reservist caught up in the panic of the general mobilisation. He was from a different unit of the Local Defence Force to myself and Harry, however . . .'

The old man fell silent, staring back across fifty-eight years, into a distant past.

'Why did he do it?' Halpin wondered.

'I beg your pardon?'

'Rosen,' Halpin said. 'Was it simply lack of familiarity with the ritual? Because he was Jewish? Or was it a personal protest against the assumption that all Irishmen must be Roman Catholics?'

'Does it matter?' Manning asked.

'I think it does, yes.'

'Why?'

'His action defined him as dangerously different.'

'Certainly different,' Manning accepted. 'But why impute danger to it?'

Halpin thought of Cormac Lowry, the skinhead who spent his afternoons trying to distribute racist literature in Galway's main city park. Not that Lowry himself ever had much joy in his mission. He wasn't the face of prejudice in Ireland. He was too extreme. And far too *public*. He suggested mass meetings and shouted slogans, and promised only strict adherence to rigid rules and to order and discipline.

The face of prejudice in Ireland could have nothing to do with rules and nothing to do with regulations. It had to be private. Concealed. Never admitted. And therefore never spoken about.

So Halpin also thought of the Rosens' legal practice declining through the early 1940s. Just as he thought of Harry Fame calling frequently on the Jewish family in that period, hunting Alan.

'Rosen left home in March 1941, didn't he?' he said finally.

Manning nodded. 'Yes. To rent the house on the North Strand. Where he was killed, of course, a few months later.'

'Do you know why he left?'

'No. I actually lost touch with him when he moved. Or he with me. I think, perhaps, that he was slightly embarrassed about accepting money from me.'

'How often had you met him?'

'Oh, not frequently. It was, as I've suggested, an uneasy relationship. You can understand my reluctance to claim any credit from what little assistance I gave the family.'

'Did you ever get the sense that he was pursued?'

'You mean, the victim of racial prejudice?'

'Yes.'

'But then the entire family would have suffered also, wouldn't it?'

'Presumably.'

'And it didn't, of course.'

'No. Could I ask you a question that might seem absurd, that might even offend?'

'Of course. I am too old to take offence, Mr Halpin.'

'Have you ever had the suspicion that there was something ... something *convenient* about Alan Rosen's death in the bombing of Dublin? The circumstances are peculiar. He made no contact with his family during the previous week, for instance. You knew that, I believe.'

He thought he saw a tremor passing over the old man's clouded face.

The cause wasn't fear, he decided, however. It was loyalty.

'Is this why you were asking about Harry Fame earlier?' Manning enquired. 'Is this why you are worried about your sister interviewing Harry?'

Halpin saw no point in denying it. 'Yes.'

He wondered if Manning knew about Fame's pursuit of Alan Rosen through the early months of 1941.

What would make a man like Manning protect another like Fame over a lifetime, he asked himself in the silence. They were

Friday, 13 November

opposites. Fame was vain and self-interested. Womanising. Flashy and parasitic. The very antithesis of everything that the charity Crastina stood for.

Wasn't there a point where the Christian embrace became too indiscriminate? Where blind love finally created injustices elsewhere?

Manning had risen from the chair. He wasn't excited or offended, however. He was calmly helpful.

'Look,' he said. He took his stick in one hand and Halpin's elbow in the other and walked across to a section of the photographic display mounted on the south wall. When they got there, he released Halpin's elbow to tap a number of the photographs with his fingers. 'Look,' he invited again.

All the photographs here had been taken in the aftermath of the bombing in 1941. All had the same figures, although in varying positions. A solitary and slightly dishevelled policeman, guarding the bomb crater in front of the ruined buildings. The young Manning himself, his uncovered head bowed in prayer. The young Harry Fame, looking bereaved and distraught.

Halpin had no desire to disturb the old man's illusions. The beliefs and affections and memories of a lifetime.

Or not yet, anyway.

'I understand,' he said. 'I understand.'

But he thought otherwise.

The external show was easy, he reminded himself. The acceptable emotions. The genuine lies. They were always the easiest. And particularly for a practised performer like Fame.

The camera couldn't help but distort.

FIVE

1

From the pier at Kinvara, beyond the *Prince Killeen* whose crew were unloading in front of her, down the main road to the small headland where the castle had been built, Charlotte Rainey watched the extraordinary dance of visitors and residents at St Kieron's House.

For this entertainment, Rainey had deferred complying with the instructions of her chief superintendent.

Which was stupid, she accepted now.

If she was going to buck the orders, she should've swung Jarlath Burke behind her for support and advice. If she was going to pass Burke's office without whispering in his ear, she should've followed her orders to the letter.

Doing neither, she'd left herself exposed, without any back-up.

But that was how she always wanted it, she reminded herself irritably. How she always liked to play it. Wasn't it? Dragging a reluctant world towards admitting a truth she herself had almost wearied of from overfamiliarity.

Angel? She wasn't an angel. She was too human for that. She was a fucking saint. And application in for martyr status.

Rainey had acquired her anger very early in her life.

With an intelligent, caring mother, whose only real fault was

Friday, 13 November

lack of self-belief ... *Don't make the same mistakes I did, Charlotte*. What mistake had she made, Rainey wondered furiously. Getting conceived in the wrong womb at the wrong time in the social history of the country?

In any case ... with a mother like that, it was inevitable that Rainey's anger was directed as much inwards as outwards.

Fighting her corner. Fighting her mother's corner. There were times when the sense of *continual* struggle was a burden to her.

This was one of them.

She needed to share it with someone.

Eddie Halpin would've been ideal. The only male who'd never told her to stop kicking at the world. Ideal. If only he wasn't part of her current problem.

With hindsight, she'd tried to contact the blunt, unsentimental Burke after leaving the police station in Galway. But it was too late by then. He'd already left on a case. And she couldn't afford to leave her name on a message for him.

Not that she'd done anything irreversible yet. She hadn't gone to interview Harry Fame. She hadn't returned to Cork to chase up Birdy Finnegan's lover, Kylie. Thirty minutes after failing to contact Burke, she'd rung a close colleague in Special Branch, fishing for a little guidance, a little inside information on McQuaid's shielding of Crastina. The man's intense anxiety had been embarrassing. And unhelpful.

So she'd come down to Kinvara, where Joseph Manning was staying, to sit on a sharp, uncomfortable fence. And to watch. Because it was the dark, patriarchal figure of Manning who was the object of all her suspicions, the source of her unease.

She could still have left without damage at any stage, of course.

Or any stage before eight o'clock.

At eight o'clock, the door to the west wing of St Kieron's

was opened and Roger Walcott and Michael Carter stood in the light of the hallway on the threshold.

They might have been arguing. Although Walcott was relaxed and perfectly still, Carter was gesturing broadly.

They stayed less than a minute. After that, Carter seemed to push Walcott outwards and then retreat and close the door.

Walcott stayed standing outside. Without knocking. Without moving. As if he was a child, counting to a hundred before a game of hide-and-seek.

After a few minutes, however, he turned and walked to the red Nissan Micra. He sat in it. But only to release the handbrake, the gear lever and the steering lock, it seemed. Because he stood out again immediately and then pushed the small car backwards over the gravel and halfway down the driveway.

Only then did he start its engine. And only when he'd reversed onto the main road did he finally switch on its headlights.

He drove the short distance down to the village and turned onto the pier to park, less than twenty yards from where Rainey was standing.

He was waiting for Eddie Halpin. Why?

Until this point, Rainey had known Walcott only as a name and a photograph in a file. His personal history was unremarkable. The only child of Sussex farmers. An honourable career as an officer in the British Army. Immediate involvement with Crastina in England after retiring from the armed forces.

Thin material. And clearly not the entire story.

About eight thirty, when Halpin finally left St Kieron's and drove back towards Galway in his BMW, Walcott allowed a couple of other vehicles to slip between them before pulling out to follow.

And Rainey wondered if she, too, should tag along. Or stay

Friday, 13 November

at Kinvara, where Manning planned to spend the night and where the activity, to judge by the blinking lights in the buildings, was still as intense as ever.

She couldn't cover both, obviously. And she couldn't summon back-up.

The first consequence, she reminded herself, of diving alone and head first into this mess.

2

The house in Grattan Court, to the south-west of Galway city, was a three-bedroom, semi-detached residence on a middle-class estate.

Its lights were all on and there were empty beer cans and bottles in its front garden, but it seemed quiet and deserted by the time Eddie Halpin pulled up outside.

It was still early. Only a little after nine thirty.

There was no answer when he rang the doorbell.

He walked around the side, through an open wooden gate and into the garden, and from there followed the path to the rear door, which was also swinging open.

Beyond it, the kitchen was deserted.

He stepped in. He moved quickly through the kitchen and along the corridor to the bottom of the stairs, where he stopped, alerted by a noise from the living-room to his left.

Inside, in the opposite corner of the room, a slight, balding man, dressed in bright reds and greens, was kneeling by the stereo system, with the contents of the CD rack scattered around him on the floor.

He seemed to be crying. When he finally looked up and saw

Silent City

Halpin standing in the open doorway, he dabbed his nose with the back of his hand and smiled with exaggerated bravery.

'Hi,' he said. 'Are you all right? My name is Martin. Martin Trayne.'

'Eddie Halpin.'

'Hi, Eddie.'

'Sorry for barging in,' Halpin said. 'But, ah, isn't there supposed to be a party here?'

'*Supposed* is right.'

'I'm looking for my sister, Linda. Linda Halpin.'

'Oh! I see.'

'Do you know her?'

'No.'

'No? Then, ah . . . Tomkin! Do you know—'

'The Echoing Tom. Yes, I know *him*.'

'Was he here?'

'An impatient man,' Trayne complained. 'And impatience is the mother of unfaithfulness.'

'Right. But has he *been* here?'

'Oh, yes. He's been here.'

'With a woman.'

'But of course.'

'What did she look like?'

'Young? Tall? Long black hair?'

'That's her.'

'They must have left with the rest of them.'

'To go where?'

'Didn't you know?'

'What?'

'They've gone to the bride's house,' Trayne explained. 'The wedding is tomorrow, you know.'

He sniffed again. But this time he took a paper handkerchief from his sleeve and blew in it gently.

'Bride's house?' Halpin repeated.

Friday, 13 November

'To finish the party,' Trayne told him impatiently. 'Half at the groom's here, half at the bride's there. Everyone except myself. It's in Oranmore. Outside the city.'

'I've just passed through it,' Halpin complained. 'Fifteen minutes ago. On my way here.'

'Then you'll have to go back,' Trayne advised. 'On the main Galway road. A house called Merridew.'

He laughed lightly and stood up, but then grimaced with pain and showed his bare left arm, under the shirtsleeve he'd rolled to the elbow. Blood was spilling from a wound on his wrist and dropping onto the CD covers.

'I'm afraid I cut myself,' he said simply.

He walked unsteadily over. When he reached the doorway, he stumbled forward, so that Halpin had to catch and support him. 'Your clothes,' he said sadly, with genuine concern.

'It doesn't matter,' Halpin assured him. 'We'll go to the kitchen. You need to wash that off and see how badly it's cut.'

'No, no,' Trayne objected. 'There's a medicine cabinet upstairs. I know where it is.' He closed his eyes for a moment, holding back a resurgence of the tears. 'I live here, you see. By myself now.'

He rounded Halpin and left the living-room with absurd dignity, holding his bleeding left hand in front of him. As he turned past the banisters to climb the stairs, he stumbled a little, slipping on a beer carton someone had left on the carpet.

'Do you need me?' Halpin called.

Trayne picked himself up and smiled back. 'You're very sweet.'

'Right,' Halpin agreed. 'Do you want me to wait for you? I'm going to drive to Oranmore to see Tomkin and my sister. You can take a lift with me if you want.'

3

Roger Walcott didn't bother with the front door of the house.

Expecting Halpin to come back along the same route, he walked quietly around the unattached side of the building.

At the gable corner he stopped and peered into the garden, alerted by the rustling of bushes in the shadows at the back.

Only the wind?

He waited.

Most of the garden was illuminated by the lights spilling from the building itself. There was a low wall, he saw, built with unplastered concrete blocks at the end. A narrow border of plants and flowers ran along the boundary to his right. To the left stood an elm tree, its trunk surrounded by shrubs and bushes.

And it was from the base of the elm, out of the density of bushes, that a white-faced tom-cat suddenly darted and stopped to stare at Walcott before jumping the wall into the next garden.

Walcott moved on, around the back of the house, up to the open rear door.

He peered into the empty kitchen. He stepped inside. Using the wall as cover, he made his way cautiously to the interior door and then along the deserted corridor beyond, from where he could check the living-room to his left.

That too was empty.

At the base of the stairs he placed his hand lightly on the banister and got himself ready to climb.

He almost didn't catch the warning noises from above. A floorboard creaking. The first splash of water running from a

Friday, 13 November

tap and hitting an enamel sink. Both sounds heard only for an instant before being drowned again by the noise of a car pulling away from the street outside.

He silently climbed the stairs, until he could see into the bathroom that was facing him at the top.

Its door was almost half open. Inside, leaning over the sink and with his back to the door, there was a small, wiry man who had stripped to the waist and who was wrapping a bandage around his bleeding left wrist.

As the man started humming softly to himself while he worked, Walcott climbed the rest of the stairs and moved along the corridor to check the three bedrooms on the floor.

All of them were empty.

Starting to worry a little, starting to wonder now about that car he'd heard outside, he came back and used his fist to push the bathroom door fully open.

The knock of knuckles against wood made Martin Trayne jump a little.

'Go to the *party*, Eddie,' Trayne said irritably. 'I'll be *all right*. I never change my mind, you know, once I—'

He half-turned then, saw that it was a stranger standing behind him, and nervously tailed off.

Walcott looked at the slight, bony figure with growing disgust.

The manicured nails. The high-pitched voice. The effeminate mannerisms. They all triggered intense dislike.

And since he knew now that Halpin had eluded him again, since this affected specimen seemed to be responsible for his distraction, the distaste soon hardened into resentment.

'Eddie?' he repeated coldly. 'Eddie Halpin?'

Trayne now had his bandaged left hand suspended in the air. It was trembling slightly. He rested his hips against the sink and tried to keep his eyes away from Walcott's clenched fists. 'That's right,' he said warily.

135

'*What* party?' Walcott demanded.

Trayne went immediately for a show of ignorant innocence. 'I beg your pardon?'

But it was already too late for that. And the unconvincing gesture towards heroism was the worst choice.

Walcott stepped closer, into the bathroom itself. Without any further warning, he raised his right hand and smashed the fist into Trayne's nose.

Trayne's head jerked sharply backwards to make heavy contact with the glass-fronted cabinet behind him. The impact cut his skull and left his blood spattered on the mirror and starting to trickle down its surface.

'What party?' Walcott asked again.

Already half-unconscious, Trayne slipped downwards, his right arm wedging in the sink and keeping him from falling.

Walcott lifted him, grabbing him by the hair and yanking his face upwards to almost touch his own. When the eyes were almost level, he sprung his head back and smashed his forehead into the other's already shattered face.

It was the pure release of strained emotions. Nothing more calculated. Nothing more personal.

He'd already lost hope of getting the information he needed and would've continued the attack, for his pleasure, except that the short, truncated blurp of a nearby siren as it was quickly switched on and then off again alerted him to danger.

He stopped to listen.

From outside, through the open doors and windows, came the sound of a car approaching at speed and pulling sharply up.

He lowered Trayne to the floor, left the bathroom and hurried along the corridor to the front bedroom, where the main light was still on.

Crouching low to avoid being seen, he peered through the lace curtains from the bottom corner of the window. As he'd expected, the silver BMW was no longer there. In its place was a white police car with two uniformed officers sitting in the front.

Walcott moved quickly backwards again, without bothering to wonder who had called them or for what reason.

At the bathroom, he glanced in briefly at Trayne, who was lying unconscious on the floor.

Descending the stairs, he checked the front door and the panels to its sides. All wood, he noticed with relief. No glass that was going to betray his presence to the police outside.

He reached out and unlocked the door. He left it slightly ajar, without pulling it open, and then ran down the hallway, through the kitchen and into the back garden.

Around by the gable again, but still hidden from the road, he heard the doors of the police car opening and closing and the two young officers chatting to each other as they approached the house.

The two houses in the unit to his left were both in darkness, he'd already noticed.

He climbed a low wall into the garden of the first, then a higher wall to the second, and came out, back onto the pathway, through the gap between that and the next semi-detached unit.

He turned left once more and walked calmly to the Nissan Micra and drove clear of Grattan Court without being challenged or followed. And presumably without being noticed, either.

Twenty minutes later he spotted a Jaguar XJ6 and a small Fiat outside a suburban house that seemed deserted by a holidaying family. He drove on, parked the Micra in a nearby cul-de-sac, and walked back to exchange it for the Jaguar.

SIX

1

Merridew was an isolated, three-storey house on the outskirts of Oranmore, less than five miles south of Galway city.

Easy to find.

But again, although its doors were open, there was no party in progress when Eddie Halpin finally reached it.

Apart from five or six people preparing a buffet in its kitchen, the place seemed completely deserted.

'I'm looking for Linda Halpin and Tom Tomkin,' Halpin told them. 'I was expecting to meet them here.'

A blonde girl with her hair tied back in a pony-tail shook her head and shrugged. 'I don't know,' she said. 'We're only the caterers. They're all still down in the pub.'

'What pub?'

'I don't know. We're only the cat—'

'Right. OK.'

'They're probably going to be back in a while, though. Do you want to wait?'

'Yeah, why not.' He looked hungrily at the display of food. He hadn't eaten since breakfast. With Linda. He gestured and asked, 'Do you mind if I . . ?'

'Yeah, sure,' the girl said. 'Help yourself.'

Friday, 13 November

He took a cold plate and a beer and sat at the long pine table in the dining-room next door.

For three or four minutes he ate without restraint, with his head down, concentrating only on the food. Until he became aware that someone was standing in the doorway to his left, on the edge of his vision, and that they were watching him.

When he turned to look, he also frowned with irritation.

Smiling back at him was Charlotte Rainey.

He watched her warily as she pushed herself away from the door frame. She closed the door behind her with the heel of her right sneaker and walked across, carrying an open bottle of beer in each hand.

She sat directly opposite him. She placed the beers on the table between them and with a little gesture, invited him to share.

Halpin stared at her. 'We couldn't possibly still have the same friends, could we, Charlotte?' he wondered finally. 'We couldn't possibly be still arriving late for the same parties?'

She shook her head. 'I've been following you,' she told him bluntly.

'Since when?' he asked.

'Since when?' she repeated. 'You should really ask why. Anyone with nothing to hide always asks why.'

'You put the same question more directly to me this morning, Charlotte. The response is the same. I don't have anything to tell you.'

'I've been with you since Kinvara. I was there for other reasons. I saw you arriving and leaving, and I fell in behind you.'

'I didn't notice.'

'You don't notice enough, Eddie.'

'What's that supposed to mean?'

She rocked the base of her bottle on the bare pine table. 'You're involved in something you know nothing about,' she said. 'No, it's worse than that. You *think* you know what you're doing. That's fatal. You're over your head. You need help, Eddie.'

Despite his annoyance, Halpin smiled sardonically to himself.

It was a phrase she'd always used when she was really angry in argument. *You can't take responsibility for your own decisions. No, it's worse. You can't even take decisions any more. You need help, Eddie.*

The tag was totally ridiculous. When she was composed, it was the last thing she would've recommended. She thought that most professional carers had to be approached with caution and that all psychiatrists were charlatans.

But then, she was full of quirky contradictions.

He didn't look at her again for a while. He drank the first of his beers and finished his meal, putting the plastic knife and fork down and pushing the plate away from him.

When she spoke again, it seemed at first as if they were back on the same wavelength. 'Remember about a year ago?' she prompted. 'When we had a holiday in Spain?'

He nodded. The memory was pleasant.

But she seemed to have softened the mood only to shatter it again. 'We were in the mountains at Jarama, where Joseph Manning's father was killed in the Spanish Civil War. Do you remember how you described the incident?'

'The description wasn't mine. I was quoting from a letter written by another soldier to the seventeen-year-old Joseph.'

'But you remember the details, don't you?'

'According to the letter-writer, the cruellest blow was struck at the decisive moment, after Lieutenant Manning had rallied his panicking troops and led them to victory. A Republican straggler, swarthy and arrogant, sneaked from the cover of the rocks and shot the lieutenant in the back. It's a sad fiction, of course. In the only action it ever saw in the Civil War, the Irish

Brigade was attacked by another Nationalist unit from the Canary Islands. Manning was killed by his own side.'

'I know. But the boy had to have a romantic hero as a father.'

'Come on, Charlotte.'

'Just as he had to have a black widow as a mother.'

'This is just a little something you've been hung up on.'

'Argue,' she advised. 'Don't patronise.'

'Crastina is patriarchal. This has always been your point. But examine any Irish institution and you'll find the same pattern.'

'The link, Eddie, is between patriarchy and intolerance. But I'm not merely making a point now. This is actually leading somewhere.'

'Where?'

'Manning's older sister, Bridget, had a pretty grim life. No perfume. Just the stifling smell of incense in gloomy churches.'

'It was the tenor of the times, Charlotte.'

'Why did she kill herself?'

Halpin shrugged. Wearily. Impatiently.

'OK,' Rainey said then. 'Let's see if I've got this right. Manning founded Crastina in December 1941, about three months after his sister's suicide and a little over six months since the bombing in Dublin. What did he found it with?'

'How do you mean?'

'We all know the elevating legend, Eddie. How he opened his own prosperous house to the poor of the city. But during the early months of 1942 almost fifty complaints were lodged by neighbours about the use to which he was putting the family home. That summer, he bought separate premises in the inner city. What did he buy them with?'

Halpin shrugged again. 'He sold his own house.'

Rainey shook her head. 'You're wrong, Eddie.'

'It's not an opinion, Charlotte. The documents exist. The shortfall was made up by public donations.'

'I don't think so.'

'OK, let's accept that I'm wrong. What did he buy the new premises with?'

'I confirmed this two months ago. Bridget Manning inherited a generous fortune from her Aunt Peggy less than a year before her own death. Her brother received only a small gratuity. Apart from Bridget, the Mannings were broke.'

Halpin stared at her.

He remembered from a couple of years ago the experience of discovering a significant historical document. And he felt the same weak, light-headed, nerve-tingling sensation again now.

Rainey thought she was demonstrating one solution, but in fact she'd just handed him the final piece of his own puzzle.

And in his triumph, over her as much as others, he couldn't resist pointing it out.

'Where did the money go after her death?' he asked. 'Not all to her brother, in any case.'

Rainey shook her head. 'I haven't established that yet.'

He seemed to deviate. 'Alan Rosen's family were lawyers in 1941.'

She frowned. 'So?'

He pushed the beer bottles to one side. As if they were obstructing. He said, 'And Harry Fame got suddenly rich that same year, chucked in his job and quickly emigrated to England.' He raised his right hand and released a finger for each suspicious item. 'One apparent suicide. Heiress. One apparently accidental death in convenient bombing. Lawyer. One new playboy with unexplained source of income. Interesting? Or what?'

Friday, 13 November

2

In the front room of Eddie Halpin's home, Roger Walcott sat uncomfortably on the black leather couch and struggled with a sense of irony.

Walcott hated ironies.

They were life's fractures, he felt. Life's dislocations and ruptures.

They were subversive.

At the moment, however, he seemed to be weighed down by them.

He'd finally managed to break into the bungalow on Snipe Avenue, for instance. But a day too late.

The place was no longer occupied. But only because there was nothing to guard.

And he'd found and read the documents that he was supposed to remove and destroy. But there was nothing in them that compromised anything, or anyone.

Halpin knew nothing of consequence about Harry Fame. He knew nothing of Walcott himself, apart from the fact that he'd served in the British Army. And he knew nothing at all of Columbus.

The order to kill him had been unnecessary. Foolhardy. And self-destructive.

On an A4 notepad left on the writing bureau in the study, Halpin had written, *Excluding 1492, in what year did Columbus discover America? What does it mean?*

The rest of the page was covered with absurd doodles. Betraying the man's ignorance. His confusion. His inability to answer the question.

Among the papers in the study, among the files on computer, this was the only reference to Columbus.

And even this had obviously come to him quite late, *after* the attempt on his life that had been undertaken to bury the knowledge he'd never had. Because the notes on the previous page were dated Thursday afternoon, mere hours before he'd set out to travel to Kerry.

Halpin did not understand the origins of the name Columbus. He was unaware of what lay behind it. He had no idea of its promise.

Why, then, had his assassination been ordered?

Walcott stood up from the couch and paced the bare floorboards while he thought.

The order to kill Halpin had come directly from McKelvey, less than a week before. The choice of the agent and the means had been McKelvey's. McKelvey was acting on information supplied by Michael Carter. And Carter had been first alerted to the danger by Cormac Lowry, the youth Halpin thought he was exclusively using.

With a death sentence from McKelvey hanging over him, the drug-addicted Lowry could surely be trusted for loyalty? Surely it was his *judgement* that was way off centre?

But no, Walcott realised. No. Of course not.

Lowry had somehow compromised himself further with Halpin. Something more final than mere delinquency. Something that neutralised his reliability and that therefore carried the threat of instant execution.

A betrayal, of course.

But how?

Money? The large donation from the late businessman that was supposed to have flown through the bloodstream of Columbus . . ?

In any case, caught cold between the two, Lowry's only

hope of escape had been the destruction of Columbus or the death of Halpin.

He'd clearly gone for the easier option. And set Halpin up. Even to the extent of supplying his route and his schedule on the previous day's trip to Kerry.

All of which meant that Lowry had far more native intelligence than anyone had ever given him credit for.

Wearying of ironies, of the mess this operation had become, of the precise fulfilment of all his own gloomiest prophecies about McKelvey's incompetence, Walcott reached in his pockets for his cigarettes. He shook one from the pack and caught its filter between his lips.

But he didn't light it.

Clutching the lighter in one hand and a torch in the other, he retraced the route he'd taken after breaking into and searching the bungalow.

There were no ashtrays. And therefore no smokers in the house.

Coming in from the fresh air, the first thing Halpin would notice was the smell of stale cigarette smoke. The first thing he'd think of was intruders.

Replacing the cigarettes and checking again through the rooms for traces of his own presence, Walcott somehow regained a little confidence. The operation wasn't doomed, he convinced himself. It could still be salvaged. And he himself would save it.

He decided to wait in the woman's bedroom at the rear of the house and to ambush Halpin from there.

It was the best location. In it he could use the torch to read again through Halpin's notes on the life of Alan Rosen, but without the light showing to the front or side of the bungalow. From it he could still hear the sound of Halpin's approaching car.

He looked at his wristwatch. It was already a little after midnight.

He wondered if Halpin would return that night after failing to trace his sister at the party. Or would someone else come in first and force Walcott either to show his hand too early or retreat?

And what then? What if the ambush was aborted and Halpin eluded him once more?

He lay on the bed and thought again of Lowry and of Harry Fame, who was still with the youth, he hoped, keeping out of the way.

The treacherous Lowry was of little interest now. And of less use.

But Fame, he reminded himself, had clearly been capable of luring Halpin's sister to an isolated ambush. And if all else failed he might be used again, it occurred to him, to lure Halpin himself to the same fate.

3

There was a moment of stillness after Eddie Halpin asked his questions.

The kind of stillness, Rainey thought, that proverbially preceded storms.

But even as she became aware of the silence, it suddenly broke around her.

Without warning, the doors were flung open on both sides of the dining-room, admitting a lot of noise and a lot of loud and drunken people. Within seconds, the room was overcrowded. Filled with stinging cigarette smoke and the smell of food and drink, it was a place only of public pleasures again.

Friday, 13 November

Disappointed, Rainey finished her drink in silence.

She watched Halpin anxiously scanning the crowd and searching for someone. When he got up and left, without addressing her again, she stood as well and turned to follow his movements.

In the doorway to the kitchen he talked with a bearded man whose face was bruised from a recent fight and then to a black-haired young woman who was very drunk.

She saw them only for a second or two. After that they were swept away by the surging crowd.

She pushed her way through, into the kitchen, and then beyond that, to the long garden at the rear. But when she finally tracked down the bearded character again, only the woman was still with him.

She couldn't afford to waste any more time. She showed him her ID.

'The man you were talking to just now,' she said. 'Eddie Halpin. What did he want from you?'

'He wanted to know if I'd met his sister tonight.'

'Linda?'

'That's her name.'

'Why should you meet Linda Halpin?'

'She's my girlfriend.'

Rainey glanced at the drunken blackhead by his side. 'Is that right?' she asked sardonically. '*Did* you meet her?'

'No, she didn't turn up.'

'Where did you get the damaged face? Someone else's boyfriend?'

'No, Halpin assaulted me.'

'Oh? When? Why?'

'I was staying with Linda last night in Halpin's bungalow in Galway . . .'

Rainey toured the party again after hearing Tomkin's story.

But no one there knew Eddie Halpin. And she didn't see him herself.

At twelve thirty, she tracked down the advertising executive whose Mercedes was blocking her Alfa Romeo on the road outside and she drove about a mile back towards Galway before pulling in to use her mobile phone.

She rang Halpin's home first, got nothing but the answering machine, and left a fairly pointless message. 'It's Charlotte. I'll ring you again.'

She thought a long time about the second call, weighing its dangers and its benefits, but finally looked up Jarlath Burke's home number in her personal directory and dialled it.

Maybe Burke had lots of practice answering late-night calls. Or maybe his bad stomach kept him awake, anyway. He picked up the receiver before it rang a second time.

'Hello?' he growled. 'Yes?'

'Jarlath?' she said anxiously. 'It's Charlotte. I'm sorry I'm so—'

'For Christ's sake, woman! It's one o'clock in the morning!'

'I know, I know. But I thought it was better to ring you first.'

'Better than what?'

'I don't actually have anywhere to stay in Galway tonight, Jarlath.'

'You should've asked me that this afternoon, shouldn't you?'

'I know.'

'If you'd bothered to call in on me.'

'I know. I'm sorry, Jarlath.'

'Where are you, anyway?'

'Just outside Oranmore.'

'Right. Then I suppose you'd better come over, hadn't you?'

Burke lived alone on a quiet estate in the south suburbs of Galway city. By the time she reached there, he'd dressed in a track suit and had tea ready for her. But no sympathy.

Friday, 13 November

'I think I'm in a little trouble, Jarlath,' she confessed.

'What's new?' he demanded crustily.

'You remember Eddie Halpin?'

His reaction was so disgusted that he spilled the tea he was pouring. 'Not bloody romantic trouble, Charlotte?'

'No, no. You know Crastina, the charity?'

'What about it?'

'I think it might be involved in something shady. I don't know what. I think Halpin might've stumbled across whatever it is and put himself in danger. His sister seems to have gone missing.'

'There's an awful lot of mights and maybes in there.'

'No, no, Halpin's sister is definitely missing.'

Burke brought a cloth from the kitchen to mop the spilled tea off the coffee-table. 'What are you going to do about it?' he asked.

She shook her head. 'That's the point. I can't do anything. I'm not supposed to be still investigating Crastina. McQuaid's orders.'

'Come straight out with it, Charlotte,' Burke advised. He sat back, holding a cup and saucer in his lap, and stared at her. 'I always prefer honesty, you know. You want me to stick my nose into it, don't you?'

'Either that or I come clean with McQuaid.'

'But you don't trust McQuaid.'

Rainey looked at the cup of tea she was holding. A clot of milk was floating with the current since she'd stirred.

She needed a whiskey, she thought. But Burke's stomach had no tolerance of hard liquor and he didn't keep temptations in the house.

'I didn't say that,' she pointed out.

'No, you didn't,' Burke accepted. 'And you're right. Thinking it and saying it are two different things. You can't lose your job for thinking anything.'

'Well, this is between ourselves, surely,' she probed.

'Between ourselves,' he picked up, 'let me tell you that McQuaid called me in directly you were gone this afternoon. I have his orders too, you know. I have to report to him everything you discuss with me. I even have to tell him immediately you make any contact again.'

Rainey stiffened. Her hand shook as she put the untouched tea back on the coffee-table. She felt betrayed and totally without support. As alone and isolated as she sometimes feared she wanted to be.

Her voice trembled with anger when she spoke. 'I think you should have told me that before we started, Jarlath.'

PART THREE
Saturday, 14 November

ONE

1

Jimmy Kyne had never felt so uneasy or so unsettled in his life.

Fear and danger and anxiety he had all experienced before. Many times. In as many locations. But this was different, he thought.

He had no belief in ghosts, but it was as if St Kieron's House was haunted for that night.

There was the constant sense of some insubstantial threat within the castle, some unseen and unseeable presence.

Familiar sounds took on a sinister feeling. Someone turning in a creaking bed in the darkness. The stairway groaning as its wood contracted. A low moan. The breeze gently whistling around the castle's walls. A sudden cry from someone frightened by a dream.

Twice that night, Kyne was woken from a nightmare.

Twice he found himself struggling to sit up in the bed, sweating and breathing heavily, with his heart racing loudly.

Twice he got up and went to open the bedroom window to look out, across the inlet to the opposite headland, where Crastina's tall new headquarters stood out dark against the clear night sky.

But of course, everything seemed mockingly normal again by

then. The calm sea below him. The occasional twinkling of light from one of the cottages opposite. The dim shapes of trucks and diggers still on the building site across the inlet.

All the quietness and all the peace of a night in a sheltered inlet on the west coast of Ireland.

Maybe it was the weather itself that was troubling him, Kyne thought then.

The night was unusually warm for early winter, as if a storm was brewing and threatening to break. The air in the bedroom had been stuffy and oppressive until he'd opened the window.

Or maybe it was the mystery surrounding Walcott's disappearance. The struggle to understand the curator's suspicious absence. The impatience for his return. The expectation that he might be back at any moment, if only Kyne could force himself to stay awake for another five or ten minutes.

But he knew that it was more than these, disturbing as they were.

It was more like the shifting of soil as buried memories were dug up, he thought. More like the ghosts of the dead rising to walk again.

Not from his own past. He'd come to terms with his escape from that a long time before.

But ever since that interview with Eddie Halpin in the evening, Joseph Manning had been agitated and distant. He'd been excited at first by the memories and by the grip his story had on Halpin. A bit like a child rediscovering an old forgotten toy, Kyne had thought. But then he'd gradually sunk into an anxious, nervous melancholy.

He'd stopped responding to things around him. He'd started reacting to something in his own mind.

He hadn't touched his dinner. He'd tried to pray in the chapel afterwards, and then in one of the small cells set aside for contemplation. But he'd wandered from both after a few

Saturday, 14 November

fruitless minutes, unable to be at peace, either with himself or with his God.

At ten o'clock, he'd finally taken a sedative and drifted into a sleep that was still troubled and still unsettled.

Kyne blamed himself for the relapse.

Mr Manning, he knew, was already apprehensive about the ceremony in Dublin the following afternoon and about the later reception at the American Embassy.

To allow an inquisitive academic to bother him at such a time . . .

So Kyne constantly rebuked himself, and wondered if his personal guilt also explained the strange unease that had subsequently gripped him. The nightmares. The sense of an unseen menace.

A little before eight in the morning, he was again woken by some disturbance.

Again he sat upright in the bed, in a cold sweat, gasping for breath.

Again he swung from the mattress and walked across to the window to look out on the brightening landscape and compose himself. Leaning outwards, he stuck his head into the open to draw in the sharp morning air and to clear his mind.

When the scream came, he heard it only faintly, under the rush of air through his nostrils. And he was confused.

He thought at first it had come from the village or the pier, over to his left.

But as he pulled back into the room, intending to walk across to the small gable window and glance out there as well, it pierced the night again. And he knew then that it was inside St Kieron's itself.

It was the girl, he realised.

It was Josie Thomas, who was sleeping in a bedroom at the other end of the corridor.

He hurried out, still dressed in his blue pyjamas.

The girl's door was already open. Inside, in the weak light from the dawn, Josie was lying awake in her bed, slightly propped by a pillow from behind. Her eyes were wide and staring. She was desperately clutching her brown teddy bear and shivering violently.

Kyne stepped in, but stopped again immediately. She seemed to recoil in fear at his advance.

'Josie?' he called. 'It's me, Josie. Jimmy Kyne.'

She tightened her eyebrows to peer at him, and then relaxed a little, settling back on the pillow with relief.

'Can I come in, Josie?' Kyne asked.

She nodded.

He walked across and sat on the edge of her bed, looking down on her gently. There were two fresh grazes, both bleeding slightly, on the right of her pale neck, presumably from where she'd scratched herself with her nails.

'Did you have a dream, Josie?' he asked her.

She nodded again. 'The *Grey Witch*,' she whispered. 'The *Grey Witch*.'

'Right,' Kyne agreed.

But his question and his presence seemed to have triggered a need in her. She sat up slightly, propped on her left elbow. Her eyes grew wide again, but now with the urgent effort to gain his attention.

'The fat man,' she said anxiously. 'The beard.'

Kyne was confused, uncertain whether to encourage or banish her ghosts.

A fat man with a beard. Was it some terrible figure from her past, he wondered. One of her mother's more brutal lovers? Or was it just her image for a sea captain?

'It's all right,' he assured her hopefully. 'You don't have to worry about him now.'

'Something the matter?' she demanded suddenly. But her

Saturday, 14 November

voice was strange now, clipped and deeper, as if she were trying to imitate another's.

Kyne shook his head. 'No,' he said slowly, thoughtfully. 'No, nothing's the matter, Josie.'

He stood up as he spoke, deciding finally that his presence was only prolonging the effects of her nightmare. He stooped to pat her arm and to cover her fully with the duvet.

'It's all right, Josie,' he said again. 'You don't have to worry now. All right?'

She smiled slightly, with what seemed like gratitude.

The room was already brightening with the dawn, but he thought that a little more light might ease her fears and help her settle. He switched on the bedside lamp and turned its beam away from her, down towards the floor.

She lay back on the pillow, closed her eyes, and seemed already comfortable again by the time he left the room and closed her door behind him.

Outside, Joseph Manning's secretary, Michael Carter, was also awake and out of bed. Wrapped in a red dressing-gown, he was standing in the corridor near his own bedroom door, deathly pale and shivering violently.

'What are you up to, Kyne?' he demanded suspiciously.

Kyne stopped. He stared into the secretary's queasy little eyes, intending to react. But what he saw in them wasn't accusation or anger. It was fear.

So he thought at first that Carter too had been the victim of bad dreams that night . . .

Until the secretary asked, 'Something the matter?'

In that clipped, nervous delivery that Josie had so accurately echoed.

Kyne frowned. But he said nothing. Not having anything but worries to support an argument.

He walked past Carter and returned to his own bedroom,

leaving his door open behind him. He lay on his back in bed. He closed his eyes. He thought about a fat man with a beard. He thought about the thin and balding Carter, who was clean-shaven and wore glasses . . .

Five minutes later, before he could possibly have fallen asleep again and dreamed it, his thoughts were disturbed again by a loud thud from directly below.

2

A slight, rhythmical knocking, merging with and then breaking the dream he'd been locked in, finally woke Eddie Halpin at eight thirty.

When he opened his eyes, it was with the guilty sense of being summoned to a neglected duty. He felt anxious. He felt burdened with a sense of failure and a fear of weakness. Apologies and explanations, along with inadequate and unwanted excuses, were on his lips.

Under his face, the pillow was damp with his sweat and slightly warm from his agitated breathing. He had a sharp headache. And there was a tender bruise on his left temple, where he must have taken a blow or a knock.

He looked cautiously around, without rising from the narrow bed he was lying on.

He was in a small room that seemed no bigger than a cell and that was now brightly lit by the morning sun through its thin curtains.

Apart from the bed, there was space only for a small locker on the floor. A door and a pine-effect, built-in wardrobe dominated the wall opposite him. The wallpaper had recurring images of Dennis the Menace and matched the duvet that had

Saturday, 14 November

fallen off him during the night. Above him, the white ceiling held a poster of the Galway hurling team. The carpet was dark green.

He doubted that he could've chosen the place to sleep in. And he couldn't remember being forced into it.

He had no idea where he was.

And that rhythmical knocking – two sharp raps followed by what seemed like a low growling – had started again, disorientating him more.

It was coming from behind the door, he figured now, next to the wardrobe on the opposite wall.

Still fully dressed in the clothes he'd put on the morning before, he swung from the bed and stepped across to investigate. It needed only two short paces.

Expecting the door to be locked, he pulled it sharply towards him. But it opened smoothly. So smoothly that the bald young woman who was sleeping in the corridor outside and leaning back against it still held her posture for a second, although there was nothing left to support her any more.

Even when she dropped limply backwards and knocked her head on the green carpet, she didn't wake. Her blue eyes flickered open for an instant from the impact and then gently closed again without seeing anything.

She seemed vaguely familiar to Eddie. Her black leather clothes. Her black gloves. The gold ring through her left nostril.

But it was only when he looked beyond her and recognised a few more of the faces that were visible among the tangled bodies along the hallway that he finally remembered where he was and realised that it was nothing more sinister than a hangover he was suffering from.

About one o'clock the night before, he recalled, after he'd talked with Tomkin and confirmed that Linda had disappeared, he'd fallen into a helpless despair.

Silent City

He might've driven the few miles down the road to check again on Harry Fame's house. It had occurred to him to try it. Or he might've travelled back to Galway and kicked Cormac Lowry out of bed for a few more answers.

He might even have confided in Charlotte Rainey.

Instead, he'd watched her search the party and then leave.

His freedom had been guilt-ridden, though, and he'd drunk to kill it off.

Part of his depression was just tiredness, of course. Exhaustion from all the worry and fear, from the hopeless searching, and from the lingering after-shock of the attempt on his life.

But part of it was also proud isolation. A foolish independence. A fault he shared with his sister.

Charlotte's tag came suddenly back to him. *You need help, Eddie.* Only it didn't seem so funny any more. Or so irrelevant.

He must've drunk a lot to push his worries into the background, he thought.

He couldn't remember how he'd ended in what was obviously a child's bedroom. And even though he had a vague image of the bald young woman playfully head-butting him, he still wasn't certain where he'd caught the bruise on his forehead.

He picked his way quickly through the sleepers in the hallway now and went downstairs into the chaotic kitchen and dining-room. The two of them were littered with discarded bottles and glasses and food.

He rummaged in the kitchen and found enough to make a simple breakfast to go with a pot of filtered coffee.

It was almost nine when he eventually left.

Others had woken in the meantime, but no one else had actually struggled up to meet the morning yet. Weren't they all supposed to be wedding guests that day?

If Linda wasn't at home or hadn't left a message, he decided, then he'd immediately notify the police of her disappearance.

Saturday, 14 November

He knew that he'd also have to reveal the connection with his research into Alan Rosen. Along with the hidden history of Crastina, the dark role of Harry Fame and the attempt on his own life in Kerry.

Charlotte already suspected the links.

It was a pity, really, having his hand forced like that, because police investigations were always cruder. Some of the present mysteries might well be laid bare, he thought. But those of the past never would now.

And a dark past meant only partial understanding of the present.

The traffic was light on the road back to the city and he drove quickly, wanting to move on to the next phase without delay and needing to escape that sensation of weakness and failure that had lingered from the morning's dream.

He had no real hopes left any more.

When he finally turned into Snipe Avenue and saw that the driveway of his bungalow was still empty, it wasn't so much that any lingering optimism was dashed. It was more that his depression just found a slightly deeper level.

3

In his bedroom, Jimmy Kyne had dressed quickly in dark jeans and T-shirt and sneakers.

Maybe it was only Walcott finally coming back, he'd thought hopefully. The noise below.

But Kyne had never taken a chance with Joseph Manning's safety. And he wasn't going to risk one now, when so much else was making him so uneasy.

He took the Walther semi-automatic pistol, its shoulder holster and a long torch from his suitcase.

He left his room and returned along the empty corridor, stopping first at Manning's door to listen to the old man praying quietly to himself inside, then at Carter's, and finally at Josie's, where everything was silent again.

At the bottom of the stairway, he checked that the front doors were still locked and bolted from the inside.

He didn't use the torch. Relying only on the early daylight through the windows, he went carefully into the small reception and the kitchen, and then through the cells and the chapel. All without finding anything.

When he came back, he stood again at the foot of the stairs. In front of him, the connecting door to the tower house was closed but unlocked. Its key, missing the night before, was now back on the nearby hook.

He stayed for a while. Staring at the door. Trying to remember if he'd left it unlocked like that after opening the tower for Halpin the previous evening with the spare key . . .

As he stepped across and reached out to open the door, he imagined he heard a slight sound from beyond, inside the tower itself.

A scraping, he thought. A scratching of some sort.

It was impossible to distinguish its character. Even impossible to be certain if he'd heard it or not, since it had coincided with the noise of his own weight settling on the door handle.

He waited, listening intently, his hand still lightly grasping the cold metal of the handle.

He heard nothing more.

He cautiously pushed the door open and listened again. He still heard nothing.

He stepped inside. He shone the torch across the floor and around the walls.

But nothing seemed alive in there. It had the stillness and the

Saturday, 14 November

coldness of any museum. Its evocation of old ghosts. Its gallery of paper figures staring always at the same angles from the unchanging photographs. Its furniture made unreal by being denied the uses it was built for.

And yet . . .

Something was wrong, he felt. Something out of its place.

He could *sense* it, without being able to see it.

Long familiarity had trained his eye to the shape of the exhibition. And there was a fracture somewhere in the image he'd expected.

He reached to his left to turn the light switch on. Still wary enough to retreat from the doorway, behind the cover of the wall, in case the sudden flash blinded him to any danger.

Once his eyes had grown accustomed to the new brightness, he stepped back in and stood for a long time afterwards, simply staring at the room.

And finally, he saw it.

He walked slowly across the flagstones to the centre of the tower.

He moved the high-backed, 1930s chair a little to the left. He stooped by the oak table and slightly lifted the hand-woven rug to expose the broken object that had been partly concealed by one of its corners.

It was the small wooden crucifix that Joseph Manning had taken with him from his original home in Ranelagh. One of its arms had snapped from the rest of it. Presumably in a fall from the table.

Kyne dropped the pistol in its holster and reached to pick up the separate pieces. But as he did so, he was summoned.

'Kyne!'

The sound was more like a warning than a threat. More like a plea than a criticism.

'What are you *doing*, Kyne?'

Standing in the doorway of the tower, again wrapped in his red dressing-gown, was the secretary, Michael Carter.

The man was a mess, Kyne saw. He was drenched with sweat and shaking uncontrollably. But he was also a mystery, Kyne decided. If he was so broken by fear, why had he come downstairs to investigate instead of calling for help? If he had gone for help and discovered that Kyne was already below, why was he still so scared?

'What are you *doing*?' he demanded again.

'What do you think I'm doing?' Kyne asked.

'You've broken Mr Manning's crucifix! You've disturbed the table and the rug! It *explicitly* states on all the notices—'

Carter stopped. Suddenly. With his mouth and his eyes wide open.

Kyne swayed back a little as he rose from his stooped position.

And bumped into someone who was standing behind him at his shoulders.

Already tense with uncertainty, he sprang away from the contact and swivelled sharply to meet the intruder, the arm of the broken crucifix still grasped in his right hand and the torch raised as a weapon in his left.

But it was only Josie Thomas again, he saw. Standing there behind him like a puzzled child with her soft toy.

She'd dressed herself in jeans and a T-shirt, although her feet were bare.

He wondered where she'd managed to conceal herself . . .

'Josie,' he panted. He made an effort to smile, while struggling to control his breathing and the useless pumping of adrenaline. 'Are you all right?'

She wasn't listening.

She was looking downwards, with a puzzled frown on her pale face, and staring at the broken crucifix.

She must've knocked it over while wandering around in the

Saturday, 14 November

dark, he realised. And now she was worried about being blamed.

'It's OK, Josie,' he told her. 'Everything's OK now. I'll fix the crucifix. You'd better get back to your room.'

When she raised her head again, she didn't glance at Kyne. She looked uneasily across at Carter, who was still blocking the doorway.

But Carter too had relaxed by now and seemed relieved to discover that only Josie was the cause of the noises that had frightened him. He stepped into the tower and moved to the side.

'Yes, yes,' he encouraged. 'You take her up, Kyne. I'll tidy and lock up here. And Kyne! Mr Manning is anxious to see you. Call in on him when you're ready.'

4

Opening the front door of his bungalow, Eddie Halpin was on the point of calling out his sister's name when he glanced down and noticed that the signal was flashing on the answering machine by the telephone.

He stopped and leaned to rewind the tape. And then, too engrossed to move, he held the awkward position, stooping over the instrument, as the tape played back.

The first of the calls was Charlotte Rainey's. And typically useless.

It's Charlotte. I'll ring you again.

She'd left no contact number. No address. No indication of what she wanted or what she had to offer.

It grated on his nerves. Because it revived an old complaint.

He reached out and angrily jabbed a button to put the machine on hold.

He used to think that her *job* had put the pressure on their relationship, he remembered. Her unexpected movements. Her unexplained absences. Her absorption in a case and her loyalty to the force.

Just as he used to feel that all these failings were captured in the single message that she'd left so often and so carelessly along the way.

The morning he was arrested and held for twenty-four hours so that a right-wing demonstration could proceed without his interference, this was what he'd come home to afterwards. Not her explanations. Her apologies. Not even Rainey herself. But her voice. On tape. On the answering machine.

It's Charlotte. I'll ring you again.

Maybe she had, too. He didn't know. Because he hadn't listened for it.

And then finally, from across the sea in London, where she was on liaison with the British police, she'd come back on a weekend while he was off on holidays in Kerry, to write a bitter note and to take away her stuff . . .

He hit the button now to run the tape again, wondering why he was still so contorted with the old arguments. The dead relationship.

He expected the next call to be Charlotte's also. And a duplicate of the first, made an hour or so later. Which was her usual pattern.

But it wasn't Rainey.

The voice that left the second message was a man's. Although at first, hardly anything else could be said about it for certain.

It was so deeply muffled and so heavily disguised, and the caller spoke so quickly and so nervously, that it was almost impossible to distinguish the words themselves.

Saturday, 14 November

Straining to catch the sounds, Halpin let it play through. He heard, or thought he heard, . . . *Halpin . . . contacting you . . . careful . . . your assistant . . . meet me in the . . . the Burren . . .*

There were no other calls.

Halpin again rewound the tape and again listened intently, squatting now to get a little closer to the miniature speaker.

And this time he picked it up. *This is Harry Fame, Halpin. I don't have any other way of contacting you. So be careful who's listening. If you want to make sure your assistant is not going to come to any harm, don't talk to anyone yourself about this. You'll have to meet me in the Blue Thatch Hotel at three thirty today, Saturday. You'll have to be alone. It's on the road to Lisdoonvarna, in the Burren. The important thing is that Lowry . . .*

But the important thing was lost in surface crackling.

Exasperated by the poor quality of the recording, Halpin loudly slapped his hands together and went to rewind the tape a third time.

As he reached out, his hand touched and dislodged the telephone.

But instead of just the rattle of the plastic receiver in its cradle, he seemed to hear two sounds. Simultaneously. And the second, a duller thud, seemed to come from one of the bedrooms down the corridor.

He stood upright.

'Linda?' he called uncertainly. 'Linda?'

He stayed standing there, listening intently, staring down the hallway.

But no one answered him.

He wondered if his nerves were playing tricks on him. He wondered if his mind was sympathetically supplying the sounds he wanted to hear, or if all he'd caught was an echo along the narrow passageway of his own clumsiness with the telephone.

5

He hadn't slept more than four hours that night and no longer than thirty minutes at a time before waking again to some fresh anxiety.

It wasn't the loss of sleep that troubled him, though.

At seventy-eight years old, Joseph Manning had no great need for lengthy rests.

But drifting as he was between dozing and waking, between dream and memory, it was hard to tell the difference after a while. And he longed for certainty.

He had a sense of something eluding him. Some stain or imperfection. Some great failing that went unnoticed while disguised as something else.

His conversation with Eddie Halpin the previous evening had stirred these fears in him.

And not only in himself, it seemed.

Throughout the night and the early morning, he had listened to the strange, distressing movements in the corridor outside his room. He'd called his secretary to explain. But Carter had deflected him with a trite story about Josie Thomas's nightmare. So he'd asked for Kyne.

Kyne he could trust.

As the morning light came through his curtains now, he heard footsteps outside his door again and called hopefully, 'Jimmy?'

There was no answer. But the footsteps stopped. The door handle was lowered and the door itself was slightly opened.

No one came in.

'Jimmy?' he called again.

Saturday, 14 November

A small brown head appeared through the gap in the doorway and stared at him with two black, unblinking eyes.

It took him several seconds to realise that it was only a teddy bear and that Josie Thomas must be standing outside and holding it. And by then the pair had disappeared again.

When he'd recovered from anxiety, he felt saddened by the incident.

His mind had been full of memories through the night.

One in particular had disturbed him.

Others brought back old wounds and old losses. On an afternoon in February 1937, for instance, when he'd found his mother crying in the drawing-room and holding an envelope with a Spanish stamp and a single sheet of notepaper, on which was written, . . . *Your husband has bravely given his life as a Christian soldier, to save his country and his faith against the tidal waves of evil* . . . His sister's suicide in 1941. His mother's early passing, broken by grief, in November 1947.

But what saddened him now was not these losses of fifty or sixty years ago. Deaths he'd long since come to accept as expressions of God's will.

It was that he could recall so little from his own childhood. And nothing at all of playing with toys or with other boys.

He remembered spending an unhappy year in a distant seminary when he was fourteen, studying intensely for the priesthood, and then being forced to leave again once it was decided that he lacked a true vocation.

The image triggered others. Because an earlier time was also vivid in his mind, when he was younger still, standing in short pants before his father in the living-room, listening with bowed head to severe reproofs. *Do not pretend that you are unaware of having fallen beneath the standards I expect from a boy of twelve who hopes to study for the priesthood. Do not make a spectacle of yourself in such a manner, Joseph. Please do not grin when you make a point, boy.*

Silent City

He remembered cycling with Harry Fame early one Friday afternoon. Two young men, both dressed in their best dark suits and both with metal bicycle clips holding their flapping trouser legs to their ankles, on their way to the military barracks in Rathmines for weekend manoeuvres.

All his memories shared a common theme. The burden of duty.

But of play and laughter and mischievousness, he seemed to have no . . .

'Did you leave the door like that, Mr Manning?'

He opened his eyes, aware that he must've drifted into sleep and into dream again.

Jimmy Kyne was standing at the foot of the bed, almost invisible in the dim light because he'd dressed himself entirely in black.

'No, no,' Manning said. 'The girl was here. Josie looked in.'

Kyne smiled.

Delayed by the telephone ringing as he'd passed reception, he'd asked Josie to go up ahead of him; and she must've tried to fill in on his duties while he was detained.

The call had been for the absent Walcott. From an excited, nervous young man who gave his name as Lowry, but said nothing more.

Kyne's amusement faded quickly, however.

He thought the old man seemed already tired, even though the day was only beginning. His eyes were slightly puffed and looked worried and restless. His lined face was washed of colour.

Kyne sat on the edge of the bed. 'You should get a little more sleep, Mr Manning,' he advised softly. 'We won't be leaving for Dublin for another three hours. That is, if you think you're still up to this journey. Because I—'

Manning raised a thin arm to stop him. 'No, no, it's not the future that weighs on me now,' he said. And then, gesturing sharply, he whispered, 'Go. Close the door, Jimmy. And come back to me.'

But in the few seconds it took Kyne to rise and cross the bedroom and return after pushing the door shut, Manning changed his mind about confiding in him.

He thought again about the lie he had told Eddie Halpin during their conversation the evening before. He hadn't previously concealed from him the story of his first meeting with Alan Rosen because of modesty or a desire for privacy. He had done so simply because Harry Fame had asked him to.

Because, three weeks before, he had discussed Halpin's proposal with Fame before agreeing to an interview.

'You might be better not to mention that you knew Rosen before the bombing killed him, Joe,' Fame had advised.

'Why not?'

'Well, it's the, ah, *symbolic* significance,' Fame explained. 'The founding of Crastina has always been presented as a compassion for . . . well, for *strangers*. No question of creed or colour. If it becomes diluted now as personal grief . . .'

All night, while other memories came and went, Manning had been constantly disturbed by one in particular. Until now, past nine in the morning, he no longer really knew whether the image was nightmare or flashback.

He had a picture in his mind of a Sunday morning in early June 1941. A picture of standing with Harry Fame on the site of the bombing in Dublin's North Strand, where Alan Rosen had died. Of standing on the edge of the huge crater in the middle of the road, praying with bowed head for the souls of those who had lost their lives. And then of Harry Fame, with a bitter smile on his plump face, turning to him and saying, 'It's an ill wind, Joe. An ill wind.'

Manning could understand the phrase itself. It had many meanings. Many applications.

What he couldn't understand was Fame's bitter laughter . . .

'Mr Manning?'

The old man didn't hear. Or confused the present summons with others from the past.

He didn't notice Kyne returning to sit again on the edge of the bed. He had drifted away, into distant reveries. Almost as if he was suddenly gripped by a dream with his eyes wide open.

'Mr Manning?'

No longer aware of anyone else, and probably no longer knowing where he was, the old man started angrily shaking his head, contradicting some claim or some speaker inside his mind. His wrinkled face showed a drama of emotions. Surprise. Reluctance. Pain. Even tears rolled from his vacant eyes and down his cheeks.

Kyne stood up and walked across to the window. He opened the curtains and looked out on the early sunrise over Kinvara Bay.

But even the morning, with its freshness and its renewed hope, now failed to lift him.

He'd slept too little, and too poorly, to welcome another day's work.

TWO

1

In his sleep, Roger Walcott's right hand had flicked outwards and knocked over a small jar of Vaseline.

The jar had fallen only on the surface of the bedside locker and not to the wooden floor below. So it wasn't the slight noise that woke him. It was the sensation of something foreign touching his skin.

He was immediately alert.

He found that he was still lying on the girl's bed in Eddie Halpin's bungalow. The scent of perfume from her pillow was faintly in his nose. The pages he'd been reading from Halpin's case histories were scattered around him on the covers. The intense dislike for the man's unhealthy politics of welfare and weakness was still lodged in his mind, and as sour as the air that had been trapped in his mouth.

He could see that it was already morning.

He moved to get up.

The bed groaned at its wooden joints.

And at once he heard a call from outside.

'Linda? Linda?'

He stopped immediately, caught in an awkward posture between sitting and lying.

It was Halpin, of course. Returning home.

Silent City

But Halpin knew nothing, he assured himself. And Halpin suspected nothing. His voice was too calm. Too hopeful.

But still . . . Halpin thought he had *heard* something.

Like all the floors in the bungalow, the one in the hall was uncovered except for an occasional small rug, and the shoes sounded heavily on the pine boards as Halpin walked briskly towards the bedroom.

Walcott wondered what to do. If he moved too sharply, the creaking bed would expose his presence. If he stayed, he couldn't launch an effective attack from the spongy mattress.

He rolled gently sideways, without a sound. He placed his left hand on the floor and gradually transferred his weight from the bed to his hands, until he was able to slip silently off the mattress.

He stood up.

Halpin might merely glance in and turn away again, he thought. So rather than hiding behind the door, Walcott preferred to stand facing it. When it was opened, he could easily overpower the startled lecturer.

He moved lightly across as the footsteps stopped outside. He glanced down. The doorknob, an old-fashioned brass fitting that had a white inlay decorated with frail pink roses, twisted a little to the left.

Tensed to attack, Walcott started violently as the bell attached to the bungalow's front door suddenly erupted in the hallway outside.

It rang loudly. And it rang insistently. The prolonged rasping of either an impatient official or someone who was desperately in trouble.

Halpin released the doorknob.

But he'd already opened the door itself and it now swung slightly inwards as he let it go and turned to answer the urgent ringing.

Saturday, 14 November

Walcott extended his left hand and stretched out its forefinger to prevent the door drifting fully open.

Through the gap, he heard Halpin opening the street door and then a man with a rough local accent introducing himself on the doorstep.

'I'm Detective Sergeant Pat Lawlor. This is Detective Garda Donahue. Is that your car in the driveway, sir? The silver BMW.'

'Yes. Is there some difficulty with it?'

'Are you Mr Halpin, sir? Mr Edward Halpin?'

'Yes. Do you need to come in?'

'No, no, this won't take a minute, sir.'

'I think it might be better if you stepped in, sergeant.'

'What? If you don't mind, so.'

'Not at all.'

They entered the bungalow and were shown into the front room.

As he followed them in, Halpin closed the interior door behind himself.

And Walcott, no longer able to overhear, was left to his worries.

He wondered if the police had come about Halpin's sister. He wondered if some sharp-eyed neighbour had reported an intruder. Or if Halpin's groping in the past had finally brought the stirred mud to the surface.

But what possible direct relevance could the man's car have to any of these?

Walcott burned with the anxiety of ignorance.

Unwilling to risk any movement, he stood stiffly and tensely. His legs tired and became irritated with itchiness.

The proximity of danger calmed him. But he also baulked at the continuing luck and elusiveness of Halpin, the persistent shapelessness of things, the malignity of fate.

The others spent five minutes talking in the front room.

To Walcott, who knew how precariously the future hung on each one of them, it seemed like an interminable stretch.

And when they finally returned to the hallway, there wasn't the same easiness about them. Their movements were broader. The noise they made was greater. And their arguments were sharper.

The sergeant was saying, 'No, no, I'm afraid you'll have to come with us, sir. As I said, now, under Section Thirty of the Offences Against the State Act—'

'I don't want to be uncooperative, but perhaps—'

'I'm sure it's all a misunderstanding, sir, and will only take a little while to clear up. We'll have you back here in no time. It won't disrupt your—'

'Can I take my own car, then?'

'I'm afraid not, sir.'

'Can you at least wait until I freshen up and change?'

'That won't be necessary, sir.'

'Whether it's necessary or not, I'd prefer it.'

'We don't think you should, sir.'

'I see. I've left something in my sister's bedroom. Can I collect that?'

'Garda Donahue will go with you.'

Hearing the two pairs of footsteps on the bare floorboards, Walcott could do nothing this time but step to the side of the door and out of sight.

Almost immediately, the door was pushed in around him.

Concealed behind it for the moment, Walcott held his breath.

But no one entered.

Halpin had merely confirmed that his sister wasn't in there. And turned away again.

'I was mistaken,' Halpin mumbled as he receded in the hallway. 'I must have left it somewhere else.'

Saturday, 14 November

No wiser, no less heated with frustration and feeling no safer, Walcott listened to the other three as they left the bungalow.

He would have to follow, he realised. Again.

But he had no idea where they'd taken him, because he wasn't familiar with the location of the police stations in Galway.

He went to the telephone table in the hall and found in the local directory that there was only one station in the city, situated in Mill Street.

The flashing light on the answering machine, where the tape was still on hold, caught his attention while he was reading. Glancing at his watch, he rewound and replayed the messages.

The first he'd already heard. *It's Charlotte. I'll ring you again.* He'd been awake at twelve forty-five when it came through.

As for the second, its quality was so poor that he had to play it through several times before understanding its meaning. *This is Harry Fame, Halpin*, he deciphered finally. *I don't have any other way of contacting you. So be careful* . . . It must have been recorded early that morning, he calculated, when he was sleeping.

He would have to talk again to Lowry, Walcott decided then. But without revealing that he was aware of the other's treachery. As if things were now as they always had been between them and he was simply a fellow foot-soldier, conveying the great McKelvey's instructions. Not yet, however, he thought. Not now. When he had seen the way to dealing with Halpin first.

He slipped to the front room to check through its window that no one was watching the bungalow. Satisfied, he went back to the hallway, opened the front door and stepped briskly onto the driveway.

He stopped immediately to light a cigarette. Inhaling deeply, he set off again and was walking quickly by the side of Halpin's

BMW, almost past its boot, when he heard the unexpected summons.

'Excuse me!'

It was a man's voice, shouting at him from his left.

He didn't look. He walked on, ignoring the call.

'Hey!' the voice cried then. And louder now. 'Hey, you! Hang on a minute!'

And after that, there was no further escape.

He looked up.

In front of him, a white police car had rolled up the avenue and was now blocking his exit at the end of the driveway. And a uniformed guard, a middle-aged, black-haired man, was leaning out the open driver's window.

2

The telephone woke Charlotte Rainey.

She rolled over on the lumpy mattress and reached out her left hand to grope along the seat of the nearby chair until her fingers closed over her wristwatch. She had trouble focusing on the digital display, but finally saw that it was already mid-morning. Late, she thought.

Downstairs, the telephone went on ringing.

'Jarlath!' she called.

There was no answer.

She swung out from under the covers. Underneath her bare feet, the worn carpet felt cold and damp. Still sitting on the edge of the bed, she took her jeans off the back of the chair and pulled them on.

She was awake enough by then to hurry herself a little more. Not bothering with socks or shoes, or a sweater over the

Saturday, 14 November

white T-shirt she was wearing, she scampered across to the door and onto the landing outside.

The telephone stopped ringing as she reached the top of the stairs.

Her momentum carried her on for a while and she'd taken four or five of the stairs before she stopped, staring down resentfully at the instrument that was sitting on the gross little wicker table at the bottom.

'Jarlath!' she called again.

Again there was no answer.

Opposite her the door to the box room was open. It was where Burke indiscriminately threw his junk, obviously. A damaged dressing-table was lying on its side in there and in its mirror Rainey caught her own reflection.

She looked as bad as she felt, she saw. Messy hair. Dried lips. Hollow eyes.

She hadn't slept comfortably. The bedroom Burke had given her was damp and stuffy. As if it hadn't been opened or cleaned for months. And the bedclothes weren't properly aired.

But the whole house had that feel of neglect to it. Along with the unpleasant smells of loneliness. Sour milk. Stale air. Rotted vegetables.

Without company, Burke was one of those who just let it drift at home.

As he was, she thought, gruff and arrogant, he would've made someone an intolerable partner. But he wouldn't have *been* like that . . .

The telephone rang again as she was working it out and somewhere along the way, as she hurried down the last few steps to answer, she seemed to lose the solution to her host's problems.

She picked up the receiver, a little breathless. 'Hello?'

The reaction of the man at the other end was astonished. His voice immediately rose to a high-pitched echo. 'Hello?'

'Yeah,' Rainey confirmed. 'Hello.'

'OK,' the caller said. 'Ah, I must have a wrong number. I was looking for Jarlath Burke.'

'This is Jarlath Burke's.'

There was a silence then. It baffled her for a moment, until she realised that he didn't actually believe her. Presumably a woman never answered at Burke's house.

'Right,' the caller said finally. 'Is he there at the moment?'

'Who is this?'

'This is Detective Sergeant Lawlor, from Mill Street station.'

Rainey laughed. All that tension, she thought. All that cautious footwork. 'Hi,' she said. 'We met yesterday afternoon, in Jarlath's office. This is Inspector Rainey, Charlotte Rainey.'

'Ah . . .'

Was it her imagination, or did Lawlor sound even *more* gobsmacked?

'I don't think he's here,' she told him. 'But I'll check. Just hang on a minute.'

She looked in the downstairs rooms. All were empty. She climbed the stairs again and knocked loudly on the door of Burke's bedroom.

'Jarlath!' she called.

When no one answered, she opened the door. But that too was empty.

Back on the phone, she told Lawlor, 'No, he's not here. Can I take a message?'

'Right,' he agreed. 'I can't raise him in his car, either. He must have stopped somewhere and . . . Well. Would you ask him to contact me at the station. Tell him it's urgent.'

'OK.'

'We have Halpin.'

'You what?'

'Tell Jarlath. We've arrested Eddie Halpin. He'll understand what that means. Eddie Halpin.'

Saturday, 14 November

Rainey hesitated, stunned by the information. For too long.

'Got to go,' Lawlor told her. 'Interview room.'

The line went dead, but she still held the receiver for a while afterwards, leaning against the wall at the base of the stairs, thinking back on her own arrangements with Burke.

'What's your position now with McQuaid?' he'd asked her the night before. 'What do you have to do?'

'Nothing,' she told him.

'Nothing?'

'Precisely that, Jarlath. I must do nothing. I've filed my report on the incidents in Kerry and Cork. I now have the weekend off. He'll come back to me in Dublin on Monday. When the American President is gone and McQuaid has time for other things.'

'You'll be dragged off the case come Monday, girl. That's all.'

'That's what I think, too.'

'You know it's not just McQuaid you're up against here, don't you? Manning is an establishment figure. Jesus, even the Minister for Justice is his personal friend.'

'Well, you know me, Jarlath. Stack the odds and roll the dice.'

'Are you sure you're telling me everything you know?'

'That's the point, Jarlath. I don't actually *know* anything. Yet.'

'Right. Because I don't mind chipping in, but I'd want to see everything out there on the table first. I'm not stumbling around in the dark. And I'm not screwing up my own patch while doing it. I'm not all that far off a pension, Charlotte.'

'I understand.'

'Like hell you do.'

'No, I appreciate it.'

'I'll do it on one condition. You stay here. Is that understood?'

'Well...'

'Well, nothing! Don't show your nose outside this door. Let me run with it today and see what I can come up with. And for Christ's sake, don't keep anything back from me.'

'Well, there's this notion Eddie has that Harry Fame is more implicated than Joseph Manning himself...'

Burke must've rung Lawlor before leaving earlier that morning, Rainey decided now.

But where had Burke gone afterwards? With his radio off? And why arrest Eddie? For his own protection? To squeeze him for more information?

She pushed off the wall and finally replaced the receiver.

And then she paced the narrow hall. Caged. Provoked by helplessness. Taunted by the unanswered questions in her mind.

She knew what she was going to do, of course.

Exactly the opposite of what Burke had asked of her.

It was irresponsible, she accepted. It was ungrateful. It was dangerous.

But...

What was it about her that made her break agreements as soon as she made them, she wondered. With McQuaid. With Burke. With Eddie.

Was it that she didn't trust contracts? Or trust people?

Or was it that, regardless of where she hid and what disguise she adopted, she was always flushed out by the exceptions to the rules?

She was already on the move again, bounding back up the stairs to finish dressing and freshen herself up a little, by the time she was formulating that last, rhetorical question.

Saturday, 14 November

3

Gerry Donahue, the younger detective, was already sitting at the table in the interview room in Mill Street station and had two photographs, turned face down, on its surface.

When Eddie Halpin was brought in, he was asked to sit opposite Donahue.

Pat Lawlor stayed on his feet, leaning against the wall close to the door.

'You can still call in a solicitor to advise you at any time,' Lawlor pointed out. 'You know that, don't you?'

Halpin gave him a wry smile.

This was Charlotte Rainey's manoeuvre, he was convinced.

He'd fed her too much the previous night. And now she'd guessed that it must have been Harry Fame who had organised the attempt on his life.

The one angle he couldn't settle on was whether she was trying to be maternal, dragging him in for his own good, or merely cynical, by taking a competitor out of the race.

A third possibility was always spite, of course. Jilted lovers have long and bitter memories.

Halpin had decided to run with this farce for an hour or so. *Then* he'd call in legal muscle, when the police had exhausted their excuses and made fools of themselves.

But Fame was obviously hatching some new scheme for him. The invitation to meet at the Blue Thatch Hotel was clearly another set-up. And Halpin didn't want to betray his own plans to exploit it by seeming in a hurry anywhere.

Lawlor shifted his position against the wall and folded his arms. 'Could you tell us where you were last night?' he asked.

Halpin nodded, already prepared for this inevitable opening. 'I was in Kinvara until close to nine, then I drove back to Galway for a party in Grattan Court here in the city.'

'Many people at it?'

'The party?'

'Uh-huh.'

'Not when I got there, no. There was no one.'

'There was *no* one at the house?'

'No.'

'So you're saying you went to a party at a deserted house.'

Halpin smiled again. 'I don't really mind you twisting my meaning, sergeant, but giving it back to me as my own is a bit too much.'

'Fair enough,' Lawlor conceded. 'What did you do then? When you found the place deserted. Did you drive back home?'

'No, I went into the house.'

'Why?'

'It wasn't obvious from the outside that the house was empty. It was only when I went in that I discovered it was.'

'But you'd driven there, anyway?'

'Yes.'

'In the silver BMW that was parked outside your home this morning?'

'Yes.'

Donahue stirred suddenly, separating the two photographs along the smooth surface of the table, but without turning them over. 'Do you have a problem with homosexual men, Mr Halpin?' he asked quietly.

Halpin raised his eyebrows. 'Homosexual men?'

'That's it,' Donahue confirmed. 'They're also called gays.'

'Right,' Halpin muttered. 'What about them?'

'Do you have a problem with them?'

'You're going to have to clarify that expression.'

Saturday, 14 November

'Do you dislike them? Would you prefer if there weren't any?'

'No.'

'What about other minorities? Jews, for instance. Or blacks.'

'What about them?'

'In one of your books it says that there'll be no order in the country until the Jews are routed out. Have I got that right?'

'No.'

'That's not in the book?'

'It's in the book. But it's a quotation. From 1943, would you believe? And originally made by a well-known Irish politician. It's not my own opinion.'

'So you reckon you don't have a problem with Jews or blacks?'

'No.'

'Or with homosexuals?'

'No.'

Donahue suddenly turned over one of the photographs and pushed it across the surface of the table.

Halpin looked at it without lifting it.

It was a ten-by-four black and white print. It showed a small, thin man who had his right arm around the shoulders of another who was out of shot.

'Do you recognise this man, Mr Halpin?'

Halpin nodded. 'I met him at the party last night. He told me his name was Martin Trayne.'

'The party at Grattan Court?'

'Yes.'

'But you said earlier that the house was empty when you got there.'

'Except for Mr Trayne.'

'But there was no mention of Mr Trayne earlier, was there?'

'It didn't seem relevant to the questions being asked.'

'Could you let us decide on what's relevant and what's not? It might get us where we're going a little quicker.'

'We understand that Mr Trayne was trying to get to a second party in Oranmore,' Lawlor put in. 'Did he ask you for a lift?'

'Yes.'

'Why? Because he knew that you were going to Oranmore, too?'

'Yes.'

'Why didn't you give him a lift?'

'He changed his mind.'

'He asked you for a lift and immediately changed his mind when you offered it?'

'I think you've started twisting my answers again, sergeant.'

'I'm sure we're sorry about that, Mr Halpin. Were those the clothes you were wearing to the party at Grattan Court last night?'

'Yes.'

'Are you sure?'

Something in the tone made Halpin hesitate. Some slight shift. A note of triumph or of glee.

He looked down, along the oatmeal waistcoat, the light blue collarless shirt and the blue jeans. And for the first time he felt a little nervous.

All his clothes were still lightly splattered with the dried blood from Martin Trayne's cut wrist.

When he looked up again, the two detectives were staring intently at him, drinking in the connections that were so obviously occurring in his mind.

'Martin Trayne,' Donahue said to him. 'The man you were alone with in the house last night? He's still in hospital this morning.'

'In hospital?'

'He has a broken nose, a fractured jaw and multiple bruising. And he's still unconscious.'

'Hey, hang on a minute here, now. When I left—'

'You might also be wondering why we were so interested in your car earlier.'

'When I left Trayne last night, he was perfectly healthy.'

'*Perfectly* healthy?'

'Apart from a cut on his wrist.'

'Is that so?'

'Whatever happened to him—'

'The fact is, Mr Halpin, someone saw you leaving the scene and driving away in your BMW shortly before a squad car arrived at the house and discovered Mr Trayne. They took your registration number.'

Halpin stared at him.

He wondered what they were preparing to lay against him. Assault? Grievous bodily harm? And if Trayne never regained consciousness . . . ?

Shit, he thought.

This wasn't Charlotte's style. This wasn't a fit-up to keep him off the road and out of murky corners. This was *real*.

4

'Is this the Island?' the policeman asked. 'This house.'

Roger Walcott had to disguise his confused half-turn as a shrug of indifference. As if the answer was too obvious to merit the original question.

He hadn't known what Halpin called his bungalow. But he could see now that the name was on a small plate in the open gate. The Island.

'Yes,' he muttered.

'Right. Wait there a minute.'

The policeman reached across and took a notebook from the passenger seat. He studied its open page as he stepped out of the car and stood in front of Walcott. 'You must be Mr Halpin, are you? Mr Edward Halpin?'

It was easier to agree, Walcott decided instantly, than to get entangled in dubious explanations. The policeman had seen him leave the house. 'Yes,' he said again.

The policeman raised the peak of his cap with the forefinger of his right hand and put a sympathetic expression on his plump face. 'I'm afraid I have a bit of bad news for you, Mr Halpin. Would you mind if we stepped back in? You might be more comfortable.'

Linda Halpin's key was on the ring that Walcott had taken from her car. The front door was no obstacle to him.

But he was conscious of the photographs inside the bungalow. Most of them featured Halpin himself. Some had been taken with his sister.

'No,' he said. 'It's quite all right. I'm in something of a hurry, you see.'

The policeman gestured slightly to his right, where a neighbour had come out to clean the brass fittings on her door. 'Well, if you don't really mind, I suppose . . . You're English, are you, Mr Halpin?'

Again Walcott hesitated. Did the man already know that Halpin was Irish, he wondered. 'Educated in England,' he said finally.

'And do you have a sister, sir?'

'Sister? Yes.'

'Linda Halpin. Is that correct?'

'Yes, yes,' Walcott muttered impatiently.

'I'm afraid I have to tell you that she was involved in an accident yesterday afternoon, when a vehicle struck her as she was walking in the car park of a shopping centre in Gort. She was transferred to Galway University Hospital afterwards, sir, where she underwent emergency surgery. She hasn't yet regained consciousness. Her condition is described as serious, but stable.'

'Hasn't regained consciousness?' Walcott repeated.

'She's under sedation at the moment, sir.'

'I see. Yes. Is it possible to visit her? Where—?'

He stopped. Because Halpin would clearly know where the university hospital was, he realised.

'Oh, you can visit her, sir. Of course. But they tell me she won't wake now for several hours at least. Can I offer you a lift over there, sir?'

Walcott vigorously shook his head. 'No, no. Thank you. I'll make my own arrangements.' Thinking that the last thing he needed when confronting Linda Halpin again was a police escort. 'You said yesterday afternoon. Have you tried to reach me earlier?'

'We had a problem with that, sir. Would you believe, some bowsie seems to have stolen her bag while she was lying injured on the ground? I'm very sorry, sir.'

'I see.'

'She had her name and address written in indelible ink on— But, sure, you'd know that already, wouldn't you?'

'Yes. Quite.'

'No one noticed until last night. And then the address was in Dublin. Is that where she lives?'

'Of course, yes.'

'On holiday over here with you, is she?'

'A short break.'

'So we had the lads in Dublin call to her flat and it took them a while to find out that she was actually staying here with you.'

'I understand, yes.'

'I'm terribly sorry for the delay, sir.'

'No, no, not at all. It could hardly be helped.'

'But are you sure you'll be all right by yourself, now?'

Walcott smiled. Pluckily. 'I'd like a little time alone, perhaps . . .'

5

A sharp knock on the door beside him interrupted Pat Lawlor as he started another question.

He sighed and unfolded his arms. When he turned to open the door, his body obscured the caller from Eddie Halpin.

Lawlor stooped to receive a message, listened for a while and then glanced back over his left shoulder. 'We're wanted upstairs, Gerry,' he said gruffly.

Donahue gathered his photographs together. As he stood up and followed Lawlor into the corridor outside, a young uniformed guard stepped in to take their place.

'They'll be back in a minute, sir,' the guard assured Halpin.

But they weren't.

Halpin killed the time by worrying.

He had to accept that he was now in trouble, he thought. The gaps and inconsistencies in his story were being easily shown up and exploited. The second time around the interrogation, his explanations had looked like newly invented excuses and the excuses themselves had looked thin and inadequate.

Lawlor was absent for twenty minutes.

He came back alone and stood silently for a while in the open doorway. He seemed depressed.

Looking at him, Halpin sighed and opened his mouth to ask permission to ring his solicitor.

But Lawlor edged in front of him. 'I don't think we'll really be needing you any more, sir,' he said.

Saturday, 14 November

Halpin blinked. 'Sorry?'

'Not for the moment, anyway. We might want to take a statement from you later.'

'Later? How much later?'

'Some time next week, maybe.'

'Next week? Are you telling me I can leave?'

'Uh-huh.'

'Why?' Halpin asked suspiciously. 'Has Martin Trayne regained consciousness?'

Lawlor shook his head. 'Another witness has come forward to confirm your account.'

'Who?'

'If you'll just follow me, sir . . .'

When they left the interview room, they climbed the narrow stairs and walked along the corridor above.

Neither said anything more.

At the front desk, while Lawlor finished his paperwork, Halpin stood to the side of him, waiting to sign a form. Instead of being relieved, he felt inexplicably nervous again.

Tense and edgy, he kept shifting his weight from one foot to the other and checking on the time.

He had a slight suspicion that his apparent release was part of a ruse, or part of the interrogation itself, and might be revealed as a mistake before he was actually free.

But it wasn't this that really unsettled him.

It was a sensation close to mild paranoia. He felt *watched*. There was an awareness of some sort of presence to his left . . .

Not able to resist the pull any more, he raised his head and glanced quickly to the side.

Across from the desk, on the other side of the reception area, there was a half-open door. And in the small room beyond it, clearly visible through the carefully calculated opening, Charlotte Rainey was sitting at a low table, staring back at him.

More than the view was calculated, of course, he thought.

Silent City

What did she expect of him?

The open door was an invitation. But also an admission of desperation. She knew no more now than she had the previous night.

Sitting in there, she looked simultaneously powerful and forlorn. Pulling from a distance at the strings that moved Lawlor and Donahue. And still pleading with Halpin to give her hand-outs.

But he couldn't trust her.

To confide that Harry Fame seemed to be holding Linda hostage would result in a police operation so tight that he himself wouldn't have room to scratch inside it.

'Could I use your phone?' he asked Lawlor. 'I need to call a taxi.'

'I can get a squad car to drop you back home,' Lawlor offered.

'I'm not going home.'

'They can drop you anywhere. It's a normal courtesy.'

'I think I'll settle for a taxi.'

'OK. Be my guest.'

He made arrangements for the taxi to pick him up. He signed his forms, collected his things and was already on the way out, moving quickly to avoid the inevitable argument with Charlotte, who was rising to intercept him...

Through the station window, he glanced quickly into the street outside. On the opposite pathway, there was the entrance to a second-hand bookshop. And beyond its glass-topped door, clearly visible as he hunched forward to light a cigarette, was the curator of St Kieron's in Kinvara, Roger Walcott.

Halpin stopped.

He felt Rainey closing in from behind him. Her breath was actually warm on the back of his neck as she spoke.

'He's been with you since you left Kinvara last night, Eddie,' she said.

Saturday, 14 November

He didn't turn. And although the information baffled and worried him, he didn't respond directly to her opening. He said, 'You must be the witness Lawlor was talking about, are you, Charlotte?'

'I told you last night that I was following you,' she reminded him.

'So you did. And you must've seen what happened at Grattan Court, then, did you?'

'Most of it.'

'Was Trayne really assaulted?'

'He's in hospital, yes.'

'If he was attacked after I left and you tailed me to Oranmore, why are you so certain that I didn't do it?'

'Did Trayne know where you were going?'

'He told me about the party.'

'Walcott followed you in around the back of the house while you were leaving through the front and presumably Trayne wouldn't tell him where you'd gone.'

'But you can't be certain, can you? You didn't witness the assault. You want me released now so that you can follow me again.'

'Why? Are you going somewhere?'

'Not particularly, no.'

'Why is Walcott following you, Eddie?'

Halpin shrugged. And for once, the expression of uncertainty was genuine. The question still puzzled him.

Walcott might be an associate of Fame's and Finnegan's, he thought, and tailing him with the same murderous intention as Finnegan had shown. On the other hand, of course, Walcott might only be a loyal servant to Crastina and concerned about tracking down the absent Fame before the dangerous old man fatally damaged the charity's reputation.

Halpin was unsure. And because of his ignorance, he decided that the safest thing was to elude Walcott.

'Aren't you going to arrest him?' he wondered. 'Before he slips away again.'

'It's not as simple as that, Eddie.'

'It never is, Charlotte, is it?'

'Walcott is somebody's messenger. No point in shooting him. Of course, if you told us what you know that everyone's getting excited about, it would *make* it easy.'

'No, no. It's *never* easy.'

'I've got something that'll interest you, Eddie,' she offered. 'About Harry Fame.'

Across the road, Walcott had straightened back into the shadows again. Peering over, Halpin could just see the ribbon of his cigarette smoke.

'Fame?' he repeated. 'Not Manning any more?'

'I don't like what Manning is,' Rainey stressed. 'His real women—'

'Charlotte,' Halpin interrupted.

'What?'

'Do you have a point to make,' he asked, 'that I haven't heard a hundred times before?'

She drew a breath. 'Yes, Eddie,' she said with slow irony. 'I actually have.'

'Let's hear it.'

'I think you might be right about Harry Fame.'

'Is that so?'

'I heard last night – just between us – that Fame's unexplained wealth is already the subject of an investigation . . . Jarlath Burke. You know Jarlath?'

'We've met,' Halpin remembered sourly.

'The point is, as a director of an international charity, with unlimited foreign travel—'

Halpin suddenly swivelled to face her. He wasn't really interested in what she was saying. He knew that, at best, it had only secondary relevance.

Saturday, 14 November

The crucial thing, he thought, was that Fame seemed to be holding Linda. He could only guess at the reasons. Just as he could only guess at the relationship between Fame and Walcott. But he was convinced that his best chance lay in confronting the old man alone. So he was interested now in getting rid of Rainey. And in using her to get rid of Walcott as well.

A ruse had occurred to him.

'Where are you parked, Charlotte?' he asked.

She stopped talking and stared at him. Uneasily. 'Why?'

'My taxi,' he said. 'It's just cruised past and pulled up at the end of the street.'

'I'm in the car park behind the station. Why?'

'Good,' he exclaimed.

She reached for him vainly as he moved. 'Hold on, Eddie . . .'

THREE

1

Eleven thirty, as the sun broke weakly through the clouds outside, Jimmy Kyne stepped into the tower house at St Kieron's in Kinvara, searching for Josie Thomas.

The girl wasn't there. But her brown teddy bear was sitting on the bare flagstones, facing the oak display table from which the wooden cross had fallen and broken early that morning.

Guarding it, Kyne thought. The toy had no fingers to grasp with, but a hazel twig, apparently intended as a weapon, had been tucked under its right arm.

Kyne went up the spiral stone staircase to check the upper chambers and the battlements. He didn't find the girl. When he came back down, Michael Carter was waiting for him at the bottom. The secretary held the teddy in his right hand.

'You'd better leave it,' Kyne suggested.

Carter pushed his glasses in place with the fingers of his left hand as he looked upwards. 'I beg your pardon?'

'Leave the teddy the way it was. Josie will be back for it.'

'The tower is being locked when we leave. She won't be able to get in.'

'Leave it, anyway.'

Carter shrugged and carelessly dropped the toy to the

Saturday, 14 November

flagstones. 'I didn't come here to tidy up, in any case,' he said petulantly. 'I came to look for you, Kyne.'

'Well, you've found me, haven't you? What do you want?'

'*I* don't want you. Mr Manning does.'

Kyne stooped to slowly replace the toy by Carter's feet, and only then left the tower, turning right outside and climbing the stairway to the upper storey of the west wing.

The old man had dressed in his white robe and brown sandals, and was sitting in an armchair in his bedroom, reading a book of religious poetry.

He was more alert and less troubled than he had been earlier. He smiled as he greeted Kyne. He carefully placed a bookmark in the volume and laid the poetry aside, on top of the cabinet by his bed.

But he had a strange request.

'I don't want you to drive me to Dublin today, Jimmy,' he said.

Kyne immediately misunderstood. 'You'll have to go to Dublin, Mr Manning. You have—'

'No, no. Of course I'm going. But I want *you* to stay in Galway. Can you find a substitute driver? At such short notice? Is it possible?'

'I can get Bill Foley, I suppose. You know him, don't you?'

'Yes, yes.'

'He drove for you before, so—'

'Yes, of course. But without anyone else knowing our plans in advance, Jimmy. Can you do *that*?'

Kyne nodded. 'I can get Foley to take over somewhere on the route. That's no problem. But why?'

'I've been trying to contact Harry Fame all morning, Jimmy. You must forgive the locked door the last few hours. I didn't want anyone to know. Particularly Carter.'

'No, that's OK.'

'But Harry is not at home, unfortunately. And I need you to find him for me. It's very important.'

'Do you know where he might be?'

'I'm sure he's only out for the morning. He sometimes plays golf on Saturdays. I can't afford to wait. And I can't ring him from the car. Not with Carter beside me.'

'I'll do my best.'

'I also want you to bring Harry to Dublin.'

'Today?'

'Today, yes. I must see him today. You can use his car, or take one from the pool at headquarters. But it must be today.'

'Transport's not the problem, Mr Manning. But I don't know if I'm going to be able to convince him to travel at such short notice, especially when you're coming back down here yourself tomorrow.'

'Tell him that I need to ask him something about my sister's death, Jimmy. Will you remember that? I need to ask about Bridget's death. I know he'll respond to that.'

'OK.'

'And one more thing, Jimmy. You mentioned tomorrow. Tomorrow morning. Did Carter tell you anything about it?'

'What?' Kyne asked. 'The official opening of our new headquarters?'

'Did he give you any of the details?'

'No. But there's nothing unusual in that. I only need to know the time we have to arrive places.'

The old man stared. He leaned slowly forward and grasped Kyne by the hand. He squeezed. Gently. But earnestly. And seemed on the point of some worrying confidence.

But then he suddenly drew back from it. And the withdrawal was expressed as much in the reluctant release of Kyne's hand as in his words.

'Don't mention anything about tomorrow to Harry,' he said.

Saturday, 14 November

'But surely he already knows,' Kyne pointed out. 'As a director. He'll be on the platform for the opening ceremony.'

'Of course, yes. But it would be better if you didn't discuss the topic with him.'

'That's OK. If you don't want me to, Mr Manning.'

'Good,' the old man sighed. He picked up the clock from beside the telephone on the cabinet and checked the time. 'Shall we set about our preparations, Jimmy?'

Eleven forty-five, when the sky had darkened again and rain seemed to threaten, Kyne came back downstairs, closed the door of the reception room behind him, and made a single phone call to the relief driver.

At twelve o'clock, he packed the suitcases into the limousine's boot for the journey to Dublin. No one noticed that he left his own behind.

Dominick and Margaret Rushe stood outside the west wing to wave them off. There was a broad gap between the couple. As if a comforting, protective space was being left for the still-absent Josie Thomas to nestle into.

With Manning and Carter in the back seats, Kyne drove down the gravel, away from St Kieron's, and then swung east to cut across some minor roads before breaking onto the main Dublin road.

But he travelled only half the journey.

On the main street in the town of Athlone, while slowed by heavy traffic, he suddenly indicated and pulled into a hotel car park.

Carter was immediately at his back, drumming his left shoulder with that irritating finger of his. 'What do you think you're doing, Kyne?'

'Toilets,' Kyne mumbled.

He parked. Illegally. Blocking in two other cars. And he said sharply as he opened the door and stepped out, 'I'll only be a minute. You stay here with Mr Manning.'

Inside the hotel, it took him only a few seconds to find Bill Foley, exchange car keys, and agree arrangements for meeting again in Dublin.

The last he saw of Carter was the secretary's sour, contorted face pressed against the limousine's rear window and staring back in astonishment as Foley drove them out of the hotel grounds and back onto the main road to Dublin.

2

The old bookseller coughed artificially.

Over by the window, Roger Walcott turned from the barrow of hardback novels he was pretending to browse through. Behind him, the old man had his white eyebrows arched in disapproval and was tapping with his finger at a *No Smoking* sign above his head.

Walcott shrugged his apologies.

But he was irritated by the lapse. It drew unnecessary attention to him.

He quickly searched for a bin to crush the cigarette in and then came back to flick through the novels again.

Five minutes later, while Walcott had a book club copy of *The Clergyman's Daughter* open in his hands, Eddie Halpin suddenly appeared alone on the front steps of the police station opposite.

Halpin didn't linger once he was in the open. He hardly even seemed to check right and left before hurrying down the steps and away. At the corner of the street, he picked up a waiting taxi.

Walcott replaced the novel and left the bookshop.

Saturday, 14 November

Once he was clear of its windows, he sprinted back to the stolen Jaguar he'd parked illegally a little down the road. He took a pair of tickets from under its front windscreen wipers, crumpled them in his hand and dropped them in the gutter by his feet while he opened the unlocked driver's door. He fired the ignition with the exposed wiring and pulled away.

Saturday lunch-time, and the traffic was already clogged in the city's narrow streets. An articulated lorry had impaled itself on a sharp bend at Shop Street and the tailback was dense. Halpin's taxi had travelled little and was less than ten cars ahead by the time Walcott slipped after it out of Mill Street.

They moved in slow spasms, north and north-west across the city, until they reached Halpin's home on Snipe Avenue.

Halpin didn't enter the bungalow. And therefore gave Walcott no chance to attack. He paid the taxi fare and immediately sat into his own BMW and drove off, leaving Galway by the outer ring road and then swinging south, towards Kinvara.

Somewhere on the open road, where the traffic was thinner, he must have finally noticed that he was being followed. Beyond the village of Kilcolgan, about five miles short of Kinvara, he turned suddenly left, onto a minor road, and accelerated sharply.

Walcott, a safe distance behind, struggled to respond. He wondered briefly if the move was part of a ruse, if Halpin had arranged with the police to lure him into a trap. But he knew that no one had followed them from the station in Galway. There was no helicopter in the air. And it was simply improbable that the police could have organised a roadblock on a specific minor road at such short notice.

No, he decided. Halpin was trying to elude both himself *and* the authorities.

By the time Walcott had reached the turning, all he could see was the rear of the BMW disappearing in a cloud of dust through a second junction a couple of hundred yards ahead.

The new road was no more than a tarmaced track. Little used. With grass growing in its centre. And wide enough to take only a single car. Worse, it came almost immediately to another T-junction. And when Walcott got there, he saw only blind bends to right and left and no sight at all of the silver BMW.

He guessed to the right, calculating that another left would only complete a rough square and that Halpin's intention was surely to break again onto the main Kinvara road rather than double back.

He was already turning the steering-wheel when he saw a cloud of dust on his left kicked up by a speeding silver car.

Walcott adjusted.

But the Jaguar was now so badly positioned that its bonnet wouldn't clear the ditch on the opposite side. He had to reverse. The tyres spun as he surged forward again. He worked quickly upwards through the gears, pushing the car to its limits on the narrow winding stretch and not even thinking of the possibility of anything coming against him.

He wondered now if Halpin had gambled or had panicked. Out here, after all, isolated in the middle of deserted countryside, was the perfect spot for a conclusive struggle. And the odds were all in Walcott's favour.

Confident of his reading, convinced that Halpin had made a tactical blunder, Walcott gained quickly on the car in front and was nudging the tail of the BMW within five or six bends.

The difficulty then was overtaking.

About a hundred yards ahead of them, he noticed, near the summit of a steep hill, two houses sat directly opposite each other.

From a narrow, overgrown lane, the road bulged for a while between them to more than double its usual width.

Saturday, 14 November

As they reached the bulge, Walcott dropped into second gear and sharply swung the steering-wheel. First to the right. And then, as Halpin swerved to counter, immediately to the left.

He cut through on the inside and powered ahead of the wavering BMW.

Once in front, he pulled across the other's bonnet and violently hit the brake pedal.

3

Eddie Halpin had a blurred, irrelevant glimpse of a lace curtain being pulled slightly aside to show a woman's wide-eyed face at a window of the bungalow facing him as he skidded out of control. Then the rear of the BMW slapped into the back wing of the Jaguar and the two cars bumped and separated, and met again and crashed apart once more, and finally came to rest side by side, blocking the entire road as it narrowed abruptly at the brow of the hill. Their front wheels were touching. Their rear bumpers about five metres apart.

Halpin had already released his seat-belt and thrown himself down and across the gear stick, expecting glass or metal to come flying in at him.

He slithered over towards the passenger door. Hoping to escape through there. Assuming that Walcott would come for him from the opposite direction.

He stretched his right hand out in front of him. He felt his fingers touch the door panel. But not in the right position. His hand was too far to the left. And too high. And too near the glass in the window. He squirmed a little further sideways, towards the front of the car, and managed to grasp the handle to release the lock.

But the door was suddenly yanked away from him before he could open it himself.

Trapped on his stomach, he raised his head and looked over. Outside, Walcott was stepping quickly backwards, away from the rocking door, and gesturing wildly.

'Get out, Halpin!' Walcott was shouting. 'Now! Get out!'

He waved and pointed only with his left hand. In his right, he carried a wheel brace as a weapon.

Halpin closed his eyes and feigned more damage than he'd actually taken. Groaning slightly, he brought his hands back down and under his body, pretending to clutch at his stomach. While he lay there, he explored the levers underneath.

The car's handbrake was still off. And its gear stick was in second.

As he pulled himself across and dragged himself upright in the passenger seat, he knocked the gear lever back into neutral without being noticed.

But the car didn't roll as he'd expected, even though it was facing up a hill.

'Out!' Walcott repeated impatiently. 'Now!'

Halpin swung his feet outside and planted them solidly on the lane. He pressed against the back rest of the passenger seat and put his hands above his head to reach the hand grip.

'Stand up!' Walcott ordered.

Halpin nodded, grimacing painfully. And then suddenly pushed down and back as violently as he could manage.

The BMW wrenched itself clear of the Jaguar's front left wheel and jerked away, gathering a little speed on the hill and creaking loudly with the effort. Loosened again by the movement, the door slammed shut across Halpin's shins, making him yelp with pain.

Surprised, Walcott foolishly ran after the car instead of waiting for it to come to rest.

Halpin kicked the swinging door back into him, catching the

Saturday, 14 November

other's outstretched hands at first and then, as something cracked in one of the fingers and Walcott buckled with pain, slamming the metal into his lowered face as well. Walcott went down while still in motion and fell heavily on his face. He screamed again with pain as he landed. And the wheel brace spun from his hand and away towards the ditch on the opposite side of the lane.

Even before Halpin could jump from the BMW to take advantage, though, Walcott was up and on his feet again, shaking off the pain and lunging forward.

Halpin knew that he had no chance in a lengthy fight.

He feigned a play for the wheel brace, still lying in the grass to his left. And when Walcott shifted in mid-attack to cover the move, he instantly swerved back and swung at Walcott's jaw with a hook.

The contact almost broke bones in Halpin's hand. It snapped Walcott's head back as his body kept driving forward, brought sweat and blood and mucus flying from his face and then a glassy look to his eyes.

Halpin watched the Englishman going down.

He wanted to keep going. To step beyond Walcott and disable the Jaguar. To prevent the other from following him again.

But through the window of the bungalow, he saw that the woman was now talking on the telephone. Contacting the police, he presumed. And someone else, her husband or her brother or her son, was already opening the front door and thinking about stepping out with what seemed like a shotgun.

Halpin sat back in the BMW. He twisted the ignition key. The engine turned without firing. Twice. Three times. Coughing with that awful, unproductive rhythm of a car that has taken too much damage to ever start again.

But finally, as he was despairing of its abilities, it did catch and roared into life.

Silent City

The road ahead of him was blocked by Walcott's Jaguar, of course. And where the BMW had come to rest, there was no longer enough space to quickly manoeuvre and turn.

He knocked the gear stick into reverse, released the clutch and drove backwards with as much speed as the whining engine would allow him.

His last glimpse of the scene ahead was of two men cautiously leaving the bungalow and thinking about approaching the unconscious Walcott.

After that he concentrated only on the direction in which he was going, sweating with dread at the possibility of something else – cattle, he imagined, or a tractor, or a farmer and his dog – suddenly coming to meet him on one of the narrow bends.

4

A middle-aged man, sloppily dressed in a brown cord jacket and shapeless grey slacks, was walking with Josie Thomas along the gravel in front of St Kieron's House when Jimmy Kyne came back to Kinvara a little after two o'clock to collect his suitcase.

The tower house and the west wing were both locked behind the pair. No one else was visible in the grounds. The Rushes must have closed up and left quickly, even without searching for Josie.

Kyne parked. When he stood out, he gestured irritably with his thumb over his right shoulder, back down towards the gates he'd had to unlock and open again before driving in from the main road.

'Didn't you see the sign?' he demanded. 'St Kieron's is closed for the weekend.'

Saturday, 14 November

'Why?' the visitor asked.

'What?'

'Why are you closed for the weekend?'

Kyne blinked. It wasn't a question he'd expected. And it occurred to him only now that he didn't actually know the answer. Something to do with the official opening of the headquarters across the inlet, presumably. But what precisely? And why close only St Kieron's? Other Crastina centres were still open.

He didn't know.

And his ignorance only deepened his annoyance.

'I'm afraid you'll have to leave, sir,' he said. 'This is private property. It's not open to the public at the moment.'

The visitor reached into the inside pocket of his jacket, slipped out a wallet and opened the leather to show his ID. 'Detective Inspector Jarlath Burke,' he explained. 'I'm from Mill Street station, back in Galway. You're Kyne, aren't you? Joseph Manning's bodyguard.'

'I'm Mr Manning's driver.'

'Right,' Burke drawled.

'Can I help you with something?'

Burke gestured towards Josie, who was still standing timidly by his side. 'Do you know this girl?'

'Josie Thomas. She works here. She also lives here.'

'Good,' Burke exclaimed. 'That's good. I was starting to worry. I couldn't get a word out of her.'

'It's not unusual.'

'I see. Right. I'm actually looking for Michael Carter, Jimmy. I was told by your staff in Galway that he was down here.'

'He's on his way to Dublin. With Mr Manning. They left nearly two hours ago.'

'Pity. What about the curator here? Roger Walcott, is it?'

'I don't know where he is.'

'He should be here, though, shouldn't he? I mean, he *lives* here.'

'St Kieron's is closed for the weekend.'

'So you keep saying. Harry Fame?'

'What?'

'Do you know where Harry Fame is?'

'He doesn't come down here. He works in our headquarters in Galway.'

'He's not there, Jimmy. I've just come from it. And no one seems to have seen him since yesterday.'

'It's Saturday.'

'Is that so?'

'He doesn't work on Saturday. Can *I* help you?'

'Maybe. Why aren't you in Dublin yourself, Jimmy?'

'Mr Manning has a different driver today. My day off.'

'It's Saturday, right?'

'That's it.'

'So what brings you back down here?'

'I left my suitcase behind.'

'Right. You'll look after the girl, will you, Jimmy?'

'Yes, I'll take care of her.'

'Where did you say Carter was in Dublin?'

'A ceremony on the North Strand this afternoon. There's a reception in the American Embassy tonight. He'll be there as well.'

'Good.'

Kyne stood by the car, watching the policeman walking back down the gravel and through the open gates, until Burke reached the Toyota he'd parked by the roadside and drove away.

'I'll bring you down to the village, Josie,' Kyne said then to the girl. 'You've got to stay there with the Rushes. OK? You can't keep coming back here. Do you understand? Not until Monday, anyway.'

Saturday, 14 November

The girl pouted. And imitated Burke's voice to echo the policeman's question. 'Why?'

'I don't know why, Josie,' Kyne told her irritably. 'That's just the way it is. No one tells me these things any more.'

He unlocked the front door of the west wing and went immediately to the entrance to the tower house and opened that, too. He flicked a switch to light the place.

The girl's soft toy was still sitting on the flagstones, where he'd left it earlier.

He walked across, stooped to pick it up and brought it back to where she was standing in the doorway.

She spent a long time considering the offer. And when she finally took it, she immediately carried it back and placed it again on the flagstones.

Kyne shrugged, too tired and too busy to argue with her oddities. He beckoned her to leave.

She laughed.

He said, 'Come on, Josie! Hurry up! I've got to go!'

But she did the opposite. She actually sat down beside the teddy bear and crossed her legs. She pointed at the oak display table in front of her and took a deep breath.

'The *Grey Witch*,' she said softly. 'The fat man. Something the matter?'

FOUR

1

Roger Walcott had been concussed in the fight with Halpin and only slowly regained consciousness now.

Through the darkness in his brain, he heard a voice close to him, repeatedly asking, 'Are you all right there? Are you all right there?'

He rolled painfully over and sat up.

Two old men stood directly in front of him, each dressed in a greasy black suit and cloth cap and dirtied white shirt, and each carrying a garden spade in his hands. For a moment, he thought his vision was still blurred and that he was seeing double.

But the second old man, although he asked exactly the same question, had a different accent from the other. 'Are you all right there?' he enquired.

'Bridie there can call you the ambulance,' the first suggested then. 'And the guards as well.'

Walcott quickly shook his head. 'No. No, I'm fine.'

He tried to push himself to his feet with his left hand, but the effort brought intense pain from his injured finger. He didn't cry out. He smiled grimly and said, 'I'm afraid I rather foolishly chased a young man who stole my wallet as I was sleeping in a lay-by. Although I've regained my property, I seem to have

Saturday, 14 November

suffered otherwise. I imagine it happens to tourists in every country, but somehow one doesn't expect it in Ireland.'

Whatever sense of guilt might've touched the two old men, it didn't translate itself into assistance. They watched in silence as Walcott struggled to his feet and limped around to the driver's door of his car.

He leaned on its roof and smiled at them again before he sat in. Struggling to conceal his movements, he found the ignition wires in the tangle of loose connections under the steering column and touched them together once more. The car hardly even spluttered before catching.

As he manoeuvred, he used the heel of his damaged left hand on the gear lever and kept only his right on the steering-wheel.

He'd have to strap that injured finger, he thought. It seemed to have been broken in the fight. But later. When he was clear of the police and had regained a little of the ground he'd lost to Halpin.

The two old men had stepped aside, onto the gravel margin outside their bungalow. Walcott waved when he passed them. And they seemed to nod in return.

Once he was clear, he pushed the car back up again to the limits of its speed along the narrow roads. He swung right at every junction, until he reached the main Galway road, where he turned to the south and towards Kinvara.

Almost immediately, he noticed a young couple hitchhiking ahead and pulled over to stop beside them. He lowered the passenger window. The boy looked in eagerly at first, but then drew back a little when he saw the grazing on Walcott's face.

Walcott laughed, playing again the unfortunate tourist. 'I was driving behind an Irish friend of mine,' he explained. 'I'm afraid I had something of a skid and seem to have lost him. I'm not certain of my route, you see. Have you noticed him? He's driving a silver BMW.'

'Silver BMW?' the boy repeated. 'Yeah. He just passed

through. I mean, about ten minutes ago, you know. A guy by himself, wasn't it?'

'I'm very obliged,' Walcott told him politely.

He heard the opening of the boy's next sentence. 'Hey, are you going—' But he'd pulled away again before the question was completed.

He drove more cautiously now, keeping to the speed limits.

The pace was irritating. And by the time he finally reached Kinvara, a little short of three o'clock, his frustration was intense.

But he'd been lucky, he realised. As he turned the last corner before the village itself, he saw the silver BMW immediately. It was parked on the opposite side of the road, about twenty metres short of the gates to St Kieron's, which were now locked once more.

He parked behind it and got out to peer through its rear window. There was no one inside.

He walked past it along the footpath. He climbed the gates and moved quickly up the gravel driveway towards St Kieron's.

There were no cars outside the tower house or the west wing. The buildings seemed deserted. And the main entrance was locked against him when he reached it.

He searched around the back of the tower and through the rest of the grounds. But these too were empty.

When he came back he fumbled with his keys at the main door.

He wondered why Dominick Rushe wasn't still on duty. He wondered if the groundsman had been lured away by Halpin. Or duped. Or overpowered, perhaps.

He pushed open the heavy oak doors to the west wing. He stepped onto the cold floor inside. The lights were all off. There were no odours from the kitchen or the chapel. The place was silent.

Saturday, 14 November

But over to his right, the connecting doors to the tower house were swinging open.

He stepped carefully across and peered in.

And what he saw there made him tense with fear.

The high-backed chair had been moved from the centre of the tower and placed untidily to one side. The oak table, with its display cabinet of relics and medals, had also been shifted. The hand-woven rug that had been permanently fixed to the floor underneath was no longer in place. But not because it had been ripped away from its base.

Because the flagstone it had been attached to was actually a trapdoor.

And that too had now been lifted and put aside.

And the hidden stairway below it lay exposed.

Walcott hesitated in the doorway. Wary of being bushwhacked.

The mess in front of him might only be a lure to trap him, he thought.

And yet . . .

Whoever had disturbed these things might still be down there now, groping around at the bottom of the stairs. And that was a danger he simply couldn't ignore.

He hurried across. He picked up the old sickle from the tower's display as he passed. He tucked his left hand inside his shirt to keep the broken finger from distracting him. He held the weapon in his right as he slowly descended the narrow stairs into the dark and echoing chamber below.

He listened intently for sounds of an intruder. But he heard nothing. By the time he'd reached the base of the stairs, his eyes had grown accustomed to the dark, and he saw then that the cramped chamber was otherwise deserted.

It was when he turned to climb again that he heard the harsh summons through the opening over his unprotected head and realised that the intruder had watched and followed him.

'Walcott!'

His instinct was to hide.

But there was nowhere left to hide.

And the voice was already threatening, already warning him against foolish movement.

'Don't, Walcott!'

2

Thirteen miles west of Kinvara, at the coastal town of Ballyvaughan, they turned south along the tourist trail through the famous Burren.

The taxi-driver said nothing.

He was a small, gloomy man, with an old-fashioned hairstyle and a sad face that was more suited to driving a hearse than a cab. He seemed uninterested as they cruised along the narrow road through this strange and almost alien landscape.

On either side, the terraced limestone pavement stretched to the horizon, like a rough foundation for some gigantic enterprise that was never built.

But even in early winter, its dark grey was spattered with the bizarre and inexplicable colour of the arctic and alpine plants that mysteriously grew in an otherwise bleak and barren land.

No houses were visible among the rocks. No animals. And no other people. Apart from the odd flora, it seemed like a place that was indifferent to the living.

The road cut through it for about ten miles. And the taxi-driver remained grimly silent for the whole journey.

Even when they finally emerged from it, into an area of bright lakes and fields that were only half-covered with the grey stone, his glum face still didn't reflect the light.

Saturday, 14 November

The route they were following forked inland then, bending back to the east.

About a mile outside the town of Corofin they slowed and turned into the car park of the sprawling, stunted development that was the Blue Thatch Hotel.

There was no thatch on any of its roofs, of course. The exterior walls were all whitewashed. And even the paint on the wood seemed to obsessively avoid any hint of blue.

The taxi pulled around to the front entrance and stopped at the base of the steps. Only then did its driver finally speak. But not to call or request the fare. The amount had already been agreed and paid. He twisted slightly to look back over his left shoulder and cautioned gloomily, 'You weren't thinking of having anything to eat in there, were you?'

From the rear seat, Eddie Halpin stared at him blankly. 'I don't know,' he said. 'Why?'

The driver simply shrugged, having obviously exhausted his quota of words for the day, and Halpin got out and climbed the steps to the hotel reception.

He glanced at his watch. It was already almost three.

He knew that he could've made it earlier in his own car, but the risk of dragging someone with him had been too great. He'd been right to abandon the BMW in Kinvara and lay a false trail, he decided.

He walked quickly to the reception desk and pressed a buzzer to summon the staff. A small, cheerful woman came immediately to help. He asked if a message had been left for him. She searched and shook her head. He asked her where the lounge was then, having already decided to simply show himself openly and to wait for the inevitable approach from Harry Fame rather than go searching blindly for the old man himself.

'Directly on your right, sir,' the receptionist told him. 'Straight through that door.'

Apart from the counter itself, the lounge was a warren of

secluded alcoves, fitted with black plastic seating and dark oak tables. Most were deserted. Two or three held young couples who were obviously on holiday. And none would've made a sensible place to wait.

Halpin sat at the counter and was thinking about ordering a coffee and sandwiches when a hand fell lightly on his right shoulder and a voice asked softly, 'Are you Mr Halpin, sir? Mr Eddie Halpin?'

Halpin turned to look. A young porter stood behind him, his eyebrows raised.

'Yes.'

'I have a message from Mr Harry Fame for you, sir.'

'What is it?'

'A car is waiting outside for you, sir. At the front entrance.'

'Car?'

'Yes, sir. At the front entrance.'

'Right,' Halpin muttered.

He slid off the bar stool, left the lounge, and walked again past the cheerful woman behind the reception desk.

Outside, at the base of the steps, a red Toyota Corolla had pulled up, its engine idling.

Halpin stopped. Waiting for a summons. Waiting for the driver to show himself.

He wondered if he should be playing it a bit more cautiously than he was. Shouldn't he have given the porter a return message? Insisted on meeting inside, in the lounge?

But it was unlikely that anything immediately dangerous was planned, he decided. The location would've been different. Names wouldn't have been announced to the hotel staff.

So he made up his mind, quickly descended the steps and stooped to look in through the open passenger window of the Toyota, intending to open a conversation.

But he was too surprised to talk.

Hunched behind the steering-wheel, and dressed in a heavy

Saturday, 14 November

combat jacket, was the shaven-headed figure of Cormac Lowry.

Halpin straightened, hoping to retreat. But someone else had closed in behind him, cutting off his escape.

'Get in the back of the car, Mr Halpin!' Lowry called from inside. The politeness of his address sat oddly with the aggression in his voice.

'Or what, Cormac?' Halpin wondered.

'Or you don't see Harry Fame.'

Halpin shrugged. And stooped again to open the door.

A thin youth, about seventeen years old and carrying what seemed like a small revolver in his right hand, slid in beside him along the rear seat and groped backwards to close the door as Lowry pulled away with unnecessary noise.

The youth with the revolver was extremely nervous. He had close-cropped hair and small ears and a wide scar along his left cheek. A gold-plated ring through his right nostril was gathering some of the sweat that kept trickling off his forehead and down the bridge of his nose. His dark eyes seemed both hazy and artificially lit at the same time. His sweating hand had trouble holding the gun straight. And he didn't seem too familiar with handling the weapon.

Halpin kept staring at him calmly. It was safer to do this, he felt. The youth was too jittery. And might easily mistake the purpose of even the slightest movement.

'Cormac?' he called.

Lowry crudely tugged at the steering-wheel, throwing them carelessly around a shallow bend. 'Yeah, what?'

'You want to let me in on what the arrangements are?'

Lowry laughed. Bitterly. 'I don't have to answer any of your questions now,' he crowed. 'Not any more. Not like yesterday.'

'Well, you should always think of tomorrow also, Cormac,'

Halpin cautioned. 'The future belongs to you. Wasn't that one of the theme songs of the Hitler Youth?'

'Fuck off!' Lowry swore. He swung them through another bend and then snapped at the youth, 'If he opens his fucking mouth again, just shoot him, Tony.'

The youth looked half-paralysed and half-animated by the instruction. He raised the revolver and growled softly, but then immediately frowned with confusion.

Halpin smiled at him, with closed lips, and turned gently to look out the rear window.

They were deep into the Burren again, he saw, and on a minor road. Again the limestone terrace climbed on either side until it made the horizon. Except for the lines of coloured plants that interleaved the steps, the scene was grey and grim. And totally deserted.

The light was fading when they eventually slowed.

Lowry leaned to his left, away from the steering-wheel, and looked out and up through the passenger window for a few seconds. Then he grunted with what seemed like satisfaction and accelerated again.

Halpin had to wait until they'd passed on before he could check through the rear window. He caught only a brief glimpse before it was obscured by another bend.

But it was enough.

On the summit of the limestone hill to their left were the ruins of one of the ancient ring forts that dotted the landscape in the area. And standing inside its low wall and staring after them, with his palm raised to his forehead to shield his eyes from the setting sun, was the white-haired figure of Harry Fame.

Halpin turned to ask Lowry a question.

But the car suddenly picked up speed and he was thrown back against the seat instead.

There was an instant when he might've surprised and

overpowered the youth as they collided. And an instant when the youth might've panicked and squeezed the trigger of the gun he was still desperately clinging to.

It wasn't so much that the moments passed. More that they were swallowed up as Lowry roughly negotiated another couple of left turns and screeched to a halt behind the rear bumper of Harry Fame's gold Mercedes.

3

At first, Walcott could see nothing but a shadow above him, blocking the narrow opening from the tower house to the chamber below.

He waited. He didn't respond to the summons.

He hoped that the man would impatiently descend and cut out the light, leaving Walcott himself in a darkness he might take advantage of. But his hopes were quickly crushed. Almost immediately the beam of a powerful torch struck his face and he had to twist away from its glare.

'Put down the sickle, Walcott,' the voice ordered then.

Walcott was confused by the accent. 'I beg your pardon?'

'The sickle in your right hand. Put it on the ground in front of you. Then step back.'

Walcott stooped to release the weapon. Once he'd let it go, he rose again and pressed back against the damp wall of the narrow chamber. Shielding his eyes from the torchlight, he watched the man coming slowly down the stairs.

It took him only a moment to confirm that it was Jimmy Kyne who had surprised and trapped him.

Kyne stopped on the steps before he reached the floor of the chamber and then slightly tilted the torch beam to reveal the semi-automatic pistol he was carrying in his right hand. 'What are you up to, Walcott?' he asked.

The phrase. The choice of words. The slightly puzzled tone. They all gave Walcott hope.

Kyne knew nothing yet!

'Ah!' he exclaimed. 'Kyne! You startled me. I saw the items disturbed in the tower above when I returned. Naturally, I came to investigate. Thought it was intruders, actually. Hence the sickle.'

But his own words and reactions were being as closely read.

'You don't seem surprised to find this here,' Kyne pointed out. 'This cellar.'

'Oh, no. I assure you. Quite astonished.'

'I've been working for Mr Manning more than twenty-five years now.'

'So I understand, yes.'

'I didn't know it was here. I don't think even Mr Manning knows. He never said it to me.'

'Precisely my own thoughts.'

'What happened your hand, Walcott?'

'Hand?'

'You've got your left hand inside your shirt.'

'Oh! I stumbled in the dark on the way down. I'm afraid I may have sprained my wrist.'

'You look all in, Walcott.'

'I beg your pardon?'

'Knackered. Roughed up.'

'Ah, yes! Had a slight skid on the way here, you see. Hadn't the seat-belt on, I'm afraid.'

'You look like you've lost an argument with someone.'

'No argument, no. Except with the steering-wheel.'

Kyne waited then, saying nothing for a while.

To him, the other's answers reeked of convenience and invention. They smelt like lies.

Saturday, 14 November

But Josie Thomas's thin, unsteady voice from above broke in on his suspicions. 'Mr Kyne?'

When he didn't answer, she came down the steps and tugged at his sleeve from behind. He didn't want to risk turning. She tried to go past him, but he held an arm out to prevent her.

He came off the steps and walked to the right of the chamber, covering any move Walcott might make to attack or capture the girl.

'Now, Josie,' he said softly. 'What is it?'

She jumped down, turned sharply at the bottom and started pointing excitedly at the wall under the stairway itself.

Walcott lunged at that moment. When it seemed that Kyne's attention was distracted and his concentration had slipped.

But Kyne was actually ready to take the attack. He was waiting for it, in fact. Without having to move his position, he brought the heavy torch across and into the Englishman's jaws.

Walcott's momentum still carried him forward, a little beyond the contact. He staggered for a moment. And when he finally crumpled, it was at the girl's feet. He was already unconscious before he reached the floor.

The girl's expression became suddenly animated at the sight of the blood and the suffering on Walcott's face. Her eyes grew bright with joy.

And her pleasure was so open, and so intense, that Kyne felt faintly embarrassed.

'What is it, Josie?' he asked again. 'You'll have to hurry now.'

Absurdly, she wiped the back of her jeans before sitting on the ground. As if the dirt naturally clung to *her* and she was concerned about transferring it.

Bracing herself with her hands by her sides, she pressed her feet against the wall under the stairs and loosened a small arc of stones that had been cut away at ground level and wedged back in the wall. She sprung quickly to her feet then, beamed at him to receive his praise and immediately dropped back to her hands and knees to crawl through the opening, into the passageway beyond.

'No, Josie,' he whispered to her. 'Hang on.'

She slunk back with a bowed head and a slight pout on her lips. He tried to humour her.

'I need you to stay here, Josie. I'm relying on you. I've got to go through with Walcott first, then I'll call for you. Do you understand? You have to stay here until I call you.'

He brought her back behind him and used the gun to rouse the Englishman below. 'Walcott! Walcott!'

Walcott stirred, responding to the pain of his broken finger when it was suddenly prodded.

Under Kyne's directions, he scrambled to his hands and knees and started to crawl through the opening in front of the gun.

He feigned continuing weakness. And continuing ignorance.

'I don't quite understand what you're up to, Kyne,' he said faintly, 'but if this is your—'

The cold touch of the gun barrel across his lips silenced him as they emerged on the other side.

They stood.

Kyne had brought the torch, but kept it extinguished now.

They waited until their eyes had grown accustomed to the darkness. Then they moved slowly along the dank passageway, keeping close to the wall.

Kyne tensed as they approached what was obviously an underground cell at the end of the passage.

Beyond its slightly open door, light was clearly visible from what must have been a battery-operated lamp.

He didn't ask how many were hiding inside. He didn't ask what crimes they were concealing or running from. Because he didn't trust Walcott to help him with the answers.

It hardly mattered, in any case.

Better to anticipate the worst, he decided. Better to calculate overwhelming odds. Better to back off and simply notify the police.

He had played his part, he accepted. It had come to an end. And it wasn't worth the risk, pushing it any further.

But Walcott moved before Kyne himself could manage it, although the action itself was neither dramatic nor threatening. In fact, he seemed to be doing only what he thought was now expected of him.

With Kyne's gun still poking at his ribcage from behind, he merely pushed the unlocked door in front of him.

The door creaked as it opened fully.

Beyond it, Kyne saw that there was a camp-bed against the opposite wall of the cell and that a fat and bearded man was stretched along it.

The man had pulled his blankets to his shoulders and was almost completely covered.

His eyes were open. He saw the visitors. But he didn't move. He simply stared at Walcott and at Kyne behind him.

Kyne had no choice now. He acted quickly. Judging by the position of the fat man on the bed, he figured that even if there were others in the cell, then they weren't prepared for any intrusion.

He pushed Walcott violently in and to the left. He followed closely behind, covering to the right with his pistol.

Finding that clear, he caught the swinging door at his back and swivelled to check behind it. There was no one there.

He turned again, releasing the door. The door creaked once more as it swung back on its hinges.

And the fat man still stared at him. And his eyes still held no fear. No hatred. And no surprise. He simply watched.

'If I see the smallest movement under that blanket,' Kyne told him quietly, 'I'll kill you.'

The fat man gamely tried for a crude bluff. '*Comment?*'

'Just make sure you don't move,' Kyne advised. 'You can practise your languages all you like, but just make sure you don't move. When I tell you to do something, you do it immediately, but very, very slowly. You understand?'

'Sure. I understand.'

'You want to introduce me to your guest, Walcott?'

Walcott seemed eager to oblige. Thinking the name might distract. Might disconcert.

'This is Shane McKelvey,' he said slowly.

And Walcott had been right.

'McKelvey?' Kyne repeated. He frowned. And stared a little harder. 'Half the police forces of Europe are—'

But as he spoke, he heard a noise behind him, at the entrance to the cell.

He turned sharply again.

His right hand dropped a little with the weight of the pistol he was holding. His left reached out to grapple with anyone coming through.

But it was only the girl who was framed in the doorway.

He started to caution her. 'Josie . . .' he said.

The fat man, he remembered suddenly. It just echoed unbidden in his mind. *The Grey Witch. The fat man. The beard.*

Not her notion of a sea captain at all, he realised now, but her description of the stranger she must have seen coming in off the trawler.

She stayed only for an instant now. And not long enough to hear or heed his warning. Then she screamed and darted away again, back down the darkened passageway.

But everything was changed by that moment.

On the camp-bed, McKelvey raised the Browning automatic he had held concealed beneath the blankets and fired two shots as he swung his legs to the floor and raised himself to a sitting position.

The first of the bullets embedded harmlessly in the wall.

Saturday, 14 November

The second passed in front of Kyne's chest as he was twisting back from the doorway and it shattered the crooked elbow of his left arm.

The impact spun him around again.

His own first shot went hopelessly wide, ricocheting off the wall to McKelvey's right.

Before the other could manage to fire again, however, he adjusted his aim and his posture and squeezed the trigger once more.

And his second found the target.

The fat man was jerked violently backwards by the impact. He met the wall behind him, shuddered for a moment and then slowly tipped forward again. The Browning he'd been holding slipped from his hand and clattered to the flagstones.

But Walcott, too, had moved on the first shot, charging desperately at Kyne.

Kyne tracked him now, stepping back to avoid the contact as he fired again.

But the pain of moving his left arm distracted him and his aim was poor.

Walcott didn't offer him a second chance. The Englishman sprang again, but launched himself at the doorway this time. He hit the ground inside the threshold and rolled from there into the darkened passageway outside.

Kyne had to secure his own back before leaving to follow him.

He crossed quickly to McKelvey.

The fat man was still alive, he saw. But not by much, it seemed. He'd taken the bullet under his ribcage and had now tipped almost completely forward, as if he was bowing.

Kyne took the Browning from the floor at McKelvey's feet. Unable to carry it in his left hand, he dropped it into the right pocket of his jacket.

Satisfied then that the fat man couldn't rise without support, he crossed again to the doorway. He stopped at the opening for a second, gathering himself and dealing with the pain in his arm, and then stepped quickly into the passage.

Walcott wasn't visible.

He went cautiously along the corridor, covering every alcove and every shadowy bulge, until he reached the dividing wall.

The stone was still out at the ground-level entrance. And he had to assume that Walcott was waiting on the other side of it.

So he was trapped, he accepted. He couldn't crawl through while holding the pistol. His left arm wouldn't support him as he went. And he couldn't risk it unarmed.

It seemed an impossible choice.

But he heard a groan just then from the cell behind him and something else occurred to him. The fat man, he thought. The fat man could be used as cover. He could be made to crawl backwards through the opening while Kyne himself hung safely behind, waiting to shoot Walcott in the legs on the other side.

Kyne went carefully back along the passageway.

He checked again in every alcove, in every shadow.

He stepped into the cell's open doorway.

The fat man still lay sprawled along the bed. His eyes were wide. He stared at Kyne. His mouth was hanging slack and starting to seep some blood. The wound to his stomach was uselessly covered with his right hand.

But there was a strange expression in his eyes. Something that rose above his agony. Something that glinted and even mocked a little.

Kyne stepped in and stooped to study it.

And had time only to recognise it as triumph.

From behind the door, Walcott shot him twice in the back. Both of the bullets lodged between his shoulder-blades. He was kicked forward by the impact, across the cell and down to the cold flagstones. And he was already dead before he made contact with the ground in front of the camp-bed.

Saturday, 14 November

Walcott hadn't twisted right after rolling from the cell. He'd slipped left, into the darkness where the passage ended in a narrow cul-de-sac, and then come back to get the second Browning that McKelvey had brought with him.

He moved quickly now from the door of the cell.

He bent to see if Kyne was finished.

Satisfied, he rose again and called across towards the bed. 'McKelvey? McKelvey?'

But there was no answer.

Because McKelvey, too, was dead.

Walcott allowed himself a slight smile. Of sour triumph.

There had been a moment in the passageway, he knew, when he could have sacrificed himself for McKelvey.

A noisy struggle with Kyne. A gunshot. Either would've alerted McKelvey to the threatened danger.

But Walcott did not want to die like that. Throwing his life away on a mere chance. Gambling on the dubious skills of a crude agitator.

And he did not want to save McKelvey.

He wanted to salvage what was left of Columbus.

FIVE

1

Eddie Halpin was certain that he was going to be killed.

The scene suggested it as the inevitable outcome.

Without warning or explanation, Cormac Lowry had left the car and climbed the hill towards Harry Fame. And Halpin had been left alone in the rear seat with the sweating youth who was holding a gun on him.

There was nothing he could do. The space was too cramped to struggle with any hope of success. The gun barrel was pressing tightly against him, into the loose clothes around his stomach.

He tried to hold the youth's look. Intimidating the boy with the sense of the life he was threatening. But he couldn't decide whether this was helping him or not. His stare seemed only to irritate the other. Seemed to make him edgier, and angrier, and even more uncomfortable.

So he waited for the youth to make a move.

But the youth didn't move.

Five or six minutes must've passed since Lowry abandoned them.

From behind them then, along the route they'd already taken, Halpin heard another car approaching. Noisily. In low gear. Moving slowly along the narrow country road.

Saturday, 14 November

It wasn't anyone expected, because the youth glanced quickly back and then nudged him not to look himself.

He had to wait until the car passed on his right and he finally caught a glimpse of it on the edge of his vision.

His heart skipped a beat with astonishment. And with joy, he supposed.

It was Charlotte Rainey's black Alfa Romeo cruising by out there. With Rainey herself behind the wheel.

He watched her as she braked and then pulled in ahead of the gold Mercedes. When she got out, she was struggling with a huge, unwieldy map. She stared at a section of the map. She looked around, into the gathering dusk. She shook her head. She glanced down at them. Smiled. And then wandered towards them.

'Keep your fucking mouth shut!' the youth warned Halpin. 'I'll do the talking.'

Rainey crossed in front of the bonnet and came round on the youth's side.

He tried to ignore her.

But she stooped and rapped on his window.

He lowered the glass a little. 'Yeah, what?' he growled.

'I think I'm actually lost,' Rainey confessed, in a voice that seemed to be wavering towards tears. 'Here! Look!'

She raised her huge map and fed the top of it through the gap in the window before the youth could object. Behind it, she herself was no longer visible from inside the car.

The youth swore and ducked to prevent a corner of the paper sticking in his eye. He swatted at the map with his left hand. When the thing kept growing, and kept coming at him, he wound the window a little lower to give it more space.

It was a mistake.

Around his face, the map was suddenly knocked aside; and instead of paper, he found the barrel of a Smith & Wesson .38 pressing against the side of his head.

'Armed garda,' Rainey told him. 'You're under arrest.'

Halpin took no chances. As the youth froze with terror, he pushed the arm that was holding the revolver away from him and into the open.

'Drop the weapon, son,' Rainey ordered.

The revolver clattered to the floor of the car.

'Put your foot on that, Eddie,' Rainey instructed. 'Don't pick it up. Just hold it down. Now, son, I'm going to go back a pace or two. When I do, you slowly open the door and slowly step out. Got that?'

She moved back, taking her invaluable map along with her. The youth kept his hands on his head as he followed. Behind him, Halpin's feet were already touching the road before he remembered to warn Rainey that others were about.

Too late.

They heard the bullet ricocheting off the low stone wall beside them first, and only then the sound of the gunshot reverberating through the limestone hills.

Rainey ducked underneath the cover of the wall.

Halpin, his right foot on the road and his left still in the car, launched himself forward and dived beneath the wall as well.

But the youth scarpered. Swivelling sharply, he dodged between the bonnet of the Toyota and the boot of the Mercedes and sprinted away once he was in the clear.

Rainey thought of following. She raised herself slightly. But another gunshot forced her back down again.

She took a deep breath and swore violently.

'Armed garda!' she cried out then. 'Put your weapons down and your hands in the air!'

From his prone position, lying on his stomach across the margin of the road, Halpin looked up at her dubiously. 'Does that usually work, Charlotte?' he wondered.

She glanced down at him impatiently. But she didn't answer.

She didn't have to.

Saturday, 14 November

Another bullet, cutting into the road by Halpin's leg, did it for her.

Halpin scurried to better cover and sat up, leaning back against the wall. 'Not that it makes any difference,' he said, 'but how did you manage to get here? How did you know where I was?'

'When you dropped me in Galway, I went back to your place,' she told him. 'I thought you were heading there, too.'

'I was. I didn't stay.'

'You left the tape in your answering machine. I was already inside the Blue Thatch when you came in. I watched them pick you up and I followed. And here I am.'

'Answering machine?' Halpin repeated. 'How did you get to the answering machine? Did you break into the bungalow?'

'I still have a set of keys, Eddie. Remember?'

'You kept a set of keys?'

'I'm an optimist.'

'Jesus!'

'Hadn't you better tell me what's going on?'

'That I don't know myself.'

'Come on! It's not the time for coyness any more, Eddie.'

'I don't *know*, Charlotte! Fame knows. Linda got close to him yesterday. I haven't seen her since then. It's why I want to meet him.'

'OK.' She nodded slowly, thinking about it. 'Look,' she said then, 'I'm going down a bit, where they won't be expecting me to pop up. You stay here.'

She moved away without waiting for his answer.

When she stopped again and looked over the wall, she could see nothing of their attackers. The hill above her was deserted. The ruins of the fort at the top were empty.

She climbed the wall and ran to her right. And found them on the other side of the hill.

The youth who'd been holding Halpin was already waiting

for the others on the road below. Lowry and Fame were descending towards him.

But the old man was having trouble moving across the limestone ridges. His cane kept snagging in the holes the rainwater had corroded in the rocks. His legs were too weak to take his weight as he descended.

While Rainey watched, Fame stumbled and almost went down. Lowry grabbed him by the shoulder of his overcoat, hauled him up and pushed him on. But the old man stumbled again. And this time he did lose his footing and fell to his knees.

Standing above him, Lowry raised the gun he was holding and pointed it at the old man's upturned face.

It wasn't Rainey who shouted.

She'd meant to. But she was too slow.

It was Halpin who called. From the ruins of the fort above her, she saw. Having obviously ignored her orders and abandoned his position.

Lowry swivelled at the sound. His finger squeezed the trigger as he twisted. And the shot went harmlessly between his various targets.

He looked quickly down at the terrified old man. He clearly thought about finishing the job. But must've decided that flight was the better option. A corpse wouldn't delay his pursuers, after all. Whereas a helpless old man would.

Halpin and Rainey both reached Fame together.

It was almost dusk by then.

Below them, they could barely make out the shadows as Lowry and the youth escaped along the road.

Halpin helped the old man to his feet and retrieved his cane. 'Can you walk?' he asked.

Fame, ashen-faced and shivering violently, shook his head. His ankle had been sprained. Or broken.

Halpin offered himself as a crutch. Slinging the old man's

arm around his shoulders, he guided him carefully down the limestone ridges, back towards the cars.

And of course the revisions slowly sank in as they went.

The old man was being hunted by Lowry, he realised. He wasn't being helped, or served, or protected by the thugs. He was being hounded and threatened. And therefore, it was unlikely that he had kidnapped Linda.

'In the message you left on my answering machine,' Halpin remembered. 'You said that you wanted to make sure my sister didn't come to any harm.'

The old man was still breathing heavily. 'Sister?' he gasped.

'My sister. Linda.'

'Your assistant. I said your assistant was in danger.'

'She's my *sister*! It was why I was supposed to meet you. You told me—'

'I also told you not to bring anyone.'

'I didn't,' Halpin grumbled. 'Not intentionally. This is Detective Inspector Rainey, by the way. She has a tendency to follow me.'

Rainey smiled. The old man grunted an acknowledgement.

'But where's my sister?' Halpin demanded impatiently again. 'Where's Linda?'

'What do you mean?' Fame muttered.

'She went to meet you yesterday.'

'I never saw her yesterday.'

'I was there when she made the arrangements, for Christ's sake!' Halpin exploded. 'She rang you in Crastina's headquarters in Galway. She made an appointment to meet you in the afternoon.'

'I talked to her, yes. I took her call. She said that she knew the truth about Alan Rosen. I realised immediately, of course, that you were behind it. It frightened me. I made arrangements to meet her that afternoon in the Aughty Mountains, past the village of Ardrahan. But I didn't go there. I rang Roger Walcott in Kinvara after I talked to her. I told Walcott that I thought she knew everything about Alan Rosen. It was Walcott who went to meet her.'

'Was it Walcott who suggested that?' Rainey wondered. 'Or did you?'

'It was Walcott. He told me to stay at home and—'

'Knew what?' Halpin interrupted.

'Eh?'

'You said that you told Walcott that you thought Linda knew everything about Alan Rosen. What's *everything*? What were you talking about?'

The old man stopped, dragging the others to a halt with him. He looked upwards and stared into Halpin's eyes. There was an expression of despair on his pallid face.

'Don't you know?' he asked.

Halpin shook his head. 'I don't think I do. And I don't think Linda did, either.'

'But then . . .'

'What?'

'Walcott still went after her.'

'That's because you sent him.'

'No, no. Don't you see? Don't you understand . . . ?'

'Take your time,' Halpin advised.

'Yes, yes. You see, I rang Walcott and I told him exactly where the girl had arranged to meet me in the mountains. He asked me to stay at home until he had dealt with the girl himself and until I was contacted by Cormac Lowry. He maintained that she was a journalist. He stressed that it was too dangerous for me to risk being interviewed by her. But I was restless. I thought he couldn't possibly mean confinement to the house, so I took the dog for a short walk. Quite luckily. When I came back, Lowry had broken into my house.'

Halpin nodded. 'I saw him.'

'You did?'

Saturday, 14 November

'He took old photographs of you and Bridget Manning and a letter written to you by Bridget.'

The old man bowed his head. 'He found them, did he?' he said sadly.

'On your instructions, he said.'

'No,' Fame explained. 'Walcott sent him. I know that Lowry's orders were to bring me to St Kieron's in Kinvara and to hold me there until Walcott himself was free to deal with me after meeting your sister. That's what he told me just now. Along with the boast that there's a chamber underneath the tower house in St Kieron's.'

'Chamber?' Rainey echoed. 'What sort of chamber?'

'I have no idea. I'm not sure if Lowry was also ordered to take the photographs and letters. Lowry, you see, always suspected that there was something concealed about Alan Rosen. He often asked me about it, but he could never find the proof. His hope was blackmail, I suppose. Lowry seems unattached to anything except his own needs.'

'Did you tell him that you discovered the body of Bridget Manning?' Halpin wondered.

'No. I told Walcott.'

'Why Walcott?'

'I've spent a good deal of my life in England. I knew Walcott's family over there. When you started investigating the circumstances of Rosen's life some weeks ago and when I needed someone to share the burden of my knowledge with and someone to advise me, he seemed a natural ally. I realised that something was wrong, however, when I came back from walking the dog and found that Lowry was waiting for me after breaking into my home. He would never have risked that without explicit instructions from Walcott. I fled down here. I rang your home a number of times to warn you, but always got your answering machine. This morning I decided I had to risk leaving a message. I had to meet you.'

'The message was garbled,' Halpin complained. 'I got the impression that you were *threatening* my sister, instead of trying to warn both of us. And it ended without explaining what the important thing about Lowry was.'

'The important thing is that Lowry and Walcott can't be trusted,' the old man recalled. 'That's what I said.'

Wrong trail, Halpin realised. Wrong scent. The old man was a tangent. He had nothing to do with the attempt on Halpin's life in the Kerry mountains. He had nothing to do with Finnegan. And he had no collusion with Walcott or Lowry.

And yet . . .

'What was Linda *supposed* to know that made her so dangerous to Walcott?' he asked again. 'What was concealed about Alan Rosen? What's this knowledge you've been burdened with?'

The old man ruefully shook his head. He said, 'I thought it was only Alan Rosen . . .' He tailed off. He shifted his weight. And started again. 'Fifty-eight years,' he said quietly. 'I've kept it to myself for fifty-eight years now. I've never told anyone except Walcott, and that was only a few weeks ago, when your research brought you back to Joseph Manning. Oddly, Walcott seemed to know most of it already. He knew about Columbus, you see . . .'

'Eddie,' Rainey interrupted.

'What?'

'Hadn't we better get to the cars? Apart from the risk of the other two doubling back, Mr Fame here shouldn't really be standing on that ankle.'

'Sure, yeah. You're right. Mr Fame . . . ?'

Saturday, 14 November

4

All that afternoon, after leaving Jimmy Kyne in Athlone, while travelling in silence on to Dublin with Michael Carter and the new driver, Joseph Manning dwelt on the memory of that Sunday morning early in June 1941. Of standing with Harry Fame on the site of the bombing in the North Strand, where Alan Rosen had died. Of Fame, with a sour smile on his plump lips, suddenly turning to him and saying, 'It's an ill wind, Joe. An ill wind.'

Until he'd finally understood the reasons for Fame's bitter laughter.

It wasn't a structured story that brought him the terror of knowledge, though. Not a logical plot or a sequence of events.

More flashes of insight. Disparate scenes and fractured images.

They came like waves of pain and then receded. Goading him for a moment before passing once more beyond his control.

He remembered the parade-ground again, of course. And the sight of Alan Rosen still standing in the rain while all the other soldiers knelt.

But his own response to that image, he knew now, was much more complex than the simple fascination he had admitted to Eddie Halpin. Much stronger than the innocent admiration he had always believed in himself.

What he had exorcised from his memory, he realised, was the *attraction* he had felt.

Attraction.

To the courage of the gesture. To the young man's vigour and rebelliousness.

And also, he had to accept, to the young man himself. His good looks. His *beauty*.

But Manning had been too weak ever to publicly admit to that attraction.

He had always been too weak, he thought bitterly.

His entire life, and particularly the founding and the building of Crastina, had only been an elaborate expression of that weakness.

If he'd been stronger, he would've pulled down the temples of the rich, who created the poverty he so much hated.

Instead, he'd drawn on the charity of the wealthy. He'd taken their money. Salved their consciences with their spare change. And built comfortable prisons for the poor, where they might be kept quietly out of sight.

He wasn't whole, Manning realised suddenly.

He wasn't one. But two people.

There were parallel biographies.

Here was the self-sacrificing altruist who had created Crastina as an expression of his love for humanity. And here also was the coward who had built Crastina to conceal his own guilt.

He had always been weak.

Even the very clothes he'd adopted betrayed that weakness. The simple white robe and brown sandals. In themselves, they were powerful Christian symbols. But taken on by him only after his early failures with other uniforms. The blue shirt and black beret, so proudly worn by his father as one of General O'Duffy's Irish fascists. The grey-green uniform and red leather boots that Manning himself had put on, perhaps in imitation, as an army reservist in the early 1940s. The dull suit of the civil servant.

Like his mother, he had always been weak. Always crushed by events.

Saturday, 14 November

Unlike his father, who had fought for the Church in Spain. Unlike his sister, Bridget.

He remembered again that day in February 1937, when he had received news of his father's death. He was sixteen years old. Returning home from school. His mother crying in the drawing-room.

'*It is with great sadness that I must inform you . . . pride . . . a sense of honour . . . be assured this tragedy has a higher purpose in the scheme . . . has bravely given his life as a Christian soldier, to save his country and his faith against the tidal waves of evil . . .*'

His mother had never physically or mentally recovered from that loss.

In the years that followed, it was Bridget's strength that had carried the family through the trauma.

He had always envied her power. And always been baffled by her inexplicable suicide in 1941.

The sight of Alan Rosen standing in the rain came back to his mind again. His black hair and dusky complexion. His deep-set, dark brown eyes.

The very image he had carried around with him for four years of the Republican soldier who had killed his father in Spain.

He wasn't whole, he thought again. Even in his attitude to this single man.

He remembered sitting in the back room of a popular Dublin restaurant in March of 1941. With Alex Condon. And Tony McCann. And Stephen Baldwin. All members of the Legion of Mary. All dedicated to working for the poor of the city in their spare time.

The talk that evening had been of hardship and starvation in Dublin's slums. Of hunger and disease, of squalor and drunkenness. But also of the war in Europe. And of Germany's noble crusade.

Was it Condon who had spoken . . . ?

'You know that something has to be done to give these decent poor people a better life. And you know that the thing that has to be done is to make life hard for the bloodsuckers that are living on them. There are twenty thousand Jews in the country right this minute . . .'

Someone had called the group Columbus. And the name had stuck.

They were proud to describe themselves as Christian explorers. As discoverers of the new world. And the new order.

'*There are twenty thousand Jews in the country right this minute . . .*'

Manning had been too weak to do anything but allow his silence to pass as agreement.

And this at the very time, he remembered, when he had asked Harry Fame to seek out Alan Rosen for him.

With a view to what? With what intentions?

He no longer knew.

And he was afraid now of uncovering the truth.

3

'A day in 1941,' Harry Fame recalled, 'Alan Rosen cycled down from his home in Terenure to Joseph Manning's house in Ranelagh. He'd only just recovered from pneumonia, I think. But it was a short journey. He'd called to see Manning. But Manning wasn't there, of course. He was in work. And it was his sister Bridget who opened the door . . .'

The old man stopped and looked sadly out through the window of his gold Mercedes, into the darkness that now

Saturday, 14 November

cloaked the surrounding Burren. Leaving the obvious unspoken. The lovers' intense and sudden passion. His own lingering romantic disappointment.

He said simply, 'I carried messages between them after that. They had good reasons, of course, to keep the affair a secret. He was Jewish. Both their families would've made a fuss. That's how things were at the time.

'Bridget wouldn't have minded. She had the courage to carry it through. It was Rosen himself who wanted to keep it quiet. And whatever else she had, she never had the strength to refuse him anything.

'I found the house on the North Strand for them. That's where Rosen went to live after he left home in April that year. And that's where the two of them used to meet afterwards.

'It was Bridget who paid the rent, you know. She'd inherited from her aunt the year before, when she was twenty-one.

'Manning was always pestering me to find out where Rosen had gone. I pretended I didn't know. But he must've suspected. Maybe he followed me. Maybe he followed Bridget. He was always prying into her private life, always jealous of her.

'There were three . . . three apes he knew from the Legion of Mary. Dockers, I think. Or brewery workers. Condon. McCann. Baldwin.

'The last time I saw Rosen alive was Tuesday evening, 27th May 1941. He gave me a letter for Bridget. A final one. He was tiring of the novelty, you see. Tiring of the game. That's all it really was to him. He wanted to go back to his own people.

'I cycled from the North Strand that evening, through O'Connell Street, up Dame Street, out to Bridget in Ranelagh. Manning was off somewhere on charity work. Their mother was an invalid in the bedroom upstairs. We talked in the drawing-room. Or Bridget talked, I should say. She told me she was pregnant.

'I couldn't bring myself to give her the letter. Not then. Rosen would have to change his mind or tell her himself.

'I cycled back to him the next night. It was late. Along the North Strand, who stepped out of a doorway and put his hands on the bicycle to stop me only Manning's friend, Alex Condon. He had some . . . some mysterious advice. I wasn't to bother coming that way again. There was no one to call on any more.

'I went on, anyway. But I couldn't find Rosen. Neither did anyone else, I discovered later. I thought he'd skipped off on Bridget, you see. Not wanting to face her. But no one ever saw him alive again.'

'What are you saying?' Eddie Halpin asked. 'That he was attacked and roughed up? That he was killed before the bombing? Already dead?'

Fame looked out again into the darkness. 'Who knows?' he wondered. 'Who knows? They're *all* dead now. Except for Manning himself.'

Halpin was still inclined to be dubious. 'The letter Cormac Lowry took from your house yesterday,' he said. 'It was written by Bridget Manning in March 1941, wasn't it? I read and memorised it. It struck me as odd. *You can't torture me like this, Harry Fame. You simply can't. You can have what you want. Don't make me despair.*'

The old man smiled and slowly shook his head.

'Haven't you ever heard of irony, Mr Halpin?' he wondered sadly. 'Haven't you ever heard of hyperbole? Don't they teach you these things in university any more?

'You have an impression of Bridget as grim and joyless and sexually oppressed. Because that's your impression of the times. She wasn't like that at all. She was full of life. Full of humour. Full of exaggeration. Always larger than she needed to be. When you knew her. When she was at ease with you. *Get me that or I'll kill myself*, she'd say.

Saturday, 14 November

'The letter was a joke. And I've forgotten now what it was even about.

'She had her father's spirit.

'You have an impression of her father, I suppose, as all cramped and authoritarian, because he went to fight for Franco in Spain, because you're a liberal and disapprove of the cause. But he wasn't like that, either. He was full of life, too.

'Bridget had his spirit. But she was destroyed by Rosen's death. She lost interest in everything afterwards. Not even the child inside her occupied her mind. I watched her wither away in the months that followed . . .'

He stopped and swallowed back his tears. When he spoke again, his voice was trembling.

'I thought at first I might replace him myself. But she never felt like that about me. I thought then that if I showed her the letter I still had, that the shock of knowing he had rejected her might jolt her out of the depression. Might make her angry again. She used to get very angry at things. It seemed the only hope.

'I went to show her the letter that day in September. The street door was already open. The door to Bridget's bedroom was open. She was hanging by a curtain cord she'd tied to brass centrepiece in the high ceiling. Probably already an hour or two dead.

'So I never got a chance to give it to her. The letter. I still carry it. I brought it along with me today. You see, I knew that you wouldn't really believe me. But look . . .'

He reached to the inside pocket of his heavy overcoat. But took out first a cloth handkerchief to wipe his eyes and blow his nose. And only afterwards removed a plain, yellowing old envelope.

Charlotte Rainey, sitting in the front of the Mercedes, turned on the interior lights as Halpin removed the single sheet of folded notepaper and started to read aloud.

'Dear Bridget, I will always remember the precious times we had together as the very . . .'

Halpin stopped. Embarrassed by the cruelty of platitudes. Thinking about the sad irony of Fame carrying two dead loves for the same woman through a long and lonely life. His own. And Rosen's.

He folded the paper, replaced it in the envelope and silently returned it to the old man.

Rainey seemed to understand his emotions. And took up the questioning for him.

'Why did you arrange to meet Linda Halpin in the mountains, at such an isolated location?' she asked.

'That was her own choice. She picked the location.'

'But you were quite happy at that stage to allow Walcott meet her instead?'

'He insisted that he could persuade her not to research or write about Alan Rosen's death.'

'How?'

The old man shrugged. Wearily. 'He didn't say.'

'Linda Halpin has disappeared,' Rainey told him. 'She hasn't been seen since yesterday.'

'I didn't get the impression that he intended any violence or coercion. Not at that point. It wasn't until I saw Lowry breaking into my own house that I realised the girl might also be in danger. That's when I rang Mr Halpin.'

'But Linda Halpin knew nothing of the story you've just told,' Rainey persisted. 'And besides, it's doubtful if Walcott was really concerned about its exposure. That was a ruse to keep you out of the way. There must be something else. Why did Walcott want Lowry to bring you to St Kieron's and keep you there?'

The old man shook his head. 'I don't really know.'

'You said that Walcott already knew about Columbus. What *is* Columbus?'

Saturday, 14 November

'It was what they called themselves. Condon and McCann and Baldwin, and the rest. Columbus. God knows why.'

'Were any of them involved with Crastina during the early years?'

'They all were. Crastina was founded by Manning, but it couldn't have survived without the voluntary work of the others. Most of them gave their lives to it.'

'But none of them had a very high profile within the organisation,' Halpin put in. 'Not one of them was ever a director, for instance.'

'No. That wasn't their way.'

'What you're saying is that there was always a strong, semi-secretive, anti-Semitic group active within Crastina?'

'More an influence than a group, I think. But it was there, yes.'

'How was Crastina funded initially? Apart from Manning's sale of his own home.'

'When Bridget was declining during that summer,' the old man recalled again, 'I believe she passed her inheritance to her brother to finance the charity he was already planning. She had no interest in money. The donations were recorded as anonymous.'

'You were poor, then, when you left Ireland after Bridget's death. You returned a wealthy man.'

'I married quickly in England, Mr Halpin. Out of disappointment, I suppose. My wife was a good deal older than I was. And considerably wealthier. I came home when she died in 1969.'

'Why did you become a director of Crastina?'

'Joseph Manning asked me personally. As a favour to himself.'

'Why? You'd had no contact either with him or with his charity for twenty-five years.'

The old man drew a breath and sighed heavily. 'We never

245

spoke about the past. Or not until your questions about Alan Rosen forced us to a few weeks ago. I advised Joe not to mention that he knew Rosen before the bombing.'

'Why?'

'The past lay buried between us, Mr Halpin. My concealment was deliberate. Perhaps his was more suppression. I agreed to leave it buried by accepting his offer to become a director of Crastina. My reasons have always been the same. I don't think his mind could withstand a sudden revelation.'

'What you are saying—'

'I'm not saying anything. I have no proof.'

'Columbus!' Rainey returned to it unexpectedly. 'Do you know when Columbus discovered America?'

'Of course, yes. Unless it has some meaning other than the obvious.'

'Probably.'

'Then I don't, no.'

In the gloomy silence that followed, Halpin leaned suddenly forward, his elbows on his knees. And then as suddenly threw himself back again. Trying to work off his worry and his fears in the cramped space.

He said angrily, 'What each of us is thinking is that Walcott killed Linda. Isn't that right? We simply don't want to admit it openly. He's clearly capable of it. We've just been shot at. He tried to have me pushed off the cliffs in Kerry. So this is what we're thinking now. Walcott killed Linda.'

'Or took her prisoner,' Fame offered.

'Why?' Rainey demanded.

The old man explained. 'If Lowry was ordered to bring me to Kinvara, it's possible that Walcott also intended bringing Mr Halpin's sister there.'

Rainey shook her head. 'You only have Lowry's word for that. And it's not reliable.'

Saturday, 14 November

'But the chamber!' Halpin recalled. 'You said there was a chamber underneath the tower house.'

The old man nodded. 'Yes.'

'You only have Lowry's word for it,' Rainey repeated. 'Who else has heard of this chamber? Have you ever heard of it? You wrote an essay on the history of Crastina.'

'These things are quite common in the area. There are tunnels under Northampton House, for instance, about a mile and a half to the south. These passages were used for smuggling through the bay during the last century. In the War of Independence at the turn of the century, they were used for hiding IRA men. It's not unusual.'

'You're grasping at straws, Eddie.'

'No,' he remembered then, with sudden hope. 'St Kieron's was closed for the weekend. It had a sign on the gates. Why else would it be closed? And the idea makes sense. Walcott started following me after I went looking for Linda in Kinvara. If Linda was still free, he would've been following *her*.' He moved sharply, as if ready to step from the car and immediately start the hike towards Kinvara. 'But there's only one way to find out, isn't there?' he demanded.

'No, Eddie,' Rainey cautioned. 'We've got to be careful.'

'I'm not listening any more, Charlotte.'

'I don't share your hope, but I'm willing to try it. But if we're going to do it, we have to do it officially. I've got to contact my chief superintendent to organise a search warrant.'

She stopped. Thought about it. Worried that McQuaid, concerned for Crastina's reputation and Joseph Manning's influence, might block and delay, allowing Walcott time to tidy up and escape.

'No,' she said then. 'I'll do this through Jarlath Burke. He's the local man. He'll set it up.'

SIX

1

At eight o'clock that evening, as he walked back along the footpath from Kinvara village to St Kieron's House, Roger Walcott was reasonably happy.

But then, Walcott had been reasonably happy since the death of McKelvey more than four hours earlier.

There was a natural order to all things, he believed.

And a natural hierarchy of authority. God was all-powerful. Jesus was greater than man. Man was superior to woman. And woman commanded children.

Between men, the stronger and more intelligent ruled the weaker. The more culturally sophisticated exceeded the ignorant. White eclipsed blacks and Jews and other inferior races.

For that infinite wisdom of God, which hath distinguished his angels by degrees, hath also ordained kings, dukes or leaders of the people, magistrates, judges and other degrees among men.

To disturb this natural order was to invite chaos.

And chaos had almost certainly descended with the imposition of the incompetent, unsuitable McKelvey as leader.

To begin with, McKelvey should've arrived in Kinvara on *Wednesday* night. But the *Grey Witch* that had carried him in after collecting him at sea from a Spanish trawler had been delayed for almost twenty-four hours by his own inefficiency.

Saturday, 14 November

Walcott had been forced to wait for him at St Kieron's all through Thursday. And it was this delay that had prevented Walcott from getting to Eddie Halpin's house on Thursday morning, in time to understand the treachery of Lowry and therefore to prevent the absurd, unnecessary attempt on Halpin's life. And from that one failure had flowed all the subsequent trouble.

But order was slowly being restored, Walcott felt now.

There were still threats. But not as fatal as before.

Linda Halpin was obviously still sedated at the hospital, for instance. Because no one had come to question him about her accident.

And it no longer mattered now if she *did* recover. It was too late. They wouldn't find him at Kinvara when they came looking for him.

As for Halpin himself . . . The ruse of slipping down the side roads and then abandoning the BMW outside St Kieron's had been clever, Walcott accepted. It seemed as if Halpin's destination had been the tower house. Uncertain how much Halpin suspected about Columbus and about McKelvey's presence, Walcott had worried.

But it was obvious now that Halpin had travelled on by other means to keep the rendezvous with Harry Fame at the Blue Thatch Hotel. Before entering the bookshop to watch the police station back in Galway city, Walcott had telephoned Cormac Lowry, pretended ignorance of the man's treachery, and alerted him to Fame's hiding place and Halpin's possible appearance. Since Lowry desperately needed both out of the way, it had to be assumed that they were either his captives or his victims . . .

But again, it no longer really mattered. It was too late for any of them. They knew nothing. And if they came to Kinvara, they wouldn't find Walcott.

Satisfied with his reasoning, Walcott turned in off the

footpath and through the open gates of St Kieron's. He closed and locked the gates behind him and walked up the gravel driveway.

Probably for the last time, he realised.

The thought neither saddened nor pleased him. He had no attachment to places.

Opening the main doors to the west wing, he went immediately to the tower house on his right.

Everything had been more or less tidied back in place after Kyne's intervention that afternoon.

The entrance to the underground stairway was covered again by the trapdoor and concealed by the rug attached to the stone.

The oak table with its glass display case was a little to the side of where it had been, not directly above the trapdoor any more.

Its positioning was deliberate. And Dominick Rushe would make sure it remained like that.

This, apart from posting some letters he had written earlier, had been the purpose of Walcott's visit to the village. To give the groundsman his instructions.

'I'm afraid I've been called away, Rushe,' he'd explained crisply. 'Mr Carter requires me urgently in Galway. You'll have to look after things at St Kieron's in the morning.'

Rushe had been uncertain at first about the change. He was conservative and wary of responsibility. Like all devoted menials. But he was also eager to follow the freshest orders. 'I'm not supposed to be there tomorrow, you know, Mr Walcott, but if you say so, like . . .'

'I'm afraid there's no choice,' Walcott had pointed out. 'In my absence, you assume responsibility.'

'That's right, isn't it?'

'It's quite simple, I assure you. Nothing complicated. You'll have to open before seven o'clock. They should arrive a little after eight. You'll hand over the keys and make yourself available to them. If they ask about my absence, you must

Saturday, 14 November

explain that I was called urgently to Galway. I doubt if they will, however. You may find the display on the ground floor of the tower house a little altered. This is on Mr Manning's instructions. You mustn't restore it to what it was. Simply leave it as it is. Do you understand?'

'Yes. No problem.'

'Everything will be locked. All the keys are on this bunch I'm giving you now, including the key to the tower house.'

'What do I do when they're gone, Mr Walcott?' Rushe had asked.

Walcott had frowned. The situation hadn't occurred to him. 'Gone?' he'd repeated.

'When they've all left again.'

'Oh! Quite. Simply lock up. Take the keys with you. And wait for me to return. Yes. Oh! Incidentally! Have you seen Josie Thomas?'

Rushe had shaken his head. 'Not since early this afternoon. I think she stayed at St Kieron's, waiting for Mr Kyne to come back.'

'Ah! Right. If you do see her, Rushe, make sure your wife restrains her here. The girl is quite unbalanced. We don't want her disturbing our visitors with her odd terrors or disrupting the official opening in the morning.'

'No, no. You won't be there for it, then?'

'What?'

'The opening in the morning.'

'I'm afraid not, no.'

'Pity about that.'

'I'm relying on you, Rushe. Remember that. As is the whole of Crastina. The girl could destroy everything with her nonsense.'

'Oh, you can depend on me, Mr Walcott. You can depend on me.'

Which he could, Walcott was certain. Rushe was the

251

dependable type. Devout. Deferential. And devoid of illusions about his status.

Unlike...

Walcott never managed the comparisons.

He'd left the tower house and was in the hallway outside, raising his hand to lock the entrance doors to the west wing, when the doorbell, mounted on the wall to his right, suddenly rasped in his ear and startled him violently.

He wondered at first if it was the overenthusiastic Rushe. Coming to clarify his instructions. Deciding to stay the night to avoid oversleeping.

Or perhaps it was the girl, he thought then. Josie Thomas. Still looking for the late Jimmy Kyne.

But the doorbell rang again. And he decided that it was too authoritative, too insistent, to be either of these timid people.

Walcott was unarmed. All the handguns, the two Brownings McKelvey had brought and Kyne's Walther, were still below, in the chamber underground.

If he went to get them, he risked losing contact with whoever stood outside. And since the lights were on, revealing his presence, he couldn't simply ignore the caller.

He opened the door and stepped quickly back to give himself room to manoeuvre.

The man standing alone on the gravel outside was oldish, perhaps in his late fifties. He was dressed in a brown cord jacket, with grey slacks that hadn't been cleaned or pressed in a while. He had a dour face, with dark eyes and a slightly dissatisfied twist to his narrow mouth.

'You're Roger Walcott, aren't you?' he said.

Walcott nodded. 'Yes. I'm the curator here. Can I help you?'

'Something happen your hand?'

Walcott raised his left hand. The strapping around his broken finger was light, but clearly visible. 'A domestic accident, I'm afraid.'

Saturday, 14 November

'Right. The same one that put that bruise on your face?'
'Precisely.'
'Some accident.'

The man stepped in then without waiting on an invitation and wandered casually past Walcott, glancing around inquisitively. So that Walcott immediately suspected his profession. Seconds before he was told and the ID was shown to him as confirmation.

'I'm Detective Inspector Jarlath Burke, from Galway. I'm looking for Mr Carter. Is he in?'

'Mr Carter is in Dublin. As is Mr Manning.'

'Right, right. Could you contact him for me?'

Walcott glanced at his watch. 'They're at a reception in the American Embassy.'

'So could you contact him for me?'

'I can certainly try, yes.'

'Good.'

'Can I say what it may be in connection with?'

'No.'

Walcott indicated to his right. 'The telephone is in reception. Would you like to step in and take a seat while I'm making the call?'

But Burke had already drifted off in the opposite direction. Absorbed. Abstracted.

Wandering through the connecting door to the tower house, he asked without looking back, 'Is Jimmy Kyne still around?'

'Kyne?' Walcott repeated. He glanced quickly out the open front door, around the grounds. No one else seemed to be out there. Although it was impossible to be certain in the darkness. 'No,' he said. 'Kyne left some hours ago.'

He quietly closed the door and tracked the policeman into the tower house.

Burke was standing beside the rug that covered the trapdoor. Staring down. Thoughtfully rubbing his unshaven chin.

'Excuse me,' Walcott said firmly. 'This display is currently in the process of alteration. The rearrangement is for tomorrow. I'm sure you understand. It would not be wise to disturb anything at the moment.'

But Burke squatted without answering.

He reached out and took a corner of the rug and tried to lift it towards him.

But of course the rug, attached to the stone underneath, wouldn't move. Or not without greater effort.

Burke played with its tassels between his fingers. And still squatting, he looked across towards Walcott in the doorway.

'I think you'd better get Mr Carter on the phone for me,' he advised quietly. 'I would if I were you.'

2

At eight twenty-nine, approaching from the south and through the village, Eddie Halpin and Charlotte Rainey pulled in off the main road, onto Kinvara pier. It was where they'd agreed to meet Jarlath Burke at half past eight.

Rainey parked the Alfa Romeo facing the sea and glanced uneasily at the illuminated clock on the dash before switching off the lights.

Behind them, the public house was the only premises along the row of shops that was still open. But even that was empty. And silent.

To their left, a bald man and a redheaded woman sat in the front of a Mitsubishi Galant, arguing soundlessly with each other.

Otherwise the pier was deserted.

There were no signs of any police around.

Saturday, 14 November

'What do you think, Charlotte?' Halpin wondered.

She shrugged. 'He's a little late, that's all.'

'He only had to drive from Galway. You talked to him four hours ago.'

'Maybe he had a little trouble with the search warrant.'

'Do we wait?'

'Yeah. We wait. We can't do anything else.'

So they waited. Almost fifteen minutes. Through the first of the night's customers for the pub behind, and through the raging and cooling of the couple's argument in the Mitsubishi beside them. Until Halpin's restlessness finally kicked back in.

'Charlotte?' he asked in the darkness.

'Uh-huh.'

'Isn't it possible he just went in without you?'

'Why would he, Eddie?'

'I don't know.'

'Why do you *think* he would?'

'Because of the conversation between you on the radio. The two of you seemed at loggerheads.'

'Just procedural stuff, that's all.'

'Right.'

'I trust him, Eddie.'

'Right. Why?'

'Because he doesn't *patronise* me.'

'Oh, good,' Halpin accepted. But only ironically. He glanced at his watch. 'It's already quarter to nine now.'

'I know, I know.'

'Can't we at least go down there and have a look?'

'I'm not too sure we should.'

'We won't do anything. Just look around. See if anything is happening. What do you say?'

'I suppose,' she wavered.

'Inconspicuous. Just a couple out for a walk. OK?'

'Yeah, OK.'

They left the car and walked in silence from the pier, along the footpath up to the gates of St Kieron's.

They found Burke's Ford Orion where he'd parked it earlier, a little down from the entrance to the grounds. And found that it was empty.

A couple of other cars on either side of it might or might not have been police vehicles as well.

But there were no patrol cars, they noticed. No squad cars. Nothing at all to indicate an official search.

They stood together in the darkness at the locked gates. Baffled. And undecided. And frustrated almost to the point of argument.

Until, in the front reception room of the house above them, they suddenly saw a light come on and caught a quick glimpse of Burke's crumpled figure as it drifted past the narrow window.

'Hey!' Halpin cried. 'You see that?'

'Yeah, I saw it. Keep your voice down, will you, Eddie? It travels at night.'

'Sorry,' he whispered. 'But that was Burke, wasn't it? Wasn't that him?'

'I think so, yeah.'

'He's already *in* there!'

'Let's go, Eddie!'

Burke reappeared in profile at the window as they climbed the gates. He was gesticulating strongly by then. Vigorously shaking his head. Violently disagreeing with something. And with someone.

They were halfway up the gravel driveway when he turned in exasperation to look out. And he saw them immediately.

He stared. And frowned. And pressed his face against the glass, cupping his palms on either side of his eyes to peer out.

Rainey stopped. Uncertain again of the wisdom of her actions. Unsure of her haste and her impatience. Burke was

Saturday, 14 November

such a confusing figure in her life. So paternal... It always rattled her judgement, her self-confidence. What if she was blundering into a subtle manoeuvre of his? But he hadn't *told* her. Hadn't confided in her...

Halpin strode on a pace or two without her. Then he noticed her absence and stopped as well.

'Charlotte?' he whispered.

On the point of twisting to glance behind, his attention was drawn again to the window above when Burke suddenly raised both his arms and seemed to signal intently. It was a brief gesture. Sharp. And peremptory. And characteristic of the man's sour and peevish gruffness.

After it, Burke sat down. And apart from the black hair on the top of his head, he disappeared completely from their view.

'Did he beckon us on?' Rainey wondered. She stepped up to stand beside Halpin again. 'Or did he tell us to wait?'

Halpin shrugged. 'I think so.'

'What? Which?'

'He beckoned us on.'

'Are you sure?'

'No, I'm not, actually.'

'Neither am I.'

'What does it matter, Charlotte? If *he's* already in there, there's no reason we can't be as well.'

'I suppose, yeah.'

They walked quickly up the rest of the driveway.

Burke didn't move as they came. He didn't either encourage or dissuade them. He sat stiffly in the chair below the window. Staring at someone opposite. And presumably waiting for the other two to arrive.

The door to the west wing was already unlocked. They pushed it open.

The hallway inside was in darkness.

On their right, the connecting door to the tower was also

open. Through it, inside the illuminated tower itself, they could see the displaced trapdoor and the square of darkness in the floor that obviously led to a stairway below.

But they both turned left first. And then left again. Into the small reception room.

Burke was sitting alone at the table, sunk into a deep armchair beneath the narrow window. His hands were hanging loosely by his side. The telephone was on the surface of the table, directly in front of him. Its receiver was already off the hook.

'Jarlath?' Rainey called.

The man stared back at her.

But his eyes were lifeless. And his blood was flowing from between his shoulder-blades, down the backrest of the chair, and dripping through the gap between that and the seat to the wooden floor below.

He'd obviously been shot in the back as he'd stood at the window looking out.

'Jesus!' Rainey swore quietly.

She drew her own .38 Smith & Wesson revolver. She moved to the side, away from the exposure of the window. Shocked, and not particularly knowing what to do, she uselessly covered the dead Burke with her revolver.

'The phone, Eddie,' she said then. 'Ring out. Get some help.'

Halpin moved carefully along the opposite wall and reached around Burke to pick up the receiver. He tried for a dialling tone, but shook his head. The line was dead.

'See if it's cut in here,' she told him. 'Follow the lead. You can patch it together again.'

He was on his knees, tracing the cable to the connection box, and finding it all intact, when they heard a door slamming shut outside.

Saturday, 14 November

But which door, they wondered. The front? Or the one to the tower? They weren't sure.

Rainey felt along the wall beside her for the switch and turned out the lights.

'Wait here!' she whispered to Halpin.

Crouching low, she left the reception and darted through the hallway outside.

The front door had been closed. The connecting door to the tower was still open. But it was now dark inside the tower.

It was clearly a trap, Rainey decided.

But which was the decoy, she wondered. And which was the snare?

If she went first through the tower, the gunman might be already outside the building. If she went out, the gunman might still be in the tower.

She waited.

But if she waited too long, of course, and the killer was already escaping outside . . .

Footsteps, crunching across the gravel outside, broke in on her thoughts. She moved immediately. And she relaxed until she'd reached the front door itself.

It was a fatal assumption.

There was sudden movement in the shadows on her right.

Before she could react, before she could understand her own mistake, the butt of a pistol came heavily down across her wrist and knocked the Smith & Wesson from her hand. The gun clattered to the flagstones by her feet. She stumbled and cried with pain. And as the pistol caught her again across the head, she looked up, had a brief glimpse of Roger Walcott's face behind his raised arm and simultaneously heard Halpin rushing foolishly from the reception to help.

And then, of course, unarmed and unprepared, Halpin was trapped as well.

Although he still thought otherwise for a while.

As Walcott stooped to collect the .38 and drew back from the fallen Rainey, Halpin stepped protectively between the pair.

'It's no good, Walcott,' he warned. 'There's no point. That's a detective you killed in there. The rest of them are already on their way, with a search warrant.'

Walcott only laughed. Very briefly. And very cynically.

Rainey struggled to her feet behind Halpin. 'Let it go, Eddie,' she advised.

Halpin turned to stare at her. 'What?'

'Let it go,' she repeated. Her voice was sad. Defeated.

He couldn't understand. He asked, 'What does that mean, Charlotte? Let it go. What does it *mean*?'

'Burke came here by himself, Eddie,' she told him. 'He came alone. Without any back-up. Without being part of a team. Without even telling anyone else, I'd guess.'

He shook his head. 'I don't . . .'

'Remember you once warned me to be careful about what colleagues I spoke to? That leak? Going back to your arrest? I made a mistake, Eddie. I trusted only men who were gruff. I got the wrong guy.'

'You mean Burke . . . ?'

'I'm sorry, Eddie,' she said softly. She clasped his hand from behind and squeezed it gently. 'I'm sorry. We're on our own. No cavalry on the way . . .'

PART FOUR

Sunday, 15 November

ONE

1

Eddie Halpin woke again at eight-fifteen.

It was cold in the underground cell where Walcott had imprisoned them. The night had brought frost and ice to the countryside for the first time that winter. The ground temperature had been minus two. In the ancient tower, with its bare stone walls, it had fallen a couple of degrees lower than that. And below the tower it was colder still.

There were heavy blankets and sleeping-bags, all stained with blood, on the camp-bed that had been pushed against the far wall of the cell. But Walcott had taken the gas heater and its cylinder away, worried that they might be used as weapons against him.

For warmth, Halpin and Rainey lay together under the covers on the only bed.

They hadn't slept very much. They'd talked. Angrily at first. And then with determination, and fear, and desperation. And finally only dully, without desire or conviction.

When one of them eventually dozed, the other's restlessness usually woke them quickly again.

And this was what had happened again now. Finding himself alone in the bed, with the air cooler than it had been against his side, Halpin came easily out of the thin sleep he'd been in.

Silent City

He looked across the unlit cell, staring blindly until his eyes grew accustomed again to the darkness. He was searching for Rainey, of course. But since her new location was the only thing he wasn't already familiar with, he saw everything else first. The bodies of the two dead men that Walcott had stretched along the wall to the left. The food supplies and the lamps and the two television sets opposite.

Rainey was standing by the locked door, he noticed eventually. She was facing it, with her back towards him. Her face was buried in the palms of her hands.

She might've been thinking. Or she might've been crying. But she was certainly feeling the same empty despair as himself, Halpin thought.

Their situation was hopeless, he realised now. Neither had admitted this to the other. But both accepted it.

To hold out hope, they needed knowledge.

But they knew nothing. Or nothing of any value.

'That's Shane McKelvey,' Rainey had explained the night before, searching the bearded fat man immediately after they'd been left alone in the cell, looking for clues or weapons on the corpse.

'I thought he was thinner,' Halpin admitted. 'All his photographs have him younger and leaner. And clean-shaven.'

'He hasn't been seen or photographed for more than a year. The other one is Jimmy Kyne, Joseph Manning's driver.'

'I know Kyne. I've met him a couple of times before.'

'McKelvey was obviously hiding down here. But why? Ireland should be the last place he'd come back to for refuge. He's too well-known. So what was he up to? What's Walcott up to now?'

'Does he have to be up to anything?' Halpin had wondered hopefully.

'How do you mean?'

Sunday, 15 November

'Isn't it possible that he was only protecting McKelvey all along?' But then why try to kill me last Thursday? I knew nothing about McKelvey. Why go after Linda? She knew nothing about McKelvey, either.'

'What Walcott feared was the exposure of Columbus, the revelation that an extremist group still exists within Crastina.'

'I was getting close to that, I suppose. But is it enough to kill for?'

'I doubt it. Not by itself.'

'But what else did I know? What did they *imagine* I knew?'

Knowledge of Walcott's plans might've allowed them to put some pressure on the Englishman. It might've given them the space to pretend that the information was more widely available and that his schemes were threatened from other angles. But without it, bluffing was futile.

They could find no obvious weakness in either Walcott himself or in the cell he'd locked them in.

And they couldn't even dream of some dramatic rescue from outside.

The last hope of that had died at three in the morning, when Rainey had woken with a start, sat up in the bed, and roughly shaken Halpin.

Halpin's eyes were already open. He hadn't been asleep.

'Last night,' she said urgently. 'Eddie! Eddie!'

'I'm awake, Charlotte.'

'OK. Are you listening?'

'I'm listening. What?'

'Last night. I heard someone on the gravel outside. It was why I was caught off guard. I thought it was Walcott. Did you see anyone?'

For a moment, Halpin's hopes flickered also.

But then he remembered.

'It was only the girl,' he explained dully. 'I forget her name.

I've seen her here before. She lives here. But she's quite simple.'

'Could she get word out?'

'She would've already if she was going to, wouldn't she? I don't think so. I'm not even sure she'd understand what was happening.'

Unwilling to let it go so easily, Rainey's mind played on the same theme for an hour or so afterwards.

Who could save them?

Harry Fame? They'd left him at *The Blue Thatch*, in the care of a doctor who was treating the torn ligaments in his ankle. They hadn't told him where they were going. He might've easily guessed, of course. But if they didn't return, he wouldn't immediately suspect anything. He wasn't expecting them back.

Neither was anyone else expecting them, for that matter. Not on Sunday, anyway. Halpin's absence from the university on Monday might raise a few eyebrows. Rainey's failure to keep the appointment in Dublin with her chief superintendent would set a few alarm bells off.

But that was Monday.

And by then . . .

'What about Burke?' Halpin had asked.

Rainey shook her head. 'He wouldn't have told anyone where he was going. He's probably off duty Sunday. No one's going to miss him until Monday, either.'

'You have to wonder, though. Why did Walcott kill him? Why not us as well?'

Rainey gestured at the two dead men who were keeping them company for the night. 'Because Burke's co-operation obviously stopped somewhere short of accessory to murder. He gave a little inside information to Walcott's organisation, and a little cover when it was needed. Maybe he stretched to tearing up the occasional warrant or two. He didn't do it for money,

Sunday, 15 November

though. I don't think he was like that. It was where his sympathies lay. As for us . . . I don't know, Eddie. Maybe we're hostages.'

With the prospect of outside help exhausted, the final hope lay with themselves. With their own strength and their ingenuity. With the depths of their resourcefulness and their courage to tackle Walcott.

But Walcott had never returned to the cell, although they'd heard him throughout the night in the passageway outside. And morning had come and found Halpin and Rainey tired and defeated.

So when Halpin had been woken again at eight fifteen, he no longer thought about rescue or escape. By then, he'd simply accepted his captivity.

2

Eight thirty.

And everything was ready. Everything was lying neatly in its place.

Or so Walcott thought.

Sitting on the bedding in the passageway outside the underground cell, where he'd spent the night, he surveyed his preparations.

For the last time, he imagined.

The body of Jarlath Burke was lying at the base of the stairway outside. And since Walcott had been unable to clean the bloodstains from its fabric, so was the armchair the policeman had died in.

Burke, he knew now, had been a sympathiser, a mole within

the police force recruited by Carter. But he was unable to say when Columbus discovered America. And his ignorance of the coded password had marked him off as unreliable and potentially dangerous if released. He wasn't a *trusted* activist.

Without the chair, the small reception room in the west wing now seemed a little bare and unfinished. But only to the eye already familiar with its details. To Rushe, for instance.

Rushe . . .

At six forty-five, Walcott had woken to the alarm on his wristwatch. He'd walked back along the passageway, crawled through the gap in the wall, and climbed the stairs to stand underneath the concealed trapdoor and listen for Rushe's arrival.

The groundsman had been a little late. He'd turned up about ten minutes after seven. And he seemed to be a little flustered because of it.

At least he was alone.

He came into the tower house after unlocking the connecting door to the west wing. But only to stand there, glancing around.

As instructed, he didn't move anything.

When he left again, Walcott remained on the stairs. Silent. Unmoving. Not yet at the end of his vigil.

Seven fifty-five, the others arrived. *They* were five minutes early.

Three or four of them came into the tower with Rushe. They walked back and forth across the flagstones. Keeping themselves satisfied. And never suspecting that anything breathed below them.

When they left, they locked the connecting door after them.

Everything ready, Walcott had thought. And everything falling neatly into place.

He'd descended the stairs, crawled back through the gap,

walked back along the passageway and sat on the bedding outside the cell.

Eight thirty.

With nothing else to do, he checked and cleaned the weapons. His own weapons. Or those McKelvey had brought in with him. Not Kyne's Walther. Not Rainey's Smith & Wesson. Just the two Brownings and the rifle.

3

Halpin crawled out of the sleeping-bag, swung his legs to the cold floor and sat on the edge of the bed while letting his mind drift again over the thoughts that had occupied him before he'd last fallen asleep.

And five or six minutes later, it was Rainey's voice that finally broke in on his reflections.

'What are you thinking of, Eddie?' she asked.

She came across from the door and sat beside him on the bed.

He didn't look at her. He looked down at the rough ground beneath his feet.

'I wasn't thinking of escape,' he said. 'Not any more. I was thinking about Alan Rosen and Bridget Manning.'

Rainey was surprised. 'Yeah?'

'I was actually thinking about us as well,' he confessed then. 'About the contrast, the . . . You know what I mean?'

'Not really, no.'

'The way Rosen and Bridget risked everything for their passion. They went against the current. His community. Her family. Her *honour*. They were puritan times. Reputation was everything for a young woman.'

'And us?'

'I was wondering . . . Do you think we were ever as reckless as all that, Charlotte? Ever as wild?'

She thought about it.

She thought about the struggle of their life together and the pain of their separation. They had parted on a misunderstanding. He had suspected her of informing. She had derided his blinkered liberal attitudes.

But that was the point, she realised now.

Ultimately, they were both cautious people.

Oh, they were courageous enough. In the usual sense. Willing to take *physical* risks.

But they couldn't just abandon everything. Not like Rosen and Bridget Manning. They couldn't wildly throw in the hand that birth and circumstance had dealt them to take a chance on pulling a better one.

She would always cling to the comforting demands of her career. In conflict with that, passion always came off a second best.

Halpin would always hold to the stability that his political activism offered him.

They both had their small crusades.

They hadn't been happier on mountains, she realised now, because the damned things were elevated, but only because they'd climbed on their holidays, away from the pressures of their working lives.

Was love a recreation to their modern sensibilities?

They weren't children of the repressive, puritan Ireland of the forties, but of the liberal Ireland of the late nineties. Things other than passion were important to them. Personal identity. Personal space. Self-esteem . . .

She shook her head.

'No,' she said sadly. 'Not as reckless as that. I don't think so, Eddie.'

Sunday, 15 November

'Neither do I,' he admitted.

In the silence, he put his arm around her shoulders and drew her towards him.

She thought of bowing her head to bury it on his chest. But then she changed her mind and turned her face upwards to his.

When they kissed, it was with intense regret.

'Shit,' Rainey lamented softly afterwards.

Thinking of the wasted six months, the absurdity of having to end as prisoners in an underground cell with only two corpses as their witnesses before they could accept that they'd made a mistake in parting from each other.

'You know what we do now, Charlotte?' Halpin asked her gently.

She leaned back to look at him, alerted by the tone of his voice. She saw that slightly pained smile that came on his lips from the effort of concealment. But she knew that it was only a joke he was keeping from her this time.

She never got to the punchline, though. Because she never asked for it.

'Eddie!' she cried suddenly. 'Eddie!' She gestured towards the television sets in the corner by the door. One was a hand-held mini-screen, the other a small portable. 'Why are the televisions here?'

Halpin shrugged, impatient to return to the softer mood. 'Maybe McKelvey was an addict. A couch potato. He looks like one.'

Rainey vigorously shook her head. 'No. They're not for entertainment, Eddie. The portable maybe. But not the mini-screen as well. No. Besides, the portable hasn't been used. See the dust on it? See the battery pack beside it? I bet there's no battery inside it now. They're not for entertainment, Eddie. They're for information. And information that had no relevance or wasn't available up to now.'

She sprang off the bed and hurried towards the television

sets. As if the closer she physically got to them, the more chance she had of extracting their secrets.

'Now, Eddie,' she said excitedly 'Now. If only we knew what information they were meant to give, then we might finally have some bargaining clout. Think! Think!'

4

Nine o'clock.

And there was just half an hour to go, Walcott thought.

If everything went to plan. If everything went smoothly. And on time.

Just thirty minutes left to go.

But *if*...

For some reason, the small word unsettled him. This tiny entrance into larger doubts.

If...

He felt a tightening in his stomach that had nothing to do with nervousness. It was a malady older than anxiety. It was confusion. A sense of incompleteness. Of not being fully in control.

He thought at first that it was only natural concern. A residue from McKelvey's dire incompetence. Or the pumping of adrenaline before the crisis.

But his mind kept playing for a while around the same set of questions. Until they finally ate into his confidence. Because he had no answers for them.

How would he *know* if everything was going to plan, he wondered desperately.

Locked down here like this. Underground. Deaf. And blind. Like a senseless rat in a darkened cage. How would he know?

Sunday, 15 November

How would he know whether the world was keeping strictly to its advertised schedule? Whether it was operating so smoothly that it was now ahead of itself. Or whether it was dragged down by unforeseen delays and was falling behind.

He *wouldn't* know.

He could assume. But he couldn't be certain.

When he himself moved, therefore, he might be fatally early. Or he might be fatally late. But he was highly unlikely to have the luck to precisely hit the target.

For twenty minutes, the problem crushed and defeated him.

5

As the picture clarified on the screen of the portable television, showing a helicopter shot of a road lined with spectators and police but without any traffic, Halpin was the first to identify the location.

'It's the main road south out of Galway city,' he said. He had come off the camp-bed and was standing close to the set after inserting its battery. 'The road you take to get to Limerick. And Cork. And here.'

The picture wavered and broke while he was talking. As if responding to his surprise and his anxiety.

Rainey passed him and knelt on the floor behind the set, adjusting its tuning and its small aerial.

Impatient with her progress, he took the hand-held mini-screen and opened the flap in its base to insert the batteries he'd found beside it.

But the sound returned to the portable before the images appeared again on either set.

Silent City

A man was talking. And because the voice was familiar, and disturbingly so, Halpin's attention was gripped by it.

'This is something we've worked towards for a very long time,' the voice of Joseph Manning's secretary, Michael Carter, was saying smoothly. Almost smugly. 'This has been many years in the planning.'

As the camera drew back, it was clear from the surroundings that the press conference had taken place in a Dublin hotel late the previous night.

'But why the secrecy?' someone asked him. 'The announcement came so late that—'

'Oh, no. No secrecy. Simply a matter of logistics . . .'

The coverage cut without warning, back to the Galway road.

The presenter's excited commentary wasn't necessary for understanding.

A cavalcade of twenty or more black limousines was sweeping south from Galway city and turning west, towards Kinvara, at the town of Kilcolgan. And the second of the limousines was flying two small American flags from its front wings.

'Oh, Jesus!' Rainey swore quietly. 'Christ!'

6

Walcott frowned as he heard the faint sound of the television from the cell beside him.

His first thought was that the noise might carry if the volume was raised . . .

But then it struck him.

The materials McKelvey had requested for the cell, he remembered. Months before. The items Walcott himself had

274

Sunday, 15 November

secretly brought down at night. The bed and the covers. The food. The lighting and the heating equipment. And the items he hadn't questioned while working off the list, and hadn't considered again in the meantime.

The two televisions. The small portable set. And the smaller hand-held mini-screen.

They were supposed to be his eyes, he suddenly realised. They were his ears. With them, he could burrow as deeply into the earth as he desired and still know precisely what was happening on the ground above him.

But along with the surge of relief and satisfaction he felt, came newer worries.

He could no longer hear the television from inside the cell.

Had Rainey or Halpin also guessed their function, he wondered. And before his own slow reasoning?

Had they already smashed the screens? Had they already set a trap for him, knowing that he'd be forced to re-enter the cell?

He cursed violently as he pushed himself to his feet.

He glanced again at his watch.

It was nine forty now. But even as he looked at it, the display changed again to nine forty-one. Less than forty minutes away.

He stooped and took one of the Brownings from the blankets on the floor. He fixed its silencer in place, lifted the keys from the hook on the wall and quickly unlocked and pushed open the door of the cell.

Inside, the two stood rooted in front of the portable set, their faces drawn and shocked.

Halpin held the mini-screen. But he held it loosely. Not concealing or protecting it.

Again, Walcott could've simply shot the pair of them. The muffled sound from the Browning wouldn't have carried to the ground above.

But as he stood there, enjoying the expression of shock and

distaste on Halpin's face, he suddenly understood his deepest reason for keeping them alive the night before.

There had been other considerations, of course. And far more practical ones. He hadn't been certain that no one was following behind them, for instance, and they would've made a useful shield against attack. And they might still be useful as hostages now.

But his pleasure went deeper than these preparations.

He wanted an audience, he accepted. But not an appreciative one. Not to *admire* him. He needed an audience to be frightened and appalled. He wanted to see in microcosm, on the features of one face, the profound effect his actions were going to have.

And Halpin was the perfect gauge. A liberal. Terrified of racial strength and vigour. Riddled with the disease of equality.

There was an element of personalised conflict in all of this that Walcott had never allowed enter his work before.

But this was his final mission.

He and Halpin were representatives. Of master and inferior. Of those who saw the terminal sickness of the modern world and those who didn't. Of those who were sturdy enough to draw on their own racial purity to survive and prosper and those who were too weak and infected to do so.

For once, therefore, the personal struggle was fitting.

To this conflict, and to the fact that it hadn't yet found its resolution, Halpin continued to owe his life.

So Walcott aimed the Browning, but didn't squeeze the trigger. And he said slowly and carefully, 'Put what you have in your hands down on the floor in front of you and then step back to the bed.'

He didn't want to alert Halpin to the importance of the small television. He didn't want obstructive thoughts desperately entering the man's head.

But Halpin responded oddly. Neither complying nor refusing.

His head jerked slightly upwards and he glanced quickly beyond Walcott. As if attracted by something in the dark passageway behind.

And when he spoke, he seemed intent on delaying or distracting Walcott.

He held up the mini-screen. 'You need it, don't you?' He said it calmly, simply as a statement of fact, and apparently without any other purpose.

Uneasiness settled on Walcott. Because of Halpin's signals, he had a sharp sensation of some unexpected threat behind him.

But he didn't look.

It had *only* been prompted by Halpin, he was certain. Even if it was fed afterwards by his own tension. He had to control it.

'Put the screen down on the ground,' he ordered again slowly. 'Then step away from it. I assure you. Either give it to me or I will take it from your corpse. It really makes no difference to me.'

7

Halpin hesitated.

He knew now the details of Walcott's plan.

As he'd just learned from the television coverage, the American President, Gordon Weller, en route from Galway to his ancestors' estate in Clare, was about to stop off briefly in Kinvara to cut the ribbon at the official opening of Crastina's new headquarters across the inlet from St Kieron's House. A visit long agreed between the White House and the Irish charity, and long prepared for by both governments, but not advertised in the official schedule at the request of Joseph Manning's secretary and not publicly announced until the previous night.

Carter had explained that poor industrial relations had delayed the construction of the headquarters and made the visit more an aspiration than a certainty. But Halpin knew that the reason was more sinister.

Halpin knew a lot of things by now, of course.

He knew that Walcott was going to assassinate the President, that he needed the television and the blanket coverage of the visit provided by the national station to time his intervention properly and to breach the security protecting Weller.

He knew that Columbus was a right-wing terrorist group. Its coded riddle about discovering America presumably referred to November 1996, when Gordon Weller had been elected the first black President of the USA.

And he knew that the murder of Weller could push his country to the edge of a racial civil war.

But above all, he knew that his knowledge was now useless.

'Give him the screen, Eddie!' he heard Rainey call with sudden urgency.

He turned to look at her with surprise. She wasn't looking back at him. She was staring at Walcott, who was becoming dangerously impatient.

'Give him the screen,' she said again. 'It makes no difference, Eddie.'

But the fear and concern in her eyes suddenly reminded him of a separate loss.

'Where's my sister, Walcott?' he asked.

'Sister?' Walcott repeated.

'You went to meet her on Friday instead of Harry Fame. What happened to her?'

A slight smile rippled across Walcott's lips.

But not of amusement.

TWO

1

Five miles south of Kinvara, on a minor road that his new driver had taken to avoid the delays on the main route, Joseph Manning's troubled mind finally recovered the truth about his involvement in Alan Rosen's death.

The limousine had slowed for a farmer and his dogs herding sheep along the narrow road. When it stopped as the herd was turning into a field, Manning looked forlornly out its side window.

It must have been towards the end of May in 1941, he recalled. Alex Condon and Tony McCann and Stephen Baldwin had sat opposite him at a table in the living-room of Baldwin's house, staring expectantly at him and silently waiting for his response.

'What are you going to do about it, Joseph?' Condon had asked. 'I know if any sister of mine was walking out with a bloody Jew . . .'

'There's no proof of that,' Manning protested eventually.

'No proof? My mother saw the two of them on O'Connell Street, arm in arm, there about a week ago. Only for a second. And then they were off their separate ways, pretending they didn't know each other. But you can't keep that sort of thing a secret in Dublin for long.'

'There's no proof that the man was a Jew.'

'His name is Rosen, Joseph.'

'Rosen?'

'Why? What's wrong with you now? Do you know him yourself or something?'

'No,' Manning had lied. 'I don't. Of course not.'

'Well, the family is well-known to us, I can tell you that. Bloodsuckers, the lot of them. They have a fancy house and a solicitors' practice out in Terenure. We've had our eye on them for a long time.'

'Why don't you simply visit him at his home and question him?'

'Because he's not living there any more, Joseph. And he's not working with his father's firm any more, either. The sly bastard has himself and Bridget meeting some place in secret. Except we don't know where it is, do we? So what are you going to do about it?'

At home that same evening, he'd unlocked the front door, stepped into the dim hallway and as usual called softly up the stairs to reassure his invalid mother. There was no answer. His mother was asleep. His sister Bridget was out. Again.

In that silent, gloomy house, after a long struggle, he took the spare key to Bridget's bedroom from a drawer in the dining-room sideboard and searched her belongings, until he found among her papers the address of a house on the North Strand.

He hadn't gone there himself, of course. He was too weak for that. But he'd passed the address to Alex Condon . . .

Turning again from the shame of that memory, as he'd turned away from it throughout his life, he stared through the window of the limousine.

Three black cows stared back at him. Their heads extending over the meagre ditch that separated their empire from his.

Sunday, 15 November

Their minds indifferent to anything except the cud they were chewing.

Beyond them, for an instant of hope, he was suddenly certain that he saw Jimmy Kyne standing with a tin bucket at the door of a farmhouse and staring across.

He'd already guessed why Kyne had deserted him, of course. Kyne had located Harry Fame, he thought. Fame had told him the truth about 1941. And Kyne, unable to reconcile his loyalty with his honesty, had simply abandoned Manning.

The car moved on before he could say anything, however.

New sights sped past. And new distortions replaced the older ones.

In one moment of lucidity, as they broke back onto the main road to Kinvara, he wondered if his secretary had actually sedated him before they'd left the capital. His mind had been clouded all morning. Unconnected images had pierced the fog with the clarity and speed of dreams before vanishing again. And Carter himself had been strangely agitated throughout the journey. As if something was weighing heavily on his conscience.

But the moment passed. And with it the lucidity.

When they pulled in off the road, he hardly noticed the two strange young men guarding the entrance gates to St Kieron's House. The sound of the limousine's tyres across the gravel driveway seemed unfamiliar and puzzling to him. And when they stopped and Carter stood out to speak to three or four Americans, he caught snatches of their conversation but could understand nothing of it.

A while later, Carter sat back in again. He spoke. But the words still made little sense.

'Jimmy Kyne is not here,' he said.

Manning stared at him dully.

'You wanted to call in at St Kieron's to find Jimmy Kyne,' Carter explained impatiently. There was a nervous edge to his

281

voice. An intolerance that hadn't been heard before. 'This is why we took the detour. You wanted to come to St Kieron's.'

'Ah!' Manning exclaimed.

'But Kyne is not here.'

'I see.'

Carter glanced nervously at his wristwatch. 'They tell me that the President is quite close,' he said.

Manning nodded. 'I see.'

'And we need to be at our headquarters before he arrives. Shall we go?'

'Yes,' Manning said softly. 'Yes. We must go.'

2

Walcott would've liked to lie about Halpin's sister. He would've enjoyed confirming and describing her death. But he wasn't certain of the other's reaction. Like all liberals, Halpin's judgement was clouded by sentiment. And he might react foolishly.

Walcott told the truth.

'I followed her to a shopping centre car park . . .'

The experience was unexpectedly bitter for him.

What suddenly flashed across his mind, for the first time in decades, was the timid and naive philosophy of his own father. *Always tell the truth, son.*

He remembered the shame of his father's weakness and incompetence. An English farmer whose land was finally stolen from him by foreign industrialists.

He felt again the injustice of the world. The terror of losing control. His hatred for disorder. And for powerless sentiment.

He watched Halpin, now reassured about his sister's life,

place the hand-held television on the rough floor in front of him and step back from it to sit huddled beside Rainey on the camp-bed.

For a moment, the helplessness of his prisoners disgusted him so deeply that his own hatred detained him. But then he stooped, picked up the screen and left the cell, locking the door behind him.

Once outside, however, he forgot again about his captives. They were insignificant, he'd decided. No one had come to rescue them. No one had missed them. No one had cancelled or altered the American President's plans because of their disappearance.

As he tuned the television and caught the presidential cavalcade sweeping past the town of Kilcolgan and hurrying on towards Kinvara, he armed himself in the passageway.

Both Browning automatics he carried on him. One in the shoulder holster under his left armpit. The other in the belt holster at his left hip.

The Galil sniper's rifle that McKelvey had brought in with him for the assassination was already assembled and lying by the side of the bedding in the passageway.

An hour before, Walcott had removed the rifle's muzzle brake and flash eliminator and replaced it with the silencer. He'd checked the butt again for comfort after attaching it, adjusting the cheek piece and adding another spacer under the rubber recoil pad before he was happy with it. He'd assembled the telescopic mount and fitted the 6x40 telescope.

In practice, using this sophisticated equipment, it was said that McKelvey had been capable of placing the rifle's twenty rounds from the ammunition box into a ten-centimetre circle at more than four hundred metres.

And Walcott . . . ?

His own shooting would be just as accurate, he was sure. And far more effective.

Silent City

The night before, he had written his personal testament and posted copies in Kinvara to the newspapers and television stations.

Words without action were useless, he knew. But actions without a political context were merely vague. An individual's thrill. A momentary sensation on the front pages.

Death, he felt, should be the restoration of order.

And so he had written:

> *We live in a Europe that is terminally sick, weakened by the grotesque deformities in the growing culture of addictions, by the dereliction of its urban centres, and by the parasite of massive immigration . . .*
>
> *Columbus is the expression of the trampled soul of true Europeans, a movement for national rebirth and spiritual regeneration, dedicated to restoring that spirit of noble struggle which has gone to waste . . .*
>
> *Our faith is in heroism. Our objective is a spiritual understanding of Europe . . .*
>
> *In a shapeless contemporary world, a world without order, or style, or vigour, it is fitting that Ireland, which in the previous dark ages saved Christianity from extinction, should once again be the last outpost of an ecumenical mission that will turn back the tide of decay . . .*
>
> *But to argue with the world is only an academic exercise . . .*
>
> *To Columbus, and to its allies among the Christian parties of regeneration throughout Europe, a black American President is not merely a political enemy. He is a grotesque, a deformity. He is a symbol of chaos and of sickness. In the natural order of things, black is at the lower end of God's chain of being. And a leader cannot be inferior . . .*

With the cavalcade less than two miles from Kinvara now, the camera shifted suddenly from Weller's progress along the

Sunday, 15 November

country roads to the platform at Crastina's new headquarters across the inlet.

Walcott studied the tiny images on his little screen. He tried to anticipate where Weller would enter from. How far the President would have to travel across the platform to reach the ribbon he had to cut. How exposed he might be. How long he might linger.

But the coverage cut away again.

The first of the presidential limousines had reached the turn-off by an ancient holy well known as Tobermacduogh and was rolling smoothly over the newly-built road that led through the gated entrance to Crastina's new headquarters.

Walcott tensed. And glanced at his watch. And reached for the rifle by his side.

But for a long time, nothing happened.

Weller stayed obscured in his bulletproof car after pulling up at the back entrance to the buildings.

Outside, his Secret Service detail split into two. The ones who had to do the scurrying today were moving anxiously, in and out of the headquarters building, through the patient dignitaries and employees waiting to be presented, up and down the road the cavalcade was lined along. The ones who had to do the watching were glaring into the welcoming crowds, as if the *warmth* of the reception was what was really causing the problem.

It was already nine thirty-seven.

And it wasn't until more than ten minutes later, at nine fifty, that Weller finally stepped from the car and across the few metres of road to greet his host, Joseph Manning, and to shake hands with Manning's secretary.

In the chamber underneath St Kieron's tower, Walcott picked up the sniper's rifle and crawled through the gap in the wall.

From the detailed information left by Carter for McKelvey,

he knew that there was a single agent high on the battlements above, that there were no others within the tower itself, and that the rest of them were covering the grounds and the approaches to St Kieron's.

And the one above, he thought, would be more interested in the surrounding countryside and the bay to his left than in anything else. He wouldn't be watching his back.

Walcott climbed the steps. Without the heavy oak table on top, the stone trapdoor lifted easily now when he pushed against it.

He put the rifle on the floor to the side of the opening as he held the trapdoor with his left hand and climbed outside, trying not to create any noise or vibration as he went. When he lowered the door into place again, he kicked the edge of the rug into the opening to cushion the sound.

He took the rifle and moved across to the spiral stone staircase.

As he climbed he used the broader sections of the triangular steps and leaned against the wall with his right shoulder, until he came to the openings onto the chambers, when he had to shift to the other side. He didn't want to use his hands for anything except the guns. The rifle he held in his left. One of the automatics, with the safety off, he carried in his right.

The weak morning sun, slanting in through the tower's window slits, threw crosses of dusty light onto the steps and onto Walcott's body as he passed them.

He climbed beyond the dull display of Crastina's history on the first floor, then further up, past the attempts to recreate the sixteenth-century interior on the second and third, and on to the fourth where two dummies, dressed in Elizabethan clothes, sat on chairs by an open fire.

Beyond them, at the top of the stairs, a gate blocked his progress onto the narrow wooden walkway around the battlements. A small, cast-iron thing, painted black, just like an

Sunday, 15 November

ordinary garden gate. The night before, he'd unlocked it and left it swinging open. But someone had closed it again this morning.

He put the Browning back in the shoulder holster and raised and jiggled the small bolt on the gate. As it slid back, it creaked a little along the rust that the last coat of paint hadn't reached. He stopped and waited. The sound had seemed immense to him in the surrounding quietness. But no one came to check it out.

He worked the bolt fully free and eased the gate back towards himself, confident that the hinges weren't going to make the same complaints. He'd oiled and greased them recently. And they were soundless.

He climbed the last few steps on his stomach, crawling onto the wooden walkway.

When he was comfortably clear, he rested to get his bearings.

He knew he'd come up facing south, on the opposite side to the inlet.

So he still had two lengths to negotiate, two corners to manoeuvre round. And he had to keep on crawling. He couldn't rise, couldn't even stoop. The battlements were too low to conceal him.

Wanting to check again on Weller's progress, he reached to take the mini-screen from the deep pocket of his trousers.

But it wasn't there.

He cursed silently.

He must've left the thing deep in the cellar. It was too late to go back for it now.

3

They sat on the camp-bed in front of the portable television, watching the President of the United States striding unwittingly towards death.

But they didn't mention the images on the screen. They didn't discuss Walcott's politics. They didn't dwell hopefully on the weaknesses of his scheme or on the prospects for his capture or interception before he was settled in position.

They had chosen to protect each other. First and foremost. So had they traded Weller's life for their own? Had their own survival determined their decisions?

'He would've shot us both, Eddie,' Rainey said.

'Maybe,' Halpin answered.

'We couldn't have helped or hindered. It's the helplessness that makes you feel guilty. Not anything you did.'

But neither was convinced and they fell silent again, gloomily watching the television.

On screen, Weller embraced his host at the rear entrance to Crastina's headquarters. In contrast to the buoyant, energetic American, Joseph Manning seemed frail and disorientated. And slightly absurd in a purple robe.

To Rainey's left, a rat scurried between the bodies of Kyne and McKelvey, distracting her.

She glanced across. But then looked sharply back at Halpin.

'What did you say?' she asked.

He shook his head. 'Nothing.'

'But I heard . . . Turn the sound off, Eddie!'

She stood up as he reached out to kill the volume. She moved quickly away from him, across towards the door of the cell. Pressing her ear flat against the rough oak, she listened intently, frowning with concentration.

Halpin padded carefully across to join her. But before he reached her, she stepped back and slapped on the wood with her open palm as she shouted, 'Is there someone out there?'

There was no answer.

And the silence, accepted as natural a few moments earlier, now seemed grim and cruel because of the wild hope that had been raised.

Rainey turned to Halpin. She gestured hopelessly and rubbed her face with her hands.

'When Walcott came in . . .' Halpin started. He shook his head. He'd thought at the time that he'd seen a shadow move behind the Englishman in the passageway. But he'd dismissed it as an illusion. A trick of light from the lamps. Or his mind feverishly feeding him hopes.

It seemed too cruel to raise it again now.

'What, Eddie?' Rainey demanded.

'Outside,' he said. 'It's probably only another rat. Maybe just the wind down the passageway when Walcott lifted the trapdoor to the tower.'

'It had a voice, Eddie.'

'But—'

He cut himself off before she managed to raise her hand again to silence him.

From the passageway outside, distinctly this time, both of them had heard a sound.

It was a young woman's voice, they realised now. Thin and high-pitched. Only a little above a whisper. And very frightened.

'Mr Kyne?' it called forlornly. 'Mr Kyne?'

THREE

1

Joseph Manning's eyes were distant.

His mind had long gone past worrying about the absent Kyne and was now receding deeper and deeper into his own past.

He no longer really knew where he was.

Beside him, Carter guided him like a puppet, whispering instructions and advice and explanations in his ears.

He obeyed mechanically.

When the President was introduced, he allowed himself to be clasped by the famous man. He didn't consciously respond to the hand that was placed in his. He only suffered its pressure. And remained confused about its demands.

They turned and walked through the rear entrance of the building and then around the interior hall where Crastina's personnel were all assembled. He searched in vain for familiar faces. His dark-haired sister. Her Jewish lover. And the plump young Harry Fame in his army uniform.

He was startled by the repeated bursts of applause. He kept trying to shuffle away from it all. And he stayed always on the edge of the handshakes and the kisses and the snatched conversations.

When they came out again, through a side door, the weak

Sunday, 15 November

sun hurt his eyes with the same intensity as the dawn had when he'd woken in an army barracks on that distant December morning back in 1940.

He stumbled and almost fell.

A Secret Service agent caught him on one side. Carter supported him on the other. Between them, they helped him climb the three wooden steps to the temporary platform outside the main entrance to the building, where a green ribbon stretched across the open front doorway, waiting to be cut.

For a moment that was full of dread, he was convinced that he was mounting a scaffold, to be hung there for his crime, and he shrank back, moaning softly with fear.

But then the guests that were seated on the platform all rose at once, like an army standing to attention, and he was hurtled back in time again. By the sound. By the uniform movement. By the sheer sensation. Back again to another wooden platform, in a barrack square on a winter night, when all but one of his regiment had knelt before it to wash away their sins.

The boards creaked under his feet as he stepped forward.

And for some reason he looked up and to his left, across the inlet and over to St Kieron's House, where he noticed a lone figure standing guard on the battlements of its tower house.

He moved with Weller then, along the line of Crastina's executives and invited guests. Shaking hands. Listening to names and titles. And forgetting them instantly once they'd been replaced by the next.

Weller had stopped in front of a tall young woman who was being introduced. He held her pale and delicate hand in his own. With his left, he reached back to draw Manning forward. And then, as if suddenly inspired, he looked slightly upwards, into the clouded sky, and said solemnly, 'I am reminded of something here today.'

Behind Manning, there was a ripple in the following crowd.

Some stepped slightly sideways. Others surged forward through the gap.

Those who came on, past the nervous Secret Service agents, were the mobile camera crew covering the President's progress, eager to scoop up the great man's words.

No speech had been scheduled for this particular function. There was no podium on the platform. And no microphones around. But the crew had a boom that would pick up the President's voice once he'd settled and decided to stay in a single position.

Manning himself understood nothing of all this. He felt only that his hand was trapped and that he could not escape the sentence that was about to fall.

'I am reminded,' the President resumed, 'that Ireland has always been incomparable in keeping as her own those sons and daughters who have left the immediate family through emigration. It is a gift – this gift of belonging – which I have experienced myself these last few days. To as warmly welcome, however, those strangers, those foreigners, who may have come into this closely knit family from outside its fold . . .'

2

Walcott didn't waste any time regretting the loss of his hand-held television.

Keeping the rifle aloft, away from making noisy contact with the wood he was crawling over, he reached and negotiated the first corner on the walkway without meeting any trouble.

From there he risked a quick glance over the parapet.

He found himself looking west, into Kinvara Bay.

Across from him, the village pier was crowded. Colourful

Sunday, 15 November

crowds, hoisting their kids on their shoulders and pointing across the inlet. More Secret Service agents. More Irish police and soldiers. A helicopter flying above, sweeping the bay and the coast line.

He heard someone on the battlements around the next corner. Someone who'd moved slightly. Perhaps just by shifting quickly from one foot to the other.

He waited.

When the agent started talking, reporting on his radio transmitter that his sector was secure, Walcott took the opportunity to move again, knowing that any small sounds wouldn't be heard above the agent's voice.

He stopped again when the report stopped and restarted when it resumed, having timed the lag between them.

He tried to anticipate the next call. He tried to calculate how much time he had after taking the agent out before their central control smelt a rat and got that helicopter across and the President out of sight and some back-up into the tower.

But he didn't have to go blind, he realised then. Even though he'd left the television behind. Even though he wasn't certain of Weller's current position.

At ten thirteen, the crowd on Kinvara pier, now slightly behind and over to his left, suddenly started cheering wildly, telling him that the President had just stepped onto the platform across the inlet and was in full view.

In a couple of smooth, rapid movements, Walcott put the rifle on the wooden walkway, raised himself to a crouch, took the Browning from its shoulder holster, released its safety and sprang around the corner.

He didn't bother fretting about concealing himself. Because he didn't think that anyone's eyes were going to be drifting towards the tower at that particular moment.

And he was right.

Silent City

The only one who saw him was the agent already there. A heavy black man who turned in shock, with his mouth open.

Walcott almost lost everything then. He hesitated. Delayed squeezing the trigger for just a fraction of a second. Because he had camouflaged himself, in a dark suit and light shirt, as a *white* Secret Service agent.

When he fired, it was only after the agent had moved a little away from his original position.

He didn't hit the man's heart. The bullet struck to the side of it. The agent spun and went down heavily and had crashed through the frail roof slates and into the chamber below before Walcott could cover him and fire again.

Walcott hurried up to the opening and dropped to his stomach to look down.

He couldn't see the agent.

But the man was probably dead, he decided. He certainly couldn't still be conscious, because he hadn't sounded a warning over his radio transmitter. There was no panic across the inlet. And no more than the usual excitement on the village pier.

Walcott left the Browning on the walkway. Crouching again, he spun back and around the corner. He picked up the Galil rifle. When he returned with it, he knelt on the walkway, laid its muzzle between two stone battlements and looked through its sights across the inlet to the platform.

He tracked the President as Weller moved across the platform. And he waited for an opening. Patiently. Steadily.

But Weller himself was too heavily shielded, his agents staying close against him, not leaving a gap to be exploited from any angle.

And the target was too small, too mobile and too elusive.

The President, Walcott knew, would be wearing the usual bulletproof vest. A body shot wasn't going to be of any use. It had to be the head. And it had to be accomplished with the first

Sunday, 15 November

round. Immediately after, Weller was going to be swamped and covered and bundled off the stage.

The first one had to count. No guesses. And no uncertainties.

But there wasn't an instant when the President's head was both still and fully exposed, when it wasn't bobbing and weaving, or nodding or shaking, or obscured, or disappearing like a water hen on the surface of a lake and popping up again somewhere unexpected.

Perhaps a minute passed.

From beneath him, Walcott thought he heard a low moaning. He wondered if the agent had survived the bullet and the fall and was now regaining consciousness.

It occurred to him that the man's failure to report on his sector's security should have been noticed by now.

Why hadn't it?

The time had passed for his next report.

Why hadn't Walcott himself, exposed as he was, with his own view confined to the tunnel of the sights, been spotted by someone watching the tower?

Unaware that the President's impromptu decision to deliver an unscheduled speech had created a minor panic across the inlet, that the Secret Service radio channel was suddenly overloaded with agents frantically telling each other what all of them could obviously see, and that for the moment everyone's concern was exclusively for what was happening around Weller, Walcott could do nothing but worry about his incredible luck.

His intense anxiety bred other concerns.

He had doubts now about leaving the trapdoor to the underground chamber the way he had, with the rug jamming the stone slab just slightly open instead of concealing it fully. What if one of the agents outside had been instructed to check within the tower at regular intervals? What if . . . ?

Silent City

So when the crowd concealing Weller finally realised that the President was settling into a speech and suddenly, almost as one, quietly sat back in their seats . . .

When for a moment, devoid of cover, before his Secret Service agents could surround him again, the President's upper body was at last exposed to the tower of St Kieron's across the inlet . . .

Walcott almost missed the opening.

3

Rainey was the quicker. Quicker to spot the opening. And quicker to invent a plausible story.

While Halpin was still stumbling clumsily behind her.

'Mr Kyne is injured!' Rainey called to the girl in the passageway outside the cell. 'Do you understand? We need to get him out! We need your help to get him out!'

The lie was met with absolute silence from outside. As if the girl, despite the wall and the oak door between them, could see right through Rainey's performance.

Rainey closed her eyes and gestured with exasperation. But then controlled herself and started again.

'Are you still there?' she shouted. 'Did you hear me? Mr Kyne is seriously injured! He's been shot! The man who shot him locked me in here with him! Unless we get him to a hospital, he's going to die! If you can't open the door from out there, go and get help immediately!'

But again, there was only silence.

'What's your name?' Rainey demanded desperately. 'Can you hear me? What's your name?'

'Ask Mr Kyne,' the voice suggested timidly.

Sunday, 15 November

'What?'

'Ask Mr Kyne.'

Rainey swivelled to Halpin, the question repeated in her eyes.

He grimaced and gestured, pleading for a little time. 'I was trying to remember it this morning, when you were asking . . .'

Impatiently, she started to make the excuse that Kyne was unconscious and couldn't speak.

But he stretched out a hand to stop her. Because under the pressure, it had suddenly come back to him.

Joseph Manning and himself and Michael Carter standing outside the tower house after the interview two weeks before. The girl peering at them from behind a half-open door, clutching a soft toy in her hands. Manning gently calling her over . . .

Josie . . .

'Mr Kyne says your name is Josie!'

Rainey winced after calling out. Waiting for the next rejection. Cursing under her breath at the stupidity of the situation, at the need to humour and cajole the girl outside.

'He says there's a key hanging on the wall out there,' she cried then. 'Is it still there? Can you see it?'

The girl still didn't answer.

But they heard her movements.

They heard a slight scrape as the key was inserted and then a loud, relieving click as the lock was released.

Rainey didn't hesitate. Once the door started opening slowly towards her, she grabbed its handle, jerked it back and raced past the cowering girl, almost without a glance.

Halpin, slower and more susceptible, stayed too long and caught the emotions on the girl's pale face. Hope and fear as she came through the doorway. Worry as she saw Kyne lying on the cold stone floor. Despair as she knelt beside him and realised that he was already dead. And a look of hatred and accusation as she turned her tear-filled face back up towards Halpin.

He stared down at her helplessly.

He couldn't tell what she'd been through, of course. He had no idea how she'd come to be in the underground passageway or how long she'd been trapped in or under the tower. And he could only guess at her relationship with Kyne.

But her pain detained him.

Until he heard Rainey yelling back for him as she ran, and he finally turned away from the girl.

He sprinted then down the dark passageway and dropped to his hands and knees to crawl through the opening in the dividing wall.

Rainey was already at the top of the stairs, pushing the stone slab upwards, off the rug its edge was resting on.

He followed her up to hold the stone for her as she climbed through.

'Go and hammer on those doors!' she ordered him. 'Get the rest of them in here!'

She sprinted across to the spiral staircase, trying to take the steps at speed.

But they'd been built for defence. Designed to prevent intruders making rapid progress.

It wasn't only that the structure twisted constantly, throwing her off balance all the time. As well as that, only one section of the triangular steps was wide enough to take her foot. It forced her to place one leg almost directly in front of the other as she climbed, making it impossible to hurry.

Once, she lost her footing and slipped, struggling for a hold on the walls as she fell backwards.

Halpin, behind her again, caught her before she went down.

She turned to him. Surprised. Wondering if he'd summoned help.

But she didn't ask.

Sunday, 15 November

She launched herself upwards again.

Passing the chamber on the third floor, she caught a glimpse of the black Secret Service agent lying inside. Obviously unconscious. And possibly dead.

The sun badly hurt her eyes as she came out onto the battlements a few steps later.

She stumbled and pitched forward through the open gate, landing on her stomach against the wooden walkway.

But blind or not, she knew immediately that shots had already been fired at the President.

Everywhere there were people screaming, their voices carrying loudly across the waters of the bay. Everywhere there was panic. And confusion.

She heard the roar of a nearby helicopter.

Blinded and stranded, she struggled desperately to get to her feet, feeling now the vibrations along the wood of someone else who was moving on the tower's walkway.

FOUR

1

'To as warmly welcome, however, those strangers, those foreigners, who may have come into this closely knit family from outside its fold . . .'

Joseph Manning had no idea who was speaking these words.

He had no idea who it was that was holding his right hand. And holding it so tightly that he couldn't escape its grip. So painfully that he even felt at times that it wasn't a human limb that bound him, but a manacle. A chain. A pair of handcuffs.

The rows of people lined in front of him and the crowds around him were all strangers to him. Their role was mysterious. But their presence was ominous.

The only thing that he was certain of now was that he himself was being chastised.

In the moments during which these words were being delivered, a great many confused images flashed across his troubled brain.

He thought of the Day of Judgement that he'd always dreaded, with the blessed on the right hand of the Lord and the damned on the left.

He remembered a picture he had seen of a dethroned monarch being displayed in all his ordinariness to a jeering populace.

Sunday, 15 November

And he recalled the horror of an execution that he'd witnessed.

His head sank under the weight of impressions.

Already drained by the physical and mental demands of the last few days, he was now close to collapse from exhaustion.

To as warmly welcome . . .

The words, reverberating in his head, seemed like a stern admonition and a warning.

But they also seemed like an invitation to confession.

The one who had said them suddenly drew him closer as he spoke.

Manning yielded to the Christian invitation.

And as he wept for his sins, as he *lunged* forward to seek forgiveness in a warm embrace . . .

The bullet struck his temple.

And it killed him instantly.

He sank back against the President, knocking Weller off his balance.

'Mr Manning . . . ?'

As Weller spoke, he lost his footing and went down beneath the dead old man.

He felt something warm and moist and unpleasant splash against his face. He had no idea what it was.

Against him, Manning jerked again as a second bullet hit him. And still Weller didn't realise what was happening.

It took the more conventional signals to bring it home. A woman screamed. Quite close to him. Perhaps even the blonde young woman whose hand he'd just been holding.

On his left, an agent shouted near his ear, 'Gun! Gun!'

And then the inherent brutality of being the most powerful man in the world was revealed to the President.

As his agents crowded about him, hauling him to his feet, he saw his dignified guests being knocked aside, into the path of the assassin's bullets, to clear a passage for himself. He saw women being denied the exits and children being left to fight for themselves.

As if competing in some nightmare race, he saw the green ribbon he'd been meant to cut, now like an outsize finishing tape, hurrying towards him as he was dragged along, bent over and face down.

And then, a stride or two short of the line, an agent stumbled over Manning's secretary and brought the knot of bodies down.

And the President, feeling the heat of the sun on his face once more as he fell helplessly on his back, knew that he was exposed again.

2

The trouble with a telescopic lens, focused on a small target, was that it blinded you to almost everything else in the world.

Walcott hadn't seen Joseph Manning until it was already too late, until his brain had already transmitted the instruction to his hand and he'd started squeezing the rifle's trigger.

He knew immediately that the wrong man was going to die.

He tried to adjust his aim for the second shot, guessing that Weller's face would appear again slightly to the left as the pair of them fell. But he was wrong. And only hit Manning in the head again.

After that, of course, the President was swallowed by his Secret Service agents.

Walcott had no clear sight of him at all.

And it didn't seem as if he was going to be offered the time to find one, either. There was someone else on the walkway now. Someone who'd come up through the tower by the spiral stairway. He could feel their weight and the vibrations of their movements along the wood under his knees.

But he didn't look.

And he didn't change position.

Through the sights, he followed the tense, balding officer he'd picked out earlier as the agent in charge of Weller's detail. *He* was the one who would always be closest to the President. If another gap opened for a shot, it would be somewhere around *him*.

But Christ, they were fast. And they were organised. A mere two or three seconds, and they'd already ploughed a channel through the panicking crowd on the platform to the main entrance of the building. They already had Weller at the opening, almost safe. Without offering a glimpse. Without showing as much as the heel of a shoe.

And then Walcott's luck changed miraculously again for the better.

But not just luck, he realised.

Because it was Michael Carter who suddenly broke through the cordon of agents holding that channel open to the door and brought down the group escorting Weller.

Tense with excitement, Walcott simultaneously caught sight of the President, his face turned to the sky and his eyes squeezed tight against the light of the sun, and heard the shout to his left as someone came around the tower of the corner and saw him.

He told himself to hold his own position, to pick out Weller in the sights and finish him.

But his nerves were already reacting before the conscious instruction was finished.

He swivelled, raising the rifle to bring it in over the battlements, and fired without aiming at the woman who was racing towards him.

And as she went down and hit the walkway he fired again, without adjusting his aim, at the blurred figure who was close behind her.

3

Sprinting tight on her heels, Halpin stumbled over Rainey's trailing left leg as she went down in front of him.

It saved his life.

Walcott's bullet whistled over his bowed head.

Halpin didn't quite fall. With absurd consideration, he leaped out and over Rainey, desperately trying to avoid trampling on her.

When he landed, the momentum carried him heavily forward, directly into Walcott, before he could think of what he was doing.

Walcott swung the butt of the rifle at his face.

Halpin ducked, putting his weight again on his right foot, and took the blow on his raised left shoulder. It sent him crashing back against the sloping roof of the tower. His elbows knocked on chipped rotting slates where the black Secret Service agent had earlier fallen through.

As he staggered, his left arm accidentally hooked the rifle's shoulder strap and unbalanced Walcott.

Encouraged by the chance, he then deliberately caught the strap in his hand and yanked it towards him. Too late, as Walcott's face crashed into his own, he had second thoughts about the move.

He tasted blood and felt a searing pain above his left eye where the brow had opened. An old weakness in his boxing days. And he countered it now as he had then. He brought a swinging right cross into Walcott's face as it came away from him after the clash of heads.

Sunday, 15 November

While Walcott staggered and dropped the rifle, Halpin noticed the pistol that was lying on the walkway to his right.

But it wasn't any use to him, he decided. He had no experience of handguns. Trying to figure out how to use it effectively, or how to use it at all, would only cost him too much time. And of course his life on top of it.

And besides, Walcott had another pistol in the holster on his belt and was already reaching for it.

But he was fumbling, Halpin noticed. Uncertain of his judgement. His hand was wavering over the butt.

He was groggy.

Halpin pushed himself fiercely off the roof beam and roared as he charged.

Walcott tried to dodge while pulling desperately at the Browning in the holster. But he wasn't fast enough. Halpin caught him in the chest with his right shoulder and knocked him back against the parapet.

Walcott's spine cracked against the corner of a stone and he slid into the gap between the battlements.

Hanging over the edge, his hands struggling for a grip, he tried to kick at Halpin's face with his heavy shoes.

Halpin ducked. He felt the impact of the blow in his right shoulder this time, and then brought his hands violently up under Walcott's calves and flung the Englishman's legs high in the air.

Walcott did a backwards somersault. But there was nothing behind him any more for him to land on.

He didn't cry out as he fell to the rocks below.

It was something that Halpin would always remember afterwards.

The Englishman dropping silently like that, until he died at the base of the tower.

Halpin tried to look out and down after him. But he

couldn't. Now that the struggle was over, now that he realised how high up he was, he felt suddenly dizzy and weak-kneed.

As the pounding receded in his ears, he became aware of other things and other sounds as well. There was a helicopter loudly closing in on him. In its doorway, there were several crouching American agents, and all of them were pointing weapons at him. Handguns. Rifles. One of them was shouting through a megaphone.

'Put your hands above your head! Put your hands high in the air above your head!'

It wasn't that he was being obstructive, or even that he was too scared to comply. He really did want to keep them from killing him. But the stone he was holding was like solid ground to him. It steadied him. Every time he raised his hands a little away from it, he felt as if his dizziness was going to bring him over the edge to join Walcott on the rocks below.

To his left then, he heard Rainey's voice, shouting at him at well. 'Eddie! Eddie!'

'Charlotte? Are you all right?'

'Eddie! Put your fucking hands above your head!'

He looked across at her. Her left arm was bleeding, where she'd been wounded. But otherwise she seemed OK.

Still clinging to the battlements, he smiled his relief at her.

She closed her dark brown eyes with helpless exasperation.

He shouted at her above the noise of the helicopter and the loud American with the megaphone. 'Vertigo! I never told you. All that hill climbing you brought me on.'

She used her better arm to gesture. 'Then step back! Away from the edge! Look across! Don't look down!'

He nodded, the sweat shaking from his face with the movement. And he slowly reversed, his hands still held rigidly in front of him, but gripping nothing more solid than air now, until his back touched the slates of the roof behind him.

He looked across the inlet, where the panic had at last

Sunday, 15 November

subsided a little on Crastina's platform, and he was astonished to pick out the weaselly figure of Michael Carter staring back at him from among the dishevelled celebrities.

And he finally raised his hands then.

Partly to wave at Carter.

What was probably an odd goodbye, it occurred to him. And an even odder victory salute.

FIVE

1

They had the injured Secret Service agent on board the American helicopter with them. Along with a team of paramedics, a few healthier Secret Service agents and the head of the Irish Special Branch, Chief Superintendent John McQuaid. All keeping a very close eye on each other.

The wounded agent had another of Walcott's bullets lodged in his left shoulder and he had broken a leg in his fall from the roof. Like Rainey, he was now stuffed with a cocktail of painkillers and tended to be a little sore-headed at times and a little misty-eyed at others.

Mostly, he was silent.

But Rainey herself kept veering noisily between pain and pleasure, between irritation and affection, and between analysis and sentiment.

She wanted to know first about the girl, Josie Thomas.

'I feel guilty about the way we . . .'

But no one could ease her disquiet. Amid the panic and confusion, the girl had disappeared again after discovering that Jimmy Kyne was dead. Another passage or another chamber, perhaps, lay beneath the tower house of St Kieron's, where she had spent the previous night, hidden from Walcott.

Sunday, 15 November

'And I should've seen the problem with Jarlath Burke much earlier,' Rainey mumbled then. 'I should've . . .'

McQuaid ran his fingers through his straw-coloured hair and gently tried to deflect her. 'We'll consider all that in good time, Charlotte.'

'Yes, sir, but—'

'At the moment, I'm sure Mr Halpin would prefer to hear about his sister.'

'You have news of Linda?' Halpin asked.

'She's in hospital.'

'Yes, I know. She was knocked down while Walcott was chasing her. He said she was still unconscious.'

'No, no, she regained consciousness early this morning,' McQuaid told him. 'They wanted to sedate her again when she demanded to see the police, thinking she was feverish. They didn't succeed. Quite an assertive young woman, Mr Halpin.'

'Headstrong,' Halpin translated affectionately. 'Is she out of danger?'

'Oh, yes. Some broken bones that will take a few months to mend. If she can contain her restlessness in the meantime.' He stopped, looked out the helicopter window and smiled mischievously. 'Restlessness is a troublesome fault in a woman, Mr Halpin.'

It started Rainey off again. 'I know I made a mistake, sir—'

'Quiet, now, Charlotte,' he told her.

'I can see now how it wasn't possible to investigate Crastina, what with the American President intending . . . *You* knew that, sir, but—'

'I was only amusing myself, you know. With that remark about restlessness.'

'No, sir.' She struggled to sit up and had to be restrained by a paramedic. 'I misjudged something. You see, I thought you were—'

'Maybe not, Charlotte,' Halpin cut across her quickly, before she leaked her old and damaging suspicions about McQuaid. 'You remember what the word *Crastina* means?'

She stared at him suspiciously for a moment. 'What?' she asked.

'It's from the Latin,' he prompted.

'I know it's from the Latin,' she said crustily. 'It means, *belonging to tomorrow*.'

'That's right.'

'What about it?'

'We always thought it was only a positive stress on the future, when it was founded in the forties, in the gloom of the post-war depression.'

'But that's what I'm saying!' Rainey cried again. 'We were blind. We should've seen it was meant to suppress and distort the recent past as well. It shut off Manning's involvement in Rosen's death. People see in very narrow channels. We all do.'

McQuaid frowned, confused by what they were arguing about. But he didn't interrupt.

Not that he was given much of an opening to, really.

'No, no,' Halpin came back quickly. 'The Latin adjective is *crastinus*.'

'Christ!' Rainey groaned.

'*Crastina* is the feminine form. Why did Manning use the feminine form? That's what I'm asking. Who did he have in mind? His sister? His mother? It suggests hope and resilience. As we said. That's what the charity has offered. But it also promotes a feminine image of compassion and nurturing.'

'Jesus, Eddie!' Rainey complained.

'Hang on,' he pleaded. 'Hang on. That's Crastina. OK? Or what was intended by the name. Columbus, on the other hand—'

McQuaid couldn't contain his curiosity any longer. 'Columbus?' he repeated.

'That's right.'

Sunday, 15 November

'The explorer sometimes credited with discovering the New World, although—?'

'Well . . .'

'That's him,' Rainey interjected. 'What about it? Columbus.'

Halpin leaned forward. 'Maybe,' he said quietly, 'it's only in the subterranean world of Columbus that all the male virtues dominate. Strength and order. Discipline and rectitude. Your suspicions about Manning were justified. You said there was a link between patriarchy and intolerance. I was wrong. I said his attitude towards his sister was only the tenor of the times. It was more than that.'

Rainey lay back, smiling to herself. 'I like that,' she said. 'I like it.'

'What? Me being wrong?'

'No, no. Paradise or Armageddon. Crastina or Columbus. I like it.'

McQuaid coughed. But then he saw that Halpin had taken Rainey's hand and instead of demanding explanations as he'd intended, he only coughed again.

Halpin looked out the window by his side, down on Galway Bay, where two fishermen in a black currach were pulling furiously on the oars. Beyond them, a little to the north, he could already see the city of Galway.

His home. His career. His sister. His life.

All not far from being restored to him now.

He wondered about himself and Rainey.

Wondered if they, too, belonged to tomorrow . . .